FORGED IN STEELE

STEELE GUARDIANS SERIES - BOOK 3

SUSAN SLEEMAN

EDGE OF YOUR SEAT BOOKS, INC.

Published by Edge of Your Seat Books, Inc.

Contact the publisher at contact@edgeofyourseatbooks.com

Copyright © 2022 by Susan Sleeman

Cover design by Kelly A. Martin of KAM Design

1

Bristol Steele believed in perfect days. Today wasn't one of them. Not even close.

She raced through the big Victorian house she shared with her sisters and cousins, trying hard not to topple over in the high heels she rarely wore. Today was the most important day of her adult life, and she'd failed to set an alarm.

But she had plenty of backup. Two sisters and three cousins, all knowing this was her big day with the family business. Why hadn't one of them woken her before leaving for work?

Now she had just enough time to make it to the hospital for the press conference.

Barely.

She skidded to a stop by the back door and flung it open. She ran across the lawn, meticulously manicured by her sister Peyton. Bristol's heels sank into the soil wet from morning watering, and she hoped her hair wouldn't frizz up in the unusual morning humidity. She remotely clicked open the doors of her blue Chevy Bolt.

"No. Oh no. Not today." She came to a stop, her heels

threatening to unsettle her, and she grabbed onto a nearby cherry tree to keep from falling. She stared at her front tire.

Flat. Flat as the paper targets hanging at the end of the lanes at her favorite firing range.

This couldn't be happening.

She continued on closer just to be certain. Yep. Flat. Totally flat. This car was going nowhere without a tire change, and she didn't have a spare.

She could just hear her dad lecturing her about buying a spare for a car when the manufacturer didn't provide one. She'd claimed her self-sealing tires would do the trick, but clearly she was wrong. She must've run over something beyond the tire's limit to seal the leak.

Why, God? Why? I have to get to the hospital. Now!

Panic settled in, and she looked around for her next move.

"Get a ride. Quick. But who?"

She could call one of her sisters or cousins but their work locations were too far to get here in time. She dug out her phone and opened a rideshare app. She found a driver only five minutes away and booked the ride then tottered toward the front of the house for the pick-up.

Under the tall maple trees by the road and out of the bright sun on the warm August morning, she dialed her cousin Teagan who was the chief operating officer of the family business. For three more weeks, Bristol was still a full-time deputy with Multnomah County Sheriff's Office, but then she would join Steele Guardians as the sales and marketing manager.

"Where are you?" Teagan demanded. "The press conference starts in thirty minutes."

"I know." Bristol worked hard to keep sarcasm out of her tone. It wasn't Teagan's fault that Bristol was in this spot. "I overslept and no one thought to wake me up."

"I didn't have a clue," Teagan said. "I parked out front last night, or I would've seen your car and come to your rescue. Not sure why everyone else let you sleep."

"No matter now. But on top of being late, I have a flat tire. I called a rideshare, and I should be at the hospital within fifteen minutes."

"That's cutting it close, but you should be fine. I'll update Mr. Coglin and then meet you in the lobby, so we can arrive at the conference together." Teagan disconnected.

Bristol shoved her phone into her purse and scanned the road ahead for her ride. She tapped her foot and rehearsed her upcoming speech. After what felt like a lifetime, a small car pulled to the curb, the windshield holding a rideshare company sign.

She plunged into the backseat and rattled off the address for the hospital to confirm the driver had received it from when Bristol had booked the ride.

"I need to get there fast," Bristol said, ignoring the strong smell of coffee in the car. She hadn't gotten even one cup in her system this morning and craved the caffeine.

The driver looked over the seat, his dark eyes searching. "Are you sick or something?"

"No. I have the most important meeting of my life, and I overslept. Then I got a flat tire. So hurry. Please."

"You got it." He booked it out of the space. "You might want to try taking a few deep breaths."

"I'll breathe after I get there." She looked at her watch. Twenty-three minutes and counting.

"What kind of meeting is it?"

She really was in no mood for chitchat, but talking would keep her mind off being late. "It's a press conference, actually."

He glanced in the rearview mirror. "You gonna be on the news?"

3

"Could be."

"What for, if you don't mind me asking?" Suspicion laced his tone.

"An uptick in crime has hit the hospital lately, and they came under fire in the news for their lax security."

"Yeah, I heard about that."

"I signed a contract for our family company, Steele Guardians, to provide security guards for them. It's all part of the hospital's new focus on security. Today's our company's first day, and we're announcing it this morning at a press conference."

"Impressive." He turned onto the main thoroughfare, and she wanted to press her foot to the gas. "Sounds like it'll be a big account for you."

"My first account." She let her mind drift to the day Mr. Coglin, the hospital administrator, called to say the board had approved their contract. One of the largest contracts Steele Guardians had ever secured. She hoped it showed the family that she was more than the baby of the family and was up to the new job.

She'd learned of the hospital troubles while on duty when she'd responded to a theft call. She'd gone to her family and asked to approach the hospital as her first client. Her father and uncle, who founded the company, thought it was too big of a contract for her first one, but she convinced them to let her have it.

And now she was going to be late.

She leaned forward. "Can you go faster?"

"Sorry. I won't get a speeding ticket."

As a deputy, Bristol understood—she really did—but she didn't like it.

She sat back but kept glancing at her watch. As they neared the hospital she had seven minutes until the press conference. Just enough time to run through the hospital to

4

the room near the back. Maybe she should take her shoes off so she could move faster. Nah, that would be unprofessional and the hospital administrator put the word profession in professional. He was old school to the max.

She lifted a hand to nibble on her fingernail and jerked it away. She had to break this habit if she didn't want to have jagged nails. She made sure she was always well-groomed as a deputy, but no one getting a speeding ticket cared if her nails were bitten to the quick. As a sales manager, she had to present a much more professional front.

The hospital signs came into view on the tree-lined street.

Yes!

She leaned forward. "Go to the main entrance and drop me at patient unloading."

"You got it." He clicked on his blinker. "And hey, good luck with the conference. Hope you're on time."

She checked her watch again. Four minutes. Her heart dropped in her chest.

The driver pulled into the circular patient loading area, and Bristol bolted out, nearly getting her heels tangled in the small vehicle. She rushed inside and spotted Teagan in a wide courtyard with tall plants and a trickling fountain.

They came together and ran for the back over a slick tile floor. Bristol concentrated on her steps so she didn't faceplant. That was all she needed.

She got out the ID badge provided by the hospital, giving her access to most areas and enabling her to monitor her guards today.

Teagan focused her dark eyes in Bristol's direction. "I hope you know what you're going to say."

"That's why I slept in." Bristol wanted to groan but held it back. "I was up all night getting it just right and then fell asleep at my desk without setting the alarm."

They approached the door and slowed in unison to a clipped walk. Bristol ran a hand over her hair as did Teagan. They were cousins and both had long, near-black hair and were often mistaken for sisters. Teagan was four years older, and Bristol had always taken a back seat to her cousin. Not today. Today Bristol would shine. She had to.

If her faith wasn't so weak right now, she'd ask for help.

Teagan opened the door, and they stepped into the room. Surprisingly, the space was filled with reporters and photographers, the air humming with conversation. Bristol hadn't expected the media would find this story interesting. Maybe it was a slow news day. Either way, she felt lightheaded.

"Just breathe," Teagan whispered over her shoulder. "You'll be fine."

Bristol listened to her cousin and took a few breaths as she approached Roderick Coglin. She'd always been struck by the hospital administrator's perfect posture and stylish attire for a man nearing retirement. Today he wore a serious-looking gray suit and pale blue shirt fitting with the list he'd given her of colors that came across best on the TV screen. She'd chosen a blue suit with a blouse much the same color as his shirt from her oldest sister, Londyn's overflowing closet.

"Sorry to hear about your flat tire, but glad you could make it on time." Coglin gestured at the long table with a podium in the middle. "We'll be right over there. You and Teagan first."

Bristol hurried across the room and scooted to the far end of the table to sit in the stiff plastic chair. She settled her shaking hands in her lap as Teagan dropped down beside her, and the three hospital representatives dressed in conservative suits took their seats.

Mr. Coglin stood at the podium and adjusted the microphone, emitting a squeal from the speakers. "Ah, sorry about that. Thank you all for coming. I'm eager to share our newest security plans with you. I'll give you an overview of the plan, and then you'll hear from the representatives of Steele Guardians, the firm we chose to provide our guards going forward."

He held out a hand, gesturing at Teagan and Bristol. She forced a smile and hoped it didn't come across as stilted and wooden like the fear freezing her insides.

He continued on with his speech, his deep tone soothing, doing an excellent job of engaging the audience. He'd be a tough act to follow. Could Bristol do the same thing?

Nerves peppered her body and nausea formed in the pit of her stomach.

The door burst open, and Coglin's assistant came barreling into the room. The short blonde raced across the carpet, her sights set on Coglin like a locked and loaded missile.

No. Oh no. Something was clearly wrong, but what?

She pulled him away from the microphone and whispered in his ear. Coglin went white and gripped the podium. He took a long breath then stepped back to the microphone. "I'm sorry, but we need to cut this press conference short."

An agitated hum of conversation buzzed through the reporters and gazes locked on Coglin.

Okay. Good. Seemed like a problem that didn't involve them. Bristol sagged in relief. She didn't need to talk after all.

She breathed deeply for the first time.

Coglin whipped his gaze to her, grabbed her arm, and towed her out of the room and down the hall to an alcove. Teagan followed them.

Bristol had celebrated too soon. Her heart started beating at lightyear speed.

7

"We have a Pink Alert," Coglin whispered. "Pink Alert. Room 332 East."

"Pink, no." Bristol had memorized this hospital's codes and the facility backwards and forwards and Room 332 East was in the birthing center. "A baby is missing!"

"Shh," Coglin said. "We need to keep this quiet until your guards lock this place down. We'll see if your company is up to the task of protecting our hospital."

Bristol didn't waste time responding, but kicked off her heels, pausing to scoop them up, and charged toward the security office. She tried to breathe normally as she worked out what she needed to do, but her mind seized up.

It was the first day of their hospital contract and a baby had been kidnapped.

Kidnapped!

She couldn't imagine a worse first day in history, and she was the only person in the family to make things right.

"Pink Alert. Room 332 East," the announcement sounded over the speaker in the hospital birthing suite.

Jared Wolfe came to his feet, his gut clenching. He shoved back his suit jacket and reached for his sidearm—a movement almost as natural as breathing to him.

"Pink alert means a baby, right?" Debra, his buddy's wife, clutched her newborn son close to her chest. "Someone kidnapped a baby. But how? The hospital just revamped the security, and it was supposed to be better than ever."

"I don't know, but I'm going to find out." At least he would do his best. Not like last time when his best hadn't been good enough.

Deb blinked. "You can just do that? Go ask? What about jurisdiction?"

"No asking. Telling. They'll be glad to know an FBI agent is on scene." Or they would once he convinced them. "The sooner the bureau takes charge of the investigation, the sooner this baby is safely returned."

The door opened, and Deb's husband, Tim, rushed in. A former sailor, he'd served with Jared, and they'd become good friends. Tim now served as a Portland police officer. He carried himself with authority, and Jared didn't worry about leaving his friends and their baby behind with a kidnapper on the loose.

"I heard the announcement," Tim said. "A baby. Man. That's rough. Thankfully I was in the hallway before they locked the center down." He furrowed his forehead. "Glad it's not in our wing, but it's still too close for comfort."

"Agreed," Jared said. "You stay here with Deb. I'm going to take charge and see if I can find this baby before it's removed from the hospital."

"I should help."

"I know you want to, but your place is with Deb and your son right now."

"Yeah." He didn't sound convinced. It wasn't because he didn't love his family, he just possessed the profound sense of duty of a good law enforcement officer.

Jared pounded fists with Tim on his way past. "Pray for the family."

Jared lifted them up in prayer too as he stepped into the empty hallway.

Not a surprise. When a code of any kind was called, hospital staff responded accordingly, taking on any collateral duty as assigned in such a situation. But even before the code announcement was made, the staff and security would've taken positions at key locations in the event that panic ensued. Certain doors would've been locked down, not letting anyone in or out unless it was an emergency.

The Pink Alert was issued at the hospital, but the state police would issue an official AMBER Alert to the media and law enforcement only after a responding officer confirmed that a child had indeed been abducted. If specific additional criteria were met, this officer would call the state, and the alert would be issued.

Jared made a quick scan of the other hallway and noted a uniformed guard outside Room 332. No other movement. Too quiet for such a situation. He would've expected additional support to have arrived by now.

He marched up to the nurses' station located between the two wings. Two harried-looking nurses faced him, eyes cutting every direction as if looking for the kidnapper who had to be long gone.

Jared displayed his credentials. "I need to speak to whoever's in charge."

"That's me," the nurse with graying hair said. "But I'm sure our administrator is on the way up, and he'll take over."

"Who issued the Pink Alert?" he asked.

"All I know is Natalie—Nurse Johnson—called our supervisor. Natalie heard Mrs. Pratt screaming and went in to discover Luna had disappeared while the mother slept and Mr. Pratt had gone to get some coffee. She's still with them."

Babies didn't just go missing. Someone took the newborn. "And we're sure the father didn't, for some odd reason, take the child with him when he went for the coffee?"

"I saw him leave," the younger nurse said. "He had a backpack but wasn't carrying the baby."

"Did he have the backpack when he returned?"

They both nodded.

"And you didn't see the baby being taken?"

They both shook their heads.

"Anyone suspicious hanging around here?"

"I didn't see anyone that didn't look like they belonged," the older nurse said.

"Me, either." The younger woman picked at her nails. "But then we're run off our feet all the time with the patients and trying to staff this desk too. Sometimes it gets too much, and the patients have to come before watching the door."

"So there might've been a time today when there was no one at this desk. Say the time the baby went missing?"

They glanced at each other and nodded. There was a story there, but an agitated male voice came from outside the birthing center's door. It clicked open, taking Jared's attention.

An older man and a young woman stepped in. They had to be staff if they gained access without asking to enter. The older man wearing a gray suit looked like a stuffy business-man. The woman watched the floor as she walked so he couldn't get a look at her face, but her blue suit and high heels weren't all business looking like the man. More young, fresh, and curvy, but she seemed unsteady in the heels.

She looked up.

No! No way! He swallowed a gasp.

What was she doing here of all people?

"That's Mr. Coglin, our administrator," the older nurse said.

"Thanks for your help," Jared managed to utter and tried not to gape at the woman as he stepped into Coglin's path to hold out his ID and introduce himself.

"Roderick Coglin, administrator." He shook hands with Jared.

Jared turned his attention to the woman and forced himself to take a long look. He hadn't been conjuring her up from his past. She was here in the flesh. The woman he'd once loved and left.

"Jared? FBI? Really?" She didn't introduce herself, but she didn't have to.

Bristol Steele, his former summer girlfriend, stood before him. Just as gorgeous as she'd been that summer. All tan and toned. Now a woman. A fine-looking woman.

Words failed him. What could he say?

He resorted to a nod and gave her another once over. A bulge under her suit jacket could only be a sidearm. Did she go into law enforcement after all? She hadn't wanted to, but her family pretty much expected it.

"This is our jurisdiction." She hadn't possessed such confidence the summer when they'd served as counselors together at a Christian middle school camp.

"Our?" he asked.

"Multnomah County Sheriff's Office. I'm a deputy." She met his gaze and held it. "How did the FBI get an agent here so fast?"

"I was visiting a friend in the other wing."

"Someone who just had a baby?"

His tongue seemed glued to the roof of his mouth, so he nodded again.

She lifted perfectly plucked eyebrows over the big brown eyes that had mesmerized him under starry skies for two long months. "You're not here in an official capacity, then?"

Right. Get it together. Your brief romance was how many years ago? Nine, ten? So what? Time didn't seem to matter. She had the same ability to disarm him and turn him into a babbling idiot as she'd done back then.

You're an FBI agent for Pete's sake. Act like one.

He took a breath. "All it'll take is a phone call to my

supervisor, and we'll be offering our services. I'll also be lead agent."

She tilted her head and eyed him. Did she think the FBI didn't have a place in local investigations or was her non-verbal message a nod to their past? He would stick with the present because delving into the past would cause them both a world of hurt again.

"We have a missing baby," he said, putting the self-assurance he'd earned in his four years as an agent into his tone. "We need to throw all resources at it and quickly."

"I agree," Mr. Coglin said. "We're on our way to interview the mother. Please join us."

"Hold up." Jared lifted his hand. "No one goes in that room without booties, Can't risk scene contamination."

Coglin turned to the nurses. "One of you get surgical shoe covers, stat."

The younger nurse scurried away.

"While we wait," Jared said. "We can get started on arranging technical items. We'll need to set up our command post for the initial investigation. Do you have a conference room we can use? One with access to a printer and copier would be best."

"I can arrange that. Excuse me." Coglin dug his phone from his suit pocket and turned his back on them to make the call.

Jared kept an ear out for Coglin's conversation in case it revealed information he might need and gave Bristol a surreptitious look. Her professional suit resembled the ones female agents at his office wore, but her shoes looked like the designer types his sister liked to spend big chunks of her money on, and the heels were much higher than the women's at work. Bristol had been wobbly as she walked, telling him she didn't wear them all that often.

"You're staring," she said.

He liked her blunt approach. "Sorry. I just can't believe it's you."

"Right back atcha." Her tone dropped into the same husky pitch it had taken when they were making out down by the lake, and his heart tripped faster. She didn't appear at all flustered. Or at least not as deeply as he was. Could be because he'd hurt her when he broke things off, and she was still angry.

He sure wouldn't bring that up. He needed to get moving forward on finding out what happened here, and her lack of uniform told him she wasn't on duty. "Are you here as a deputy or some other reason?"

"Other. As of today, my family's company provides security guards for this facility."

"I remember. Steele Guardians, right?"

She nodded. "And before you tell me it's our guard's fault that this baby went missing because we're new at this site, many of our seasoned people are assigned here today." She opened her mouth as if to add something then clamped it closed.

Defensive much? He would circle back to that later, but for now, he would find out more about her and the company charged with guarding this facility. "You work two jobs?"

"I'm leaving the force in three weeks."

One of those. Stay cool. Keep your opinion to yourself.

No one needed to know how he felt about law enforcement officers who leave the job. Too many had jumped ship because of societal pressures. She likely had a good reason to go, and he shouldn't think she was bailing like he'd done when things got serious between them.

"I'm assuming your staff is already reviewing the security footage." He swallowed away the shock of seeing her and tried to impart in his tone that he believed himself in charge.

"They are." She continued to eye him and not in a good way.

So she didn't like him taking charge. If they ended up working together, they would need to have a talk to be sure their past stayed firmly there—in the past.

"The minute we finish with the parents, I'll want to see anything your staff thinks is significant," he said. "My team will also want to review all the feeds for this past week."

"We can make it available *if* you're assigned to the investigation." She shifted on her feet, her ankle giving out, and she had to grab the counter to right herself. Her feet with pink toenails constantly in flip-flops at camp came to mind.

"A week of footage will be a lot to cover," she said.

"Can't be helped," Jared said. "Unless the parents give us conflicting information, we'll start with the typical infant abduction premise."

Bristol gave a sharp nod. "Suspect will be a woman who desires to have her own child. Maybe replacing a child or lost pregnancy. Or to appease a significant other who she thinks will leave her if she can't have a child."

"Exactly," he said, impressed at her knowledge. "A typical abductor makes frequent recon visits to the hospital and birthing center before attempting the abduction. She could be recorded on earlier security footage. We'll start with this week and then go back further if needed. She likely scoped out nearby hospitals too, and we'll request footage from them."

"I'm sure we'll have the baby in hand long before that becomes necessary."

He nodded, but his past experience with abduction proved such a statement could be untrue.

"If you'll excuse me for a moment, I need to make a call." She stepped away, moving well out of earshot.

Did she need a private conversation because she was

trying to hide something from him? His trust in others hadn't been the same for years, but surely he could trust her, couldn't he?

She paced as she talked, her ankles wobbling a few times, and she shoved her hand into that thick mop of hair that he'd always loved running his fingers through. She'd had long hair back when they dated and it remained as thick and shiny.

She abruptly spun and marched back to him.

"Anything wrong?" he asked.

"Maybe." Her sharp tone warned him not to ask for additional information, and his unease grew.

He would press the issue, but Coglin ended his call and rejoined them.

The administrator shoved his phone into his jacket pocket and smoothed the pricey fabric. "You've got our executive room on the first floor. It's private and has all the amenities you'll need. After we talk to the parents, I'll get you a key card. Bristol, yours will work there."

This guy moved fast, something that could make a big difference in finding the baby.

The nurse came back with the shoe covers, and the three of them put them on while she bit her lip and watched. Coglin led them to Room 332, their booties whispering over the tile floor. He entered.

Bristol stopped near the guard. "Glad to see you assigned here, Damon."

"Zeke had me in the atrium, but Teagan repositioned me here."

Bristol gave a firm nod. "Good move on her part. She's in the security center and will remain in charge while I conduct interviews."

"Yes, ma'am."

She cringed. The woman Jared had once known

wouldn't like the formality used by the guard. She'd always been laid back and fun-loving. But she could've changed since they'd been together. She likely had. He sure had. A stint in the Navy and four years with the FBI saw to that.

"You see anything unusual while in the atrium or out here?" she asked.

"No, ma'am." He clamped his mouth closed as if he wanted to say something else but didn't.

Jared would keep that fact in mind for the formal interview that would come later.

She took a good look at him. "Let me know if something comes to mind."

Seemed as if she also thought Damon wanted to talk, but she went into the room, and an image of the last kidnap victim Jared had tried to save came to mind. Ten-day-old Wyatt. Jared drew in a long breath before stepping across the threshold. He had to wash away the pain from Wyatt's family. The pain of losing a lively baby to a kidnapper only to learn he'd died.

Not all the air in the hospital would erase such a memory from Jared's mind.

A gowned woman sat in bed, a pink and green plaid baby blanket clutched in her hands. Her eyes were red and swollen, terror mixed with the tears. She flashed her gaze to them. "Did you find Luna?"

"I'm sorry," Coglin said. "Not yet."

The woman wailed and pressed the blanket against her face as she drew her knees to her chest. The nurse whose badge clipped to her uniform read *Johnson* patted the woman's shoulder.

The man with a bracelet on his wrist, who Jared believed to be the father, stepped forward. "And who are you anyway?"

Coglin and Bristol introduced themselves.

Jared took out his ID and displayed it. "I'm very sorry this has happened to you."

"As am I," Bristol added. "And I'll bring your daughter back to you. I promise."

Rookie mistake. Never promise such a thing ever but even more so when she didn't know if she would be involved in the investigation. In fact, Jared doubted she would be. Not as a patrol deputy. She didn't mention that she worked patrol, but he doubted she was on the job long enough to have reached detective status.

The father eyed Coglin. "How could you let this happen?"

Coglin stiffened. "We have excellent security systems in place. We'll figure out how this happened and find those who did it."

Right. Spoken like an executive protecting his company's assets.

"You better do it quick." Nurse Johnson clasped her hands together. "We've been working to regulate the baby's blood sugar for three days now, and if she's not fed every few hours, it could pose a serious health issue. That's why Mrs. Pratt hasn't been discharged yet. We have to get Luna feeding right."

"Can you tell me more about that?" Jared asked, wanting to get the medical information before he split up the parents and the nurse to be questioned on their own.

Johnson nodded. "Because the baby was a larger size at birth and she arrived late, she burns through sugar at a higher rate and needs to have it replaced more frequently than many babies."

"How big is she?" Bristol asked.

"Eight pounds, eleven ounces," Nurse Johnson answered. "We've needed to give her a few sugar supplements and make sure she feeds often. If she doesn't get the sugar she needs, hypoglycemia can cause a myriad of problems that we don't want to even contemplate. And worse, it might not present with any symptoms at all, and the person who has her might not see it."

"Which means you have to find her fast." The mother's frantic cries cut into Jared like one of the big rotors on the ships he'd been assigned to in his Navy days.

So it was official. They were dealing with a missing baby.

Even worse, a ticking time clock was counting down until the child's health could put her very life in danger.

2

_____

Bristol's gut hurt as she texted Teagan, who remained in the security office manning operations.

Pink Alert confirmed. Get through that video as fast as you can.

On it, came her cousin's reply, and Bristol took just a moment to wrap her head around the situation. Seeing Jared again after nearly nine years? That was shocking enough. But the baby was truly missing, and they were likely looking at a non-family abduction. A child in such a situation should always be considered endangered. Which meant they hadn't a moment to lose.

But she didn't know how much to share with Jared about her company. She'd been shocked when she arrived at the birthing center and didn't find a guard at the door. Sure, Damon was protecting the family's room now, but Aaron King should've been at the main entrance to the center. Probably what Damon wanted to tell her, but kept quiet in front of Jared.

She didn't know Aaron well enough to know if he could be involved in the kidnapping, but her hasty call to Zeke confirmed that he thought highly of Aaron and was shocked that he'd gone AWOL. Zeke had radioed Aaron at the start of the shift to confirm his location and was now looking into where Aaron could be. Maybe he took an unauthorized bathroom break. Or spotted the suspect and took off after her. But Zeke said Aaron would've called in by now.

It was looking like he abandoned his post. Not something she wanted to admit to herself, let alone tell anyone else. She would have no choice after this interview. She had to tell Jared. A baby's life could depend on her truthfulness.

Bristol looked at Coglin. "Can you find rooms for Mr. Pratt and Nurse Johnson so we can interview them separately?"

"Now just a minute." Mr. Pratt took a step forward. "I'm not leaving my wife."

Bristol drew her shoulders back, trying to look taller than her five-foot-nine inches. "I'm sorry, Mr. Pratt, but this isn't optional."

"Why?" He crossed his arms.

Jared opened his mouth to step in.

No way Bristol would let him take over again. She moved closer to Pratt. "We find when witnesses are together during questioning that they inadvertently take on the other person's account of the incident and make it their own. We don't want that to happen here, as we might miss something vital to finding your daughter."

"But I…" Mr. Pratt shrugged.

"You want the best chance of finding Luna, right?" Bristol asked, her tone softer now.

"Yes."

"Then let's not waste valuable time arguing," Jared stated as if he was used to being obeyed. "Mr. Coglin, can you escort them to rooms?"

"Of course."

"Assign rooms next to each other if possible, and I'll tell

our guard to wait outside in case you need anything." Bristol didn't want the pair to think they were under guard when in actuality they were. "Also, please don't call anyone or talk to anyone else."

Nurse Johnson nibbled on her lip. "I'll have to tell the charge nurse that I'm not available."

"We'll do that when we ask her for the empty rooms," Coglin said. "If we have any."

"We do have two rooms closed for pending maintenance requests just down the hall from each other," Nurse Johnson said.

"I don't like to hear we have two rooms out of commission, but they'll work." Coglin stepped off.

Mr. Pratt kissed and hugged his wife, then picked up his backpack.

"I'm sorry, but I need you to leave your pack here." Bristol removed the strap from his shoulder.

He tried to tug it from her hands.

She held firm. "Anything in this room could be considered evidence, and that includes your pack."

"Fine." He released the strap and flung his hands out in exasperation.

The trio exited.

Bristol tried to block out the mother's wailing cries and followed them into the hallway while still holding the backpack. She stopped next to Damon, who was a veteran and long-term employee of Steele Guardians. "I need you to go with them. Mr. Coglin will assign them separate rooms. They said they were close together, but let Teagan know if you can't cover both locations, and she can add someone to your detail. They're not to leave the rooms or talk to each other."

"Yes, ma'am."

She cringed at the formality. No matter how many times

they'd asked Damon to use their first names, he'd continued with the formality that he preferred from his military days.

She texted Zeke and Teagan to let them know of the change and send someone up to guard Mrs. Pratt's room, then unzipped the backpack as she wouldn't search it in front of the mother. The pack didn't feel like it held a baby but Bristol squinted as she looked. Laptop, book, earbuds, and snacks sat in the bottom. She let out a long breath, but then worry set in.

The bag was big enough to fit a newborn inside. Not a living one. No, the child would cry but...

Living. Was there blood in the bag?

She couldn't dig into the bag without wearing gloves, but she saw no obvious sign of blood. Nor any other indication that the baby had been killed, and she wouldn't think about the baby potentially dying until it became a real possibility.

She headed back into the room. Jared remained in place, standing there with his shoulders back, his feet planted in a wide stance, ready to take action instead of calming down the sobbing mother. Beneath his pricey black suit and crisp white shirt, she could imagine him as a sailor before his FBI days. Or at least she thought he'd joined the Navy. He'd left her that summer to go into the Navy, and she assumed that wasn't a lie just to ditch her.

He gave a pointed look at the backpack. She signaled that the bag was clear and received a sharp nod of acknowledgment, his manner equally as pointed. This man was so different from the boy she'd known. Sure, he'd just graduated from college back then, but in so many ways the two of them had still been children. She'd gone on to her sophomore year of college, but she still knew what they'd had together was real and deep.

Her phone rang, and she set the pack on a chair to dig

out her phone. The call came from Teagan. "Tell me you have good news."

"We have something," she said. "A woman carrying a tote bag exited the birthing center via the emergency exit just before the child was reported missing."

"But the alarm didn't go off."

"She or someone else must've disabled it."

Bristol turned her back to the mother and contemplated the news. She lowered her voice. "Not the typical kidnapping then as she would have to study the alarm and have skills to disable it."

"Exactly," Teagan said. "Obviously not a spur-of-the-moment abduction."

Obviously not. "Anything else?"

"The suspect avoided the cameras with her face, so she knew what she was doing. We tracked her to the parking lot but lost her there. We'll want to get this description added to the AMBER Alert."

"I'll be right down."

The door burst open, and Bristol spun, hand on her sidearm. An experienced deputy she recognized as Craig Franz charged in and planted his feet.

His hands drifted to his duty belt. "What are you doing here, Steele?"

She explained along with giving him the details of the kidnapping then introduced everyone. "We were about to ask Mrs. Pratt some questions, but there's security footage needing immediate review."

"You have something?" Mrs. Pratt's face lit up. "Did you find Luna?"

Bristol shook her head. "There's a person of interest on one of the security videos, and we need to check it out. We'll update you the moment we know anything."

"I need a few details before we leave." Franz looked at

Mrs. Pratt. "Do you have a picture of Luna in the clothing she's wearing right now?"

"Yes. Yes. I know my husband took one before he went to get coffee." She grabbed her phone and displayed the picture. "It's hard to see her clothing because she's swaddled, but the blanket is unique. She was too big for the hospital blankets so we used ours. This pink one with bunnies should be very recognizable, right? I mean the colors are so bright."

"Could be." Bristol didn't know how long the kidnapper would keep the baby in her blanket for that very reason. She noted the mother had an iPhone as did she. "Can you AirDrop the photo to me?"

"Sure." Mrs. Pratt quickly sent it.

Bristol confirmed the arrival, and her heart ached at the sight of the precious newborn who was now in someone's hands with the power to harm her. Maybe not because they planned to do her harm, but because of the blood sugar issue.

Franz looked over her shoulder. "I'll need the photo as well."

"Of course."

Jared didn't say anything but gave her a look. She took it to mean she better plan to share the picture with him too. She gave a single nod.

He relaxed his shoulders. "Does your daughter have any distinguishing marks like a birthmark?"

"Yes," Mrs. Pratt said. "A strawberry mark near her shoulder." She tapped the location on her own body.

"And do you have a photo of the birthmark?" Bristol asked.

"I'll send it to you too." Mrs. Pratt tapped her phone's screen.

Bristol accepted that photo as well, and Franz took a

long look. "I'll need the baby's full name, and please spell it for me."

"Luna Louise Pratt," Mrs. Pratt said proudly, then spelled it out.

"And date of birth?"

"She's only three days old." Mrs. Pratt started to cry again.

Bristol wanted to give her a hug but settled for resting her hand on the distraught woman's arm to keep things professional.

"I'll also need to see your driver's license," Franz said.

She pointed at the cabinet in the corner. "My purse is in there with my license."

"I'll get it." Bristol retrieved the large hobo-style bag and handed it to the mother. She dug out her license and gave it to Franz, who took a picture of it.

"You don't think I had something to do with this, do you?" She lifted her chin.

Franz returned the license. "I have to officially establish custody of the child."

He would also need the information for National Crime Information Center Missing Persons File that the detective would create, but better not to mention such a thing to the mother as it would surely set her off.

"We'll get an AMBER Alert issued and be right back." Franz reached for his radio microphone. "Hold positions for further instructions."

He jerked the door open and stepped out but stopped by another deputy standing outside. "Don't leave this post for any reason."

"Roger that."

Jared followed Franz, but Bristol looked at Mrs. Pratt. "We'll be back soon."

"Can my husband or Nurse Johnson come back?"

"Sorry. Not yet." Bristol couldn't leave the father's backpack in the room alone with the mother, so she grabbed it.

Mrs. Pratt raised the baby blanket to her face, and Bristol escaped the room before she broke the professional barrier she needed to keep in place and gave the grieving mother a hug.

"Text me those pictures now." Franz dug out his phone and rattled off his number.

She texted them to him.

"Lead the way to the video, Steele," he said. "As we walk, I'll call my sergeant to get that AMBER Alert going."

She moved as fast as possible while walking in the spikes of death on her feet. Outside the birthing center, she noted Aaron was still AWOL, and that put a hitch in her steps as much as the shoes did.

Stupid shoes. She'd never planned to be walking all day in them. Just to show up for the press conference looking her very best then change into more sensible shoes for the rest of the work day. Of course, in her hurry to leave, she'd left the other pair at home.

She led the men down to the first floor and toward the back of the building to the security office. Franz remained on the phone with his supervisor confirming that this abduction met the AMBER Alert criteria, mainly that the victim was seventeen or younger and was in imminent danger of serious bodily injury or death. And that they had a description of the child and full name and the information would be entered into the National Crime Information Center NCIC system before requesting the alert.

He ended the call as they reached the last hallway. "I'll need to call in the suspect's description after we view the video, and then we'll be good to go on the AMBER Alert."

Teagan buzzed them into the security office and waved her over to a wall of computer monitors being watched by three techs, Zeke overlooking it all in the room that smelled like stale popcorn. Bristol introduced Franz and Jared, and Teagan shook hands, her expression intense as usual.

"Can we see the video?" Bristol asked.

"Zeke has the files queued up." Teagan stepped to an unmanned computer near their supervisor with a buzzed haircut and stern look.

"The woman and a man are the only people who leave the birthing center for the hour before the PINK Alert was issued," Teagan said. "The man wasn't carrying a baby but had a backpack. I don't think he could comfortably put a living baby in the pack and the baby not cry."

Living. There was that word again. The father might've killed the baby and discarded her body. Bristol could have the evidence of such a heinous crime on her back.

"The man is likely the father." She looked at Franz. "This is his backpack. I checked inside for the baby. Nothing and no sign of blood. But I didn't have gloves so couldn't dig deeper."

Franz fisted his hands. "Shouldn't have looked in it at all."

"You would've done the same thing in case the pack held the baby."

"I'm on duty and you aren't." He gave a huff of air and took the backpack. "I'll have another deputy bag this and secure it in his vehicle."

He went to the door and handed the pack to the deputy standing outside, giving strict instructions on how to handle it.

Bristol grabbed Teagan's arm, the soft silk jacket crinkling under her hand, and dragged her aside. "Any word on Aaron King?"

Teagan stepped closer. "No, and he's not answering his

phone. Uncle Hugh is going out to his house to look for him."

"I've held off telling anyone else until we know more. It'll look bad for Steele Guardians."

"I can't imagine anything could look worse for us." As the CEO of the company, Teagan had a vested interest in keeping this quiet too.

"But do I think he's part of the kidnapping?" Bristol asked. "And I need to tell them?"

"There's no evidence of Aaron going missing on video." Teagan curled her hands into fists. "We could wait until we hear back from the search party before reporting it."

"Anything you two want to share with us?" Franz asked as he double-timed it back to the monitors.

"No." Bristol purposefully didn't look at Jared because he knew her well enough to know when she was withholding information.

It's not pertinent yet, she told herself as she strode back to the monitors, but she didn't believe her own words and couldn't keep this under wraps. "Our guard who was on duty at the birthing center door when the baby was taken is missing."

Jared spun to stare at her. "What do you mean missing?"

"He's not at the door and not reachable by phone," she stated plainly. "We have someone out looking for him."

"You think he's helping this woman?" Jared asked. "Or she hurt him?"

"He's a good and long-term guard with us," Zeke said between clenched teeth. "If he's missing, something's happened to him."

Jared rubbed a hand over his jaw. "When did you last hear from him?"

"I check in with the guards via radio at the start of every shift. He was at his station when I radioed him at eight."

"Does he appear on video?" Jared asked.

Zeke shook his head. "The camera by the birthing suite has a narrower focus so it catches a close-up view of the people arriving. We don't see him on the other video either."

"So you have no proof other than him responding to your radio call," Jared said. "Was it a conversation or just an affirmative answer?"

"Affirmative."

"So someone could've impersonated him," Jared said.

"I suppose so, but..." Zeke's shoulders slumped.

"Or maybe he was there, and this woman paid him to look the other way and then he took off," Jared said. "In that case, he would want to avoid the cameras."

"He's not the type to take a bribe," Zeke said, not sounding as convinced now. "But then my days as a cop say anyone's susceptible to a bribe if the price is right."

Jared locked gazes with Bristol. "Tell us the minute you learn anything about him, and I mean the minute."

She nodded.

"And that goes for both of us." Franz turned back to Zeke. "Let's see what you have."

Zeke started a video playing. A woman who stood around five-six and wore a large parka with the hood up entered the birthing center stairwell at nine a.m. and carried an oversized tote bag.

"Winter jacket in August is the first clue that something's off," Jared said. "Conceals her face from everyone and hides anything on her person."

"Agreed." Bristol focused on the woman's hands. "I'm pretty sure that's the tip of a gun barrel in her right hand."

"It is." Jared's tone was deep and ominous sounding.

Teagan looked at Bristol. "Can you tell us anything about the gun?"

Bristol shook her head. "Not without enhancing the video."

Jared cast a questioning look at Bristol.

"She's really into firearms of any kind," Teagan said. "You're just as likely to find her at the firing range as anywhere else."

Jared's eyebrow went up as he studied her, but he didn't say anything. Her father and grandad taught all the siblings to shoot at a young age, so when she'd known Jared, she could proficiently handle a gun. But she didn't gain a real interest in weapons until her time at the police academy.

"The tote bag's easily big enough for a newborn," Teagan said.

"Even a nearly nine-pounder like Luna," Bristol added.

"The woman's taking a huge risk that the child could cry," Franz said. "Unless—"

"Don't say it." Jared curled his hands into fists. "She's alive until we have evidence to say otherwise. And I don't even want to contemplate that the baby was drugged so she would sleep. That could go horribly wrong."

"Maybe not if we're looking at a medical professional here," Franz said. "Which wouldn't be farfetched at all."

"Or it could be more simple," Teagan said. "The swaying movement of the bag could be keeping the baby happy."

"Or the bag is holding something else, and the woman has the baby in a body carrier hidden by the jacket." Bristol hoped she was right, but she wasn't a baby whisperer. Her only experience with kids had been as a camp counselor for middle schoolers, and her knowledge of babies was what she'd learned in a few babysitting gigs.

"Switch to the feed at the building's rear exit," Teagan said.

Zeke changed the video.

The woman stepped out, her head still down, and

hurried toward the parking lot then disappeared out of the camera's range.

"We hope to catch her on another feed." Zeke shook his head. "We're looking at the exits now to locate a vehicle. So far no luck."

"I told the deputy who's securing the backpack about this location," Teagan said. "He has deputies checking the area."

"What about the cameras where she would've entered the birthing center?"

"Nothing," Zeke said. "Looks like she came in through the stairwell. We're reviewing all footage for a woman in this coat, but cameras don't cover the stairwells."

"She could've carried the coat in the bag so it didn't draw attention to her," Bristol said.

Zeke nodded. "We're looking for the bag too, but people carry tote bags in and out of hospitals all the time so it might be a challenge. Also, she could've stashed the coat and bag in the stairwell days ago." Zeke planted his feet wide. "We'll keep going until we have her."

"Then all we have is a woman about five-six and wearing a blue parka exiting the birthing center at nine a.m.," Bristol said. "No description of her face at all."

"It's *something* to go on, though," Jared said.

"I'll call it in." Franz used his phone to update his supervisor with the woman's description then quickly ended the call. "Calling the state for the AMBER Alert."

The Oregon State Police were responsible for statewide coordination of Oregon's AMBER Alert program and issued the alert. All calls came through their special number which rolled to the tip line for the local law enforcement agency.

Bristol turned her attention back to Zeke and Teagan. "Start looking for when this woman entered the hospital."

"Already on it," Zeke said. "But we could get through the footage faster if we have more people looking."

"We'll make that a priority," Jared said, as if he planned to be working the investigation.

"I can get the rest of my team over here in thirty minutes." Bristol looked at Franz. "That is if you're okay with them reviewing the feed."

"That's really up to the detective who takes over, but I don't want to waste valuable time. Everyone you'll assign is current or former law enforcement, so it should be fine." He lifted his shoulders. "Better to ask for forgiveness later."

Bristol turned to Teagan. "Text everyone and get whoever's available headed this way."

Jared looked like he wanted to argue, but didn't. Since he wasn't officially involved, he couldn't muster the needed resources any faster, and she knew he wanted this baby found.

"Let's get a look at the father on video and check his timing out," she said to move them along.

Zeke tapped the screen. "Here he is leaving the birthing center at eight-fifteen. We can track him to the restroom and then to the cafeteria."

"He seems pretty casual and laidback," Bristol said.

"Hard to tell from the footage, but you're right," Jared said. "He's not looking over his shoulder or acting hinky, but he might just be a good actor."

Franz grabbed his radio again. "I need a deputy to cordon off the men's restroom on third floor west, just outside the birthing center."

"Deputy Pilsner," came a female's voice. "I'm nearby, and I got it."

"Roger that," Franz said.

"Let's see the rest of the footage for the father," Jared said.

Zeke changed the camera angle again. "He returns at seven minutes after nine, seven minutes after the woman leaves out the back exit. And I assume after the wife wakes up to find the baby gone."

"Does his pack look empty?" Bristol asked.

"Compare the feeds," Jared said.

Zeke ran them side by side.

"Not sure if I'd say empty," Jared said. "But the shape is different."

Her heart racing, Bristol looked at the men. "We need to get back upstairs and search that restroom now!"

Jared approached the bathroom, and his gut tightened down like the strings on his favorite guitar. The horror of finding Wyatt, a baby who hadn't survived his kidnapping, haunted him even two years after the investigation went wrong. Haunted his dreams and his waking hours too.

But he would do his job and follow Franz and Bristol through that door.

He erased little Wyatt's face from his mind and stepped into the room that held a fresh odor of orange cleaner. Franz was already checking the stalls, his bootie-covered feet rustling over the tile floors as he rushed from one to the next and left the stall doors clanging against the walls. Bristol hurled brown paper towels from the nearest garbage can to the floor, but the pile on the floor was slim.

Jared went to the back trash can and moved a couple of paper towels with his gloved hands. The space had been cleaned at some point or hadn't been used much as the can held very little.

"Nothing here." Bristol crossed to the door. "Cleaning

log posted here says the crew was here at seven fifty-five. So close to when Pratt stopped in."

"Explains the empty trash cans," Jared said.

"Nothing in the stalls." Franz frowned. "We'll still have forensics process the room. See if they can find any blood or other sign of the baby."

"Where would Pratt ditch the body other than here?" Bristol asked. "Various cameras tracked him straight to the cafeteria. And he sure wouldn't take the baby out in a public area."

"We need Zeke to look at the video outside this room again," Jared said. "See if anyone came in here after the father and could've carried the baby out."

"You mean he left the child in here and had arranged for someone else to take her," Franz clarified.

"Yes."

"Their timing would have to be exact or they would risk someone else finding her," Bristol said. "But I'll call Zeke."

Jared watched her every move as she ripped off her gloves, got out her phone, and explained their need. "I'll hold while you look, Zeke."

She tapped her foot, her expression tight with the same horror that was churning Jared's breakfast. Tim had asked Jared to stop at Deb's best-loved restaurant and arrive at the hospital early with her favorite quiche, thick slabs of bacon along with hearty wholegrain toast, the tangy smell alone mouthwatering. Of course, he couldn't resist eating the fluffy toast with the crispy bacon.

What Jared wouldn't give to go back and eat his normal egg and toast for the morning. Even better, go back to keep this baby from being abducted.

"Okay, thanks." Bristol shoved her phone into her pocket. "No one entered the bathroom between Pratt's departure and our arrival."

"Okay, so doesn't look like he took the child," Franz said.

"But we can't rule him out," Bristol said. "He could've simply left the birthing room so the woman could come and take the baby. Maybe he even was the one who disabled the door for her."

"All very good possibilities." Jared met her gaze. "Time to question the parents and especially the father."

3

Bristol was thankful when Franz got a call before they entered the mother's room as it gave Bristol time to make a quick phone call. She excused herself and hurried to the end of the hallway where she could still keep an eye on Jared and Franz, dialing her father on the way. As the founder of Steele Guardians, along with her uncle Hugh, her dad was still a vital part of the company. Even as much as she didn't want to ask for his help, she needed his connections. As a former Multnomah County detective, he had contacts she couldn't begin to access on her own, and she needed him to work a miracle for her.

"I'm on my way to the hospital to help review security footage, but you need more help, Baby Girl?" he asked.

Just like him to use his nickname for her even if she was at work, but the love oozing from his tone brought tears to her eyes. She had to fend them off for now. "A task force is forming, and the hospital account is mine and my responsibility, but there's no way a patrol deputy will be allowed on the task force. So I hoped you would call in some favors and get me on it."

He didn't answer right away and her heart fell as she knew what was coming.

"I don't know if it's possible," he said, confirming her thoughts. "We're talking kidnapping here, and like you said, it would be very unusual to have a patrol deputy involved."

"But I'd be an asset to the team. I know everything about the investigation so far. And about the hospital security and can get information in an instant that others might need a warrant to obtain."

"As lead on this contract with the hospital, you also have a conflict of interest," he pointed out as she thought he might.

"Not really a conflict. The hospital and I both want the same thing as the task force wants. To find this baby and find her fast." She waited for her dad to speak but he didn't say anything. "Please, Dad. We're talking about a newborn who might have a health issue. We have to do everything we can and do it quickly."

"Okay," he said, but it was with reluctance. "I'll make a few calls and get back to you."

Hope burgeoning in her heart, she rejoined Franz and Jared, who watched her as if he expected her to share her conversation, but she wouldn't. Not yet. Maybe never actually, as she wouldn't want him to think she got her slot on the task force due to her sphere of influence. Even if that was exactly how she got it, she'd like him to think it was because she brought much-needed skills to the team. Her confidence still stung from the way he could so easily walk away from her, and she didn't need him questioning anything about her life.

"It wasn't about the missing guard," she said to him to get him to quit staring at her.

It worked as he looked away, but not before she caught his skeptical expression.

Franz finished his call, and he led them into Mrs. Pratt's room. She took one look at them, and her crying amped up. Her deep wailing cries cut Bristol to the quick. She couldn't just let the distraught mother suffer alone. Bristol crossed the room and handed her the tissue box. Bristol wanted to assure the mother that they would find her child, but Bristol had already let the heat of the moment get to her and made the mistake of saying she would find the baby. She couldn't give the parents false hope again.

"Thanks." Mrs. Pratt blew her nose.

"I'm so sorry, Mrs. Pratt," Bristol said. "Is Luna your first child?"

"Sonya. It's Sonya. Please." She swiped at her nose again and took jerky breaths.

Bristol would love to call this mother by her first name, but formality was required in such a situation. Bristol would ignore the request, and she knew Jared and Franz would do the same.

"Luna's our first." She rubbed the baby blanket against her face. "Do you have kids?"

"No, I'm not married."

Mrs. Pratt swung her gaze to Jared. "And you?"

"No, but my close friend just had a baby. He was born last night, and I see how fiercely Tim and his wife already protect the little guy."

"I didn't know what it meant to love so deeply until Luna was born." Mrs. Pratt dabbed at her eyes. She took a few struggling breaths, and her body relaxed.

Franz turned to them. "First, I want to say how sorry I am that this happened. I'm a father myself, and I can't imagine the pain you're going through."

"Just find her," Mrs. Pratt said.

His kindness impressed Bristol, but she also understood the mother's need to move forward and quickly.

"I know you've told this story a few times now," Franz said. "But please tell me what happened."

She blew out an exasperated breath. "My husband went for coffee, and I took a nap. I woke up and Luna was gone. I started screaming for help. Nurse Johnson came in and called security."

"Did you see anyone in your room?" Franz moved closer.

She shook her head almost violently. "I didn't sleep at all last night and really zonked out."

"Do you have any idea of who might want to take Luna?" Bristol asked.

Mrs. Pratt shook her head. "Only our family knows about her. Oh and I posted a picture on Facebook so my friends do too."

"Is the photo public or private?" Jared asked.

She shrugged. "I don't really understand all of that."

"Would you look it up on your phone and show me?" he asked.

She grabbed her phone from her bedside table and tapped the screen before handing it to Jared. "It's set to public status. Which means anyone can see this picture. I'll show you how to change it to private then you need to modify your settings for all of your photos in the future."

Her face paled. "Do you think someone saw this and that's why Luna was taken?"

"Could be." So he was hesitant to come right out and tell the mother that she might have messed up. Showed the same empathy she remembered him having that ill-fated summer.

"We'll want full access to your social media accounts," Franz said.

"I only do Facebook but whatever you need." Mrs. Pratt took her phone back from Jared.

Franz handed her a notepad and pen. "Jot down your

40

login and password. And don't change the password until we clear you to do so."

Eyes narrowed, she scribbled on the pad and handed it back. "I can't believe I could've caused Luna to be taken."

"We don't know that," Bristol said. "For now, let's just focus on the details we do know."

"Yes. Yes. That would be better."

"What about other family members?" Bristol asked. "Might one of them have taken Luna?"

"It's only my and Kevin's parents. We're both only children and so were they. Plus, one great-grandfather who's in a nursing home with dementia. I doubt anyone has even told him about Luna yet."

"Have Luna's grandparents visited?"

"Last night." Mrs. Pratt gripped the bedding, her fingers tight and turning white.

"I'll need their contact details." Franz held out his notepad again.

The terrified mother snatched it from his hands as if she was relieved to have something to do.

"Add the names of any close friends who could've taken the baby," Franz added.

"No one I know would do that." She poked her chin in the air at Franz, then started writing and glanced at her phone a few times, likely looking for contact information.

"I just want to clarify," Bristol said. "Your husband wasn't here when you discovered Luna was gone."

"He came back a few minutes after I found her missing. At first, I thought I was dreaming, but then I pinched my arm to make sure I was awake and started screaming. That's when Nurse Johnson came in."

"Do you have any reason to suspect Mr. Pratt might have taken Luna?" Franz asked gently.

"Of course not." Mrs. Pratt slammed the notepad on the

bed. "He's a fine upstanding Christian man. He would never do that."

"I'm sorry, ma'am, but we have to ask," Franz said, but his statement came off as placating, not as if he believed it. "What about the nurses who've been caring for you and Luna? Was there anything off about any of them?"

"No." She shook her head violently. "They're wonderful. So helpful as we struggled to get Luna feeding right and keep her sugar levels up."

"And you haven't seen any strangers lurking in the hallway or cleaning and maintenance staff acting oddly?" Jared asked.

"I haven't left the room since I arrived and no one but Kevin, our parents, and the nurses and doctors have been in the room. And before you ask, no, our parents weren't acting weird. Just grandparents in love with their first grandchild. Now all of it is ruined." She shoved the notepad and pen at Franz. "Now tell me what you know."

He closed his notepad. "We have a female, about five-six, wearing a blue winter parka leaving via the emergency exit during the time your husband was gone from the room."

"Was she carrying Luna?"

"She had a large tote bag." Bristol stopped there to let Mrs. Pratt draw her own conclusion.

"She put Luna in a bag?" Mrs. Pratt's tone shot up like a bottle rocket.

"Maybe or maybe she had a baby wrap or carrier under the big jacket," Bristol said. "Or she might not be the person who kidnapped Luna. We don't have a lot of details at this point."

"Is there a woman in your lives who might've recently lost a child?" Franz asked.

"Oh, I get it. Someone who wants to replace her lost

child." Mrs. Pratt wrapped her arms around her abdomen. "I don't know anyone like that."

"You're sure?" Jared asked. "Maybe a coworker or someone at church that doesn't come readily to mind."

Mrs. Pratt shook her head. "No. No one."

"How about someone desperate for a child who can't have one?" Jared asked.

She shook her head.

Franz pocketed the notepad and pen. "I don't have any other questions for you."

"Good." Mrs. Pratt glared at him. "Stop wasting time and go find her."

Bristol stepped forward. "I know this might seem like a waste of time, but we have to know where to begin to look. Asking questions of the people closest to a missing child often provides the direction to proceed."

"Okay, well, good. Please just find her and do so quickly." She folded her hands and closed her eyes as if she were praying.

Bristol turned and stepped into the hallway, pausing outside the door to wait for Jared and Franz.

Franz looked at her, then Jared. "Before we talk to the father, I'm going to run a quick check on the Pratts for any priors and find out which detective caught this investigation. Once they get here, it likely means this is the end of the road for the two of you."

"Not for me." Jared got out his phone and stepped away.

Franz leaned down to his mic but kept checking around the area.

Bristol looked at the pair of men, uncertain what to say. Jared could likely end up being involved in the investigation. Probably not as the supervisor or even investigative coordinator. She suspected those jobs would remain in-house at

Multnomah County, and he would fulfill an investigator role, working tasks assigned to him.

At least he would be on the team. She didn't see herself being allowed to work the investigation at all unless her dad pulled out that miracle.

Oh, please. I have to. Just have to.

Did God even hear her? She'd basically turned her back on Him when Thomas was murdered. Why should God listen to her now?

Because a precious baby was missing, that was why.

She'd seen that baby's face in the photographs and could easily imagine her being held by someone who might want to do her harm.

What a horrible thing. Horrible, horrible thing.

Bristol needed to see this baby reunited with her parents. Of course she did, but she also had to protect the reputation of her family's business. If any blame were placed on the company, it could sink them.

All her fault. She'd talked her dad and uncle into taking on the hospital. If they lost the business because of this kidnapping, how did one live with destroying something so important to the people she loved? All the while doing it with a former boyfriend looking on. One who had devastated her heart.

Jared stepped out of earshot but kept Franz and Bristol in sight while he dialed his supervisor. As Assistant Special Agent in Charge of the FBI's Portland field office, Nathan Adair was a real taskmaster. Didn't matter right now. Jared could be persuasive when he wanted to be. And he wanted to be. Not only to find this baby, but to catch up with Bristol on her life. *If* she would even talk to him about anything personal.

"Adair," the ASAC answered, his voice as sharp as the creases he usually pressed into his clothing.

"Wolfe here."

"Let me guess. You're calling about the kidnapping?"

So he'd already heard. Not surprising. At least not fully. The FBI was immediately notified of any kidnapping. Even so, this was quick.

Jared brought his supervisor up to speed on his situation. "I'd like to offer our services to the county."

"Agreed."

Wow. Adair's easy acquiescence was unexpected.

"But it will be just that," Adair continued. "An offer. The county is quite capable of handling this investigation. If they refuse our offer, we'll back off."

"Understood." *But not necessarily agreed with.* "I'd also like to take lead on the investigation for our agency."

"Don't get ahead of yourself. They might not agree." Adair let silence linger on the phone. "I'll make the offer and get back to you."

The call ended, and Jared took a moment to get his thoughts organized before rejoining the others. Bristol had made a call to check in with her security staff, but her eyes burned into his back the whole time.

What was she thinking about him? Surely, she didn't trust him. Not one iota. He got that and understood. But it hurt. He wanted to be the opposite of his parents. To be a person everyone could rely on. Except for leaving Bristol in a lurch, he had been. But she would likely never see that.

Determined to prove she was wrong, he headed toward her, but slowed. The intensity flashing in her eyes caught him off guard. Sure, she'd been watching him, but wow! The woman could stare a guy down. He'd never experienced such a force coming from her in the past. Probably because it had been love at first sight with them, and she had no need to stare him down. But she wasn't in love with him now. That was for sure.

He dredged up a tight smile and stopped in front of her.

"Your agency on board?" she asked.

"Eavesdropping?" he asked.

"I couldn't hear you, but I'd be calling my supervisor if I were you and wanted to work the investigation."

He had to give her credit for her sharp instinct. She'd asked good questions so far too and remained cool and in control when many officers would get excited and make mistakes. She was more flighty in her younger days, but seemed quite capable now. Patrol officer or not, she might be helpful in the investigation. Not that he would suggest it. Not with their past and when she was also a distraction to him. Those gorgeous brown eyes fixed on him and pursed full lips were bringing back all kinds of thoughts of kissing her.

He cleared his throat and shoved the thoughts out with it. "You know the FBI often partners on kidnapping cases and the odds are good that I'll be involved."

"I do." She arched a brow. "We'll see if that happens here."

Why wouldn't she cut him some slack? Because he basically bailed on her, telling her he didn't want a long-distance relationship while he was learning his way around the Navy. Still, he liked that she had the guts to stand up to him now. Liked it a lot. Not that he would admit it to her.

Franz disconnected his call. "Detective Hale is on his way." He paused and stared at each of them in turn. "I don't want either of you to argue if he tosses you out when he gets here."

"Hale caught the investigation?" Bristol asked.

"You know him?" Jared asked.

Bristol nodded. "He's sharp and a real team player. And he has high case closure rates."

"Yeah, he's one of the good ones," Franz said. "Let's get to the father."

Franz led them down the hallway to the nurse's station. The nurse on duty directed them to Mr. Pratt's and Nurse Johnson's rooms. Damon stood between this room and the one just down the hall where Nurse Johnson had been sequestered. Pratt's door held a maintenance request sign, and Franz pushed it open.

Jared followed the deputy into the birthing suite where Pratt was housed. The space looked much like the room where Luna had disappeared from but was decorated in blue instead of yellow.

Mr. Pratt came to his feet from an easy chair in the corner. "Did you find her?"

"I'm sorry," Franz said. "Not yet."

Pratt slammed a fist into his palm. "What's taking so long?"

"We're still gathering facts and following leads," Franz said. "Were you having coffee when Luna was taken?"

He nodded. "In the main cafeteria."

"What kind of coffee did you have?" Bristol asked.

"Beg your pardon?" He gaped at her.

"The coffee. What kind?" She didn't wilt under his gaze, raising Jared's respect for her law enforcement skills even more.

"A mocha." He suddenly clenched his hands as if trying to control himself from punching her. "Oh, I get it. You're asking because you don't think I was having coffee. You think I took my own daughter." His eyes narrowed into seething slits.

Bristol winced this time, but in fairness to her, the harsh look would have Jared wincing too if fired in his direction.

"I don't think that, sir." Her tone was even and composed. "But it's our job to ask questions to rule things out as well as gain knowledge."

Pratt relaxed his hands. "I got a large mocha and sat at a table by the window. I shouldn't have left Sonya, but I needed a break from the crying. Luna's having trouble nursing, and she's been kind of fussy. This is all my fault. I shouldn't have gone." His voice broke.

Bristol took a step closer to Pratt. "Let's try not to place fault and concentrate on details that could help us locate her."

Pratt's shoulders sagged. "What else do you need to know?"

"Give us a play-by-play of your movements after you left the room," Jared said. "And describe what and who you saw."

"Sonya fell asleep, Just like the nurses told her—sleep when Luna sleeps. I tiptoed out. Stopped in the can outside the center. I didn't want to use the one in the room and risk waking them. Then I bolted for the cafeteria. I got the mocha and set a timer on my phone so I didn't stay more than fifteen minutes."

"What about anything unusual you might've seen?" Franz asked.

"Nada. I mean, I was focused on my mission, and I can have tunnel vision. Get there. Get it done. Get back."

"You must've seen something while you drank the coffee?" Jared said.

"Watched out the window. Honestly wished I was out on the golf course. But golf is out of the question for now."

"You're giving it up?" Bristol asked.

"For now. While Luna needs a lot of attention."

"And how does that make you feel?" Jared asked.

Pratt flashed his gaze up to Jared. "Oh, I get it. You think

I want to go golfing, so I kidnapped my own kid. That's just ridiculous."

"You didn't answer my question," Jared said, keeping his focus.

Pratt gritted his teeth. "I love to golf so I'm disappointed. But having a daughter more than makes up for it."

The guy was astute and saw through all of their questions, but Jared still believed him. And if he'd taken the child it would be on camera.

"Give me timeframes for your morning." Franz took out his notepad.

"Don't quote me on exacts. These are all about when I think things happened." Pratt rattled off times and what he'd been doing.

Jared noted the information in his phone, and Bristol seemed to be doing the same thing. They would set up a timeline for the events, including the parents, nurses, doctors or anyone else who came into their room.

"What do you do for a living, Mr. Pratt?" Jared asked.

"I'm an electrician, why?"

"Just collecting details." Jared worked hard to hide his interest over the fact that Pratt had the skills to disarm the door.

"Has Luna had any visitors?" Franz asked.

Pratt nodded. "Last night. Both sets of her grandparents."

His statement concurred with his wife's but then they could both be lying, and Jared would keep an open mind. He hated to think any parent would harm their own child, but sadly it wouldn't be the first time a child had been kidnapped or died at the hands of their parent.

Jared placed his full attention on the man. "Do you have any idea who might've taken her?"

"No." He shook his head. "That's all I've been thinking

49

about while I've been sitting here. Only our family and close friends even know she was born."

"Your wife posted on Facebook," Bristol said.

"Well yeah, but that's just our friends or people we know."

Jared didn't want to be the one to tell him that it was a public post, so he didn't. No point in driving a wedge between them when it wasn't necessary. At least not yet.

"Is there anyone in your world who lost a child recently?" Bristol asked.

"Not that I know of."

"At work, maybe?" She continued to watch him.

"Again, not that I know of."

Franz's phone rang, and he quickly answered. "Be right out."

He looked at Jared and Bristol. "Detective Hale. He's on his way up."

"We should go meet him," Jared said, as talking to the detective for the first time shouldn't be done in front of the father.

Franz looked at Pratt. "Stay put until we dismiss you."

Franz headed for the door.

"Will Hale be in charge?" Pratt asked.

"Likely," Franz replied.

Not if I can help it, Jared thought and started for the door where he hoped to hear from his supervisor before Detective Hale tried to take over the investigation.

4

Bristol's phone rang. She spotted her dad's name. The detective stood at the nursing station, phone to his ear, so she quickly answered.

She lowered her tone. "I can't talk now."

"You're in," he said.

In! She was in! She resisted whooping for joy. There was nothing joyful about a baby missing. Not even if Bristol got the chance to help find the child and restore the Steele family's reputation.

"Thanks," she said. "I won't disappoint you."

"Not in a million years, but Baby Girl, be sure you ask us for help if you need it. I know you can't share the investigation with us, but there are still things we could do if you need it."

"Thanks. Again." She ended the call when she wanted to tell him how much she loved him and really thank him. But if anyone heard her, it would come across as unprofessional when her greatest desire right now was to be the consummate professional. And that included hiding any residual feelings she might have for Jared. She'd thought she'd put all of those emotions behind her, but had she?

Argh. Stop thinking about him and start thinking about working with the task force.

If she was going to be on the task force, she needed to dress the part. With her sisters, cousins, and dad working on the video, she tapped in a text to her grandad and asked him to stop by the house to pick up her uniform, boots, and duty belt. He agreed and would text her the minute he arrived.

She strode down the hallway under Jared's watchful gaze.

"Again, not about the guard." She stowed her phone just as the detective spun in her direction. He was short, muscular, had a shaved head and a stare made of iron. He wore khaki pants and a blue Multnomah County Sheriff's Office polo shirt and windbreaker.

He shoved his phone into his pocket with extreme force and eyed her. "I don't know who you know but don't make that person regret putting you on the task force."

"I won't." She held out her hand as Jared's appraising stare burned into her. "I'm Deputy Bristol Steele, by the way, and this is Special Agent Jared Wolfe. And you must be Detective Hale." She worked hard not to come across sounding like a smart-aleck, but after her words came out she could see where the detective might mistake them.

"Oh, I know who you both are." Hale waved off her hand. "Wolfe's on the team too. But then, he has the skills and experience, and I appreciate that partnership."

A flash of surprise lit Jared's face. So he didn't know he'd made the team.

Hale planted hands on his hips. "My LT, Allen Mills, will serve as the task force supervisor along with ASAC Adair. Mills is on his way over now. Since my department is taking all of the calls from the AMBER Alert, I'll serve as search coordinator." He pinned his focus on Jared. "You'll take the investigative coordinator position."

Jared gave a firm nod. If he was glad for or surprised by the leadership position assigned to him, he didn't show it. "I already have the hospital administrator setting up a command center on the first floor and will get a keycard for you and your LT."

"You go ahead and do that. To save time, I'll have Franz update me, and then we'll meet in the command center to determine needed resources." Hale looked at Bristol and opened his mouth.

"I'd like to assist on the investigative detail," Bristol said, before she was tasked with searching or running down the many false leads that would come in on the tip line. Sure that meant working with Jared, but that's where the real action would be.

Hale looked at Jared. "You okay with that?"

"Deputy Steele has proven her skills, and I'd be glad for her help."

Bristol struggled to hide her surprise, but Hale didn't. His eyes widened, and then he shook his head as if he believed she was a liability. Fine. She would work even harder to prove her worth.

"C'mon, Steele. Let's get those keycards and the room set up." Jared marched off without waiting for Hale's dismissal or for her to agree.

Not that she had to agree to anything he said. He was, for all practical purposes, her supervisor going forward, and she had to do what he told her to do. And he was Hale's equal too, only reporting to Hale's lieutenant and his own supervisor.

On the way to the elevator, she called Coglin and asked him to meet them at the command center in case there were additional items they needed in the room.

"Thanks for calling him." Jared pointed at the elevator doors that were splitting open with a groan.

She whisked past Jared, catching his scent of sandalwood and musk. It would be no hardship working with this man, but she had to be on guard for his ability to distract her. It wouldn't do to be lost in the sight of those dark eyes when she should be working on finding this precious baby.

His phone rang even with the doors closing. For security reasons, she didn't want the hospital to have down spots in the event of an emergency just like this one and wanted her guards to have phone coverage in as many spaces as possible. So before signing a contract with the hospital, she'd recommended the installation of antennas in the elevator shafts to give a stronger signal inside the elevator cars. They'd complied.

"Sir." Jared leaned back against the wall, acting casual but his jaw was set as he listened.

"The detective is here, and he informed me." Jared ran his hand through his thick dark chocolate hair. "I'll have a list of needed resources and agents to you within the hour."

Jared ended his call. "My supervisor. Nathan Adair, Assistant Special Agent in Charge of the Portland field office. He will personally coordinate allocation of assets and additional agents. Means we won't have any downtime."

"Will you have your pick of agents?"

"In as much as they can be freed up from current assignments, yes." He stared ahead at the wall. "My second in command will be Reed Rice, a seasoned agent who's on the violent crimes squad with me."

Perfect. Someone she knew. "Reed's great."

"You know him?"

She nodded. "My family has worked with his wife, Sierra, at The Veritas Center on a few investigations lately."

"Reed told me all about the Center and how they handle forensics for law enforcement. Reed might be biased, but he said they can be counted on to provide the latest in procedures and tests in all areas of forensics from trace evidence to firearms."

Bristol nodded. "It would be great to use them."

"They'll have faster turnarounds," Jared said. "So I'll recommend we do use them. Starting with processing the Pratts' room."

"Your supervisor will approve that?"

"He said anything I need, and I need." He grinned.

The sweet grin was so reminiscent of the ones he'd shared with her at the camp, sending her heart somersaulting. The elevator dinged on the first floor, and she all but raced out of the car before she gave away her feelings.

They strode together across the large atrium with a fountain flowing, the rushing water sound calming in the past, but not today. She matched Jared's long strides step-for-step, but it wasn't easy in the spiky heels. She only wore heels of any kind when forced and hoped her grandad got here soon if she didn't want to face-plant in front of Jared. Equally as important, since she was officially on the team, she should be wearing her uniform.

"I'll bring in a few of our geek agents to review any leads on the security footage and enhance any photos that can be cleaned up. Means I'll want access to the feed in the command center." He skirted around a toddler who raced ahead of his mother.

The mother gave an apologetic look. Bristol smiled at her and wanted to tell her to be glad she had her child with her, but held her tongue. She looked up at Jared. "My cousin Teagan can arrange the video."

"I'd like to know more about Steele Guardians. More than you told me in the past, that is."

She'd expected he would ask, maybe for information only or to try to pin the blame on them. "What do you remember?"

"Just that your dad and uncle founded it after retiring from law enforcement careers. Your dad was a detective, right?"

"Right, and Uncle Hugh was a sergeant before they retired. They're now ready to fully retire, and my sisters and cousins are taking over for them. As I said, I'll be joining them in three weeks. Teagan is the company COO and has been in place since my brother was murdered."

"Murdered?" He shot her a look. "Oh, man. Thomas was murdered? That's awful. I'm so sorry. Did it happen on the job?"

"No. At his home." She didn't want to say more than that or with her emotions already raw she might start crying. "Three of us still work in law enforcement and three with the company."

"I remember your dad and uncle required five years' service in law enforcement before joining the company so you'd get a feel for how criminals act."

"Correct."

"Your insights today seem to bear that out." He glanced at her. "Your suspect questions and video interpretation says you think just like one."

"Thanks, I think. I mean I've never been complimented about something like that." She wrinkled her nose, a habit she needed to break if she wanted to come across as a hard-nosed deputy during this investigation.

"Trust me, in this case it's a compliment." He trained that smile on her again.

She looked away before it could capture her full attention and turned down the corridor leading to the conference room.

"And you're in charge of this account?" he asked.

She nodded. "The first one I signed, so in addition to finding Luna, I have a vested interest in this."

"I'll need a list of your guards on duty today."

"I'll make one when we get to the command center."

"I'll be present at all the guard interviews and you won't be involved."

"I would expect nothing less."

"And you're sure you haven't heard anything about the missing guard?"

"I'm sure."

Coglin stood outside the door, worrying his hands together. "Any news?"

"Nothing actionable," Jared said. "I'll be heading up the investigative piece of this case. I'll take a look at the room and let you know if we need anything."

Bristol followed the men into the large space set up with a long conference table and plush chairs. Whiteboards hung on the wall and projection equipment along with a computer, copier and printer sat at the far end of the room. A floral air freshener scented the air.

Jared strode to the projector. "I'm assuming this is functioning, and we're free to use it."

"It is, and you are," Coglin said.

"Does the copier or printer require a password?" Jared asked.

"Both." Coglin picked up a sheet of paper from the table and handed it to Jared. "These are the passwords you'll need and the directions to use the machines and access our secured network."

Jared took the paper. "Thank you. We'll also need keycards for additional staff who will be joining us very soon."

"I'd like to issue picture IDs. The staff is on edge, and it'll help ease their concerns if they see the ID clipped to your clothes."

"We can't waste time going to your photographer. If you can bring him here, we'll be good with it."

Coglin nodded. "Everything is electronic now so that won't be a problem. I'll have my staff on standby."

"We'll be holding an informational meeting soon," Jared said. "A perfect time to handle the cards."

"We can make that work." Coglin waved a hand at the far wall holding a small refrigerator, sink, microwave, and baskets of snacks. "Water and drinks are in the refrigerator, and as you can see there are snacks on the counter. I'll have staff replenish everything a few times a day."

"As much as that would be nice, as of this moment, no one is allowed in this room except task force members. If you want to refill the baskets just have the cleaning staff knock, and we'll give them empty baskets and trash bags. And I'm afraid you're included in the no entrance policy."

Coglin gave a sharp nod. "I understand."

"I'll also need a room to interview the staff and guards who were on duty during the kidnapping. It'll need to have a private waiting area so we can efficiently move through the group."

"We have empty offices that could work for you. I'll text you once I have the area set up and a list of staff who were working." Coglin frowned. "But I can only afford for you to have one nurse at a time. We run lean as it is, and it will be hard to pull more than one nurse from another area."

"Understood." Jared gave a tight smile. "We need to move the Pratts to another suite. Not only for their safety, but so forensics can process the room where Luna was taken."

"We're fully booked but they can move into the suite Mr. Pratt is in right now. I'll get maintenance to fix the issue with the room."

Jared nodded. "We'll interview Nurse Johnson now in

the room we've isolated her in. Then after a brief meeting here, we'll start with the other staff. Please encourage them not to talk about the incident any more than they already have."

Coglin nodded.

"I'll also let you know when the others are ready for their ID cards, and we'll take the pictures in the hallway." Jared gave Coglin a dismissive nod.

The man took the hint and headed for the door.

Bristol looked at Coglin. "Just so you know, I spoke to Teagan. She's putting the video files on the network so we can view them here. I'll need logins for the agents to access the files."

He nodded and hurried out.

"Seems like he might be upset with us for banning him from the room," Bristol said.

"Can't be helped. We need to be sure we lock down security on this room. Wouldn't do to have any leaks that could potentially put this child in more danger." He glanced at the computer. "Let's start by putting No Entry signs on the door."

She nodded but honestly his intensity was unsettling her. Sure, they needed to have top secrecy around the information and only disseminate what was needed, but this man gave a new meaning to intense right now, and she was certain there was a story behind it that he hadn't shared.

Question was, was he fully in control of his emotions or did something in his past impact his ability to lead the investigation where a baby's life was on the line?

~

Jared held the door for Bristol to the suite where Nurse Natalie Johnson sat on the bed, her hands clutched in her lap. She shot to her feet and pushed up oversized black glasses with thick lenses. Jared had to remain professionally detached from the parents and use the formal Mr. and Mrs. Not with Nurse Johnson. A casual approach would help her relax so she could do a better job of sharing every bit of information she could remember.

She shoved her hands into the pockets of her uniform top. "Any news?"

Jared moved close to her but tried to appear relaxed when he wanted to pummel her with questions and get this investigation moving faster. "Not yet."

She crumpled back onto the bed. "If I'd only come into the room sooner."

"Where were you when the baby was taken?" Bristol asked as she stepped past Jared.

"I was in the suite next door. The Bakers." She poked a thumb to her left. "They'd just delivered, and we were getting the baby settled. I heard Sonya scream and rushed in. By then the baby was gone. So I called my supervisor, and she took care of getting the Pink Alert issued."

"When you say called, do you have phones you use on the job?" Jared asked.

Natalie nodded and held up a cell phone.

"We'll want to take that for evidence." Jared held out his hand for the phone.

She planted it firmly on his palm. "You'll tell my supervisor you took it? If I lose it, I have to pay for a new one."

"We'll tell Mr. Coglin." Jared pocketed the phone, glad that he had a way to track any calls this woman had taken this morning.

"Did you stay with the family the whole time after you entered the room?" Bristol asked.

Natalie nodded and chewed on her lip.

"Did you participate in Luna's delivery?" Jared asked,

trying to get a read on Nurse Johnson. She fidgeted, which could be a sign that she was deceiving them or could just be anxious over the missing baby.

Natalie shook her head. "I started working with them when Luna had a problem latching on to feed. I do labor and delivery, but I'm also one of our lactation specialists."

All things Jared had heard Tim and Deb talking about but had tuned out. "Anything unusual about the parents?"

"Unusual? I'm not sure I know what you mean."

"Extra nervous," he clarified. "Not ready to be parents."

"You don't think..." She paused. "I mean you think they might have something to do with her disappearance?"

He forced a smile to ease the woman's worry. "We have to consider all angles."

Natalie narrowed her eyes. "Kevin's kind of a nervous guy. Not sure if it has to do with becoming a dad, but his head was often elsewhere when I was in the room. Not Sonya, though. No. No. She's a very devoted mother and wanted Luna more than anything."

The father had the skills to disarm the alarm, and he was acting nervous. Could he be involved? Didn't seem like it, but then, Jared couldn't discount the parents at this point. "Did they seem like typical parents?"

Natalie sat forward. "No such thing. All the parents are here to bring a child into the world, but no case is like the other. That's what makes this such an interesting job."

Jared kept his attention pinned to her. "What about your fellow staff members?"

"What about them?" Natalie lifted her chin.

"Is there anyone who you think might be involved?" Jared asked. "Maybe not directly taking Luna, but helping someone else to do so. Maybe someone who needs money badly enough that they'd be open to a payoff."

"I don't know of anyone who would do that. Especially

not with a baby who has blood sugar issues and needs regular feeds and monitoring. We all got into this profession to help people, not risk their lives."

Jared knew she spoke the truth, but money woes could make people do the unexpected. "What about you? How are your finances?"

"Me?" She clutched her chest. "I'm good. I mean, I have some credit card debt. Doesn't everyone? But nothing overwhelming or anything."

Time to put a little pressure on. See how she reacted. "You know we'll look into that, don't you? So if there's something we're going to find, now would be the time to tell us."

"There's nothing. Really." Her gaze cut back and forth between him and Bristol. "I'm just your average twenty-seven-year-old single girl trying to make ends meet in a city where rents keep skyrocketing."

"Are you having trouble paying your rent?" Jared pressed when if she turned out to be innocent, he would feel bad for his behavior.

"No. No. Nothing like that." She waved a hand. "But it's why I have to put some things on my credit card and carry a balance."

"Did anyone approach you about aiding an abduction?" Jared kept at her, putting on more pressure.

"No. For sure not."

"How about a woman hanging around the area asking questions?" Bristol asked. "Someone who didn't seem like she fit."

Natalie seemed to relax at Bristol stepping in. Maybe Jared had come on too strong.

"I don't remember anyone in particular. I mean, we have pregnant women ask questions all the time when we leave the center." Natalie smiled, revealing even white teeth.

"That's part of my job that I like. But maybe if you tell me what she looks like I'd remember."

"We don't have a good picture of her." Jared tried to be less aggressive but his sharp tone said he didn't manage it. "But she was a shorter woman, wearing a blue winter parka and carrying a large tote bag. Did you see her?"

"Not that I know of, and I think I would've noticed a parka in August." She frowned. "But here's the thing. We're all so busy moving from patient to patient, attending to their needs, that it's hard to pay attention to what else is going on around us. It's only when we step out on break that we notice there's life outside of our suites."

"Thank you for your time." Jared held her gaze. "I'd like you to give this more thought and let me know if you think of anything that you believe will help."

"Sure. Sure."

Jared smiled at the nurse. "And it would be best not to discuss this with others in case they inadvertently change your story."

"Okay, yeah. Sure."

"Thanks again," Bristol said and led the way out to the hallway.

Jared waited for the door to close, then looked at Bristol and patted his pocket. "We'll have an agent go through all of the calls for the staff to try to place them at the time of the abduction, but she seemed on the up and up. Still, we'll have her background run too."

"It's gonna take time to go through all of those call logs."

He nodded and glanced at his watch. "I got a text telling me Sierra Rice has arrived and is working the Pratts' room. We have enough time before the task force meeting to check in with her."

He didn't wait for Bristol to agree, but headed down the hallway to Room 332, where the door was propped open.

The space seemed cold and empty and clinical with the two white-suited techs bent over the bassinet. He'd met Sierra Rice once, so he recognized her, even if she wore her long blond hair in a ponytail today. The other person was a young guy of average build with blond hair that was gelled in a messy style.

Jared put on booties from the box inside the door and entered. Bristol followed suit.

The pair spun to look at them.

"Oh, Jared. Bristol." Sierra let out a breath.

The guy went back to work, and Sierra held up a fingerprint brush. "We were focused on this, and you scared us."

"Sorry." Bristol eased around Jared to reach Sierra at the bassinet. "We just wanted to check in to see if you've found anything."

Jared joined them. "You're using white powder. I've seen several colors but never white."

Sierra raised an eyebrow. "Do I detect a question about our abilities?"

"I'm sorry if it sounded that way." And he had no doubt it had, but he didn't mean it. "I like to learn as I go."

Sierra's eyebrow remained raised. "It's not yet available commercially. A grad student developed it when she ran out of the typical powder, and I've been testing it for her and getting amazing results."

"Like?" Jared asked, this time trying hard to curb his suspicion.

Sierra smiled. "It replaces fluorescent powders that need an alternative light source to view the prints. This powder doesn't need the ALS and recovers fingerprints with extreme detail."

All interesting information that Jared would file away, but... "Did you find any helpful prints?"

Sierra nodded. "We've already printed the parents and

64

Nurse Johnson, and we located their prints in the room, of course, but we also have a clear latent from someone we don't have an elimination print for."

"The suspect?" Jared asked hopefully.

"I couldn't say at this point."

"Can you tell the difference between a man's and woman's print?" Bristol asked.

"Not really." Sierra shifted on her feet encased in high-top tennis shoes in a bright orange color. "Women can have large hands and men can have small hands."

"A gut feel?" Jared pressed.

Sierra watched him carefully. "You sound desperate for a lead."

He might be letting his insecurities around losing Wyatt color his actions. He needed to watch for this and take a step back in his attitude if it was overpowering, but right now he had to press full force. "A baby's life could be at stake."

She grimaced, and Jared could imagine her telling Reed the next time she talked to him about what a jerk he had for a fellow agent. "I'll get the print back to the lab the minute we're finished with this room and run it against AFIS."

Jared was very familiar with the Automated Fingerprint Identification System that held criminal and law enforcement fingerprints as it was managed by his agency.

"What about the stairwell?" Bristol asked.

"It's cordoned off, and we'll do that next."

"If the woman didn't wear gloves, you should be able to get prints off the push bar and handrails, right?" Bristol asked.

"I'll do my best, but the bars and rails are curved, and depending on where she touched things, it could be a challenge."

"If anyone can lift the prints successfully, it'll be you," Bristol said. "I'm so thankful we were able to call you in."

Sierra smiled at Bristol, then cast a skeptical glance at Jared. Right, he *had* been pushing too hard.

"I'm glad to help," Sierra said. "But you should also know there's bound to be other prints on the bar. We'll need to spend a good bit of time on that and manpower on processing the prints. Still, I should have the results to you before morning."

Jared laid his business card on the bed. He didn't want her to contaminate her gloves and have to put on a fresh pair. "Then you'll get back with me the moment you know anything?"

"I will."

"Thank you for coming so fast," Bristol said.

Sierra gave a sharp nod. "As a mom, I can only imagine the Pratts' pain, and I'll do everything I can to help find their daughter."

Jared nodded his thanks and headed for the door, praying that everything Sierra could do, along with everything the rest of the team could do, would bring this little baby home alive.

5

Jared took a seat at the command center table next to Bristol, who'd changed into her deputy's uniform while he and the other supervisors formed a game plan. He had to admit it was exciting to see her taking a power position that all law enforcement officers were trained to exude, and he didn't have to see it to know she could hold her own with other officers and bad guys. But he had to ignore her. Uniform or suit. His mind had to shut her out.

His supervisor, who'd just arrived along with six agents, sat on Jared's other side. Three of them were members of the cyber-crimes squad and would handle any information technology needs, and two agents were on the violent crime squad with Jared. Maybe with Agent Piper Thorn being pregnant and due in a week, he should've claimed an extra person in the room.

Lieutenant Allen Mills from Multnomah County Sheriff's Office was taking the podium, and he'd arrived with Detective Hale and several other employees of the department, including an information officer to handle the media.

Also present were representatives from the Oregon State Police along with local law enforcement agencies and Washington agencies as well. With Vancouver just across the river from Portland, the city was for all practical purposes a suburb of Portland, and a kidnapping in a metro area like this could quickly cross jurisdictional lines. All area agencies needed to be involved and kept up to speed.

Mills introduced himself. "Thank you all for coming. I'll make this short so we can get to work finding baby Luna." He introduced Adair, then shared Hale's and Jared's roles in the search and added that Reed Rice would be Jared's second in command, and Detective Myles Waters would support Detective Hale.

"Any calls to the tip line?" Jared asked, trying to move them forward. "Legitimate ones, that is?"

Hale snapped his chair forward. "We've already had our share of crackpot calls, but we have two credible leads we're running down right now. We also have deputies canvassing the area for any witnesses."

Mills put the still shot of their female suspect on the screen. "We've distributed this photo with the AMBER Alert and in a BOLO alert."

The Be On the Lookout alert would have gone out to law enforcement officers statewide and even to nearby states.

"And my team will be showing the photo to all of the hospital staff and security guards," Jared said. "We had a change in the company providing guards for this facility, so we'll interview both the current and former guards. The suspect likely scoped the place out earlier in the week or even before. We'll be asking if she was seen then."

"Are we thinking the change in guards could be the reason the kidnapping was allowed to occur?" Adair asked.

Beside him, Bristol sucked in a breath and sat on her hands, but she didn't shrink back from the probing question. If anything, it seemed as if she wanted to defend her company, but knew better than to do so.

"A guard has gone AWOL, but there's no evidence to suggest that he or any other guard are involved at this point," Jared said. "Steele Guardians is the current company, and they have a solid reputation. That said, we're following up on that angle."

Bristol expelled a quiet breath and leaned closer to him as if offering her thanks. He didn't deserve the thanks. He hadn't said what he did because of his feelings for her. He'd said it because it was true. He'd heard about them during his time at the Bureau. Had maybe even sought out information about them. Especially after he suffered several relationship failures. He'd compared every woman he'd dated to Bristol. Sure, they'd had a relationship when they were young and it was just that, a short-lived relationship, but even back then he'd known she was a special woman.

Mills tapped the screen. "As of now, we focus on this woman. She's a strong suspect. She seems to fit the most common traits of an infant abductor—a female of child-bearing age between twelve and fifty. Frequently uses a fire exit stairwell for her escape."

"What we don't know, but should be on the lookout for, are the following." Mills turned off the projector and moved back to the large whiteboard. He slid open a wood door that covered half the board to reveal a list Jared had made of suspect traits. "She's often compulsive and relies on manipulation, lying, and deception. She's often married or cohabitating and wants to provide her significant other with a child. She often lives in the community where the abduction takes place."

"That's an important factor to keep in mind," Adair said. "When you're looking at called-in tips or any other leads, first learn where the suspect lives. Don't discount the out-of-the-area ones if they're solid, but put priority on the ones in the area."

"Good point to remember," Mills said. "Also know that she has likely made frequent recon visits to birthing centers at more than one healthcare facility where she asked questions about procedures and scoped out the layout."

"Which is why we'll be interviewing staff at all of the nearby hospitals," Jared said. "She also typically plans the abduction and often seizes any opportunity present, usually not targeting a specific infant. Odds are good that she has no connection to the Pratt family, and that'll make it harder to locate her."

"If she compromised the guard," Adair said. "She may have taken the first child on the wing where the mother was asleep."

Bristol cleared her throat and sat up straighter. "We've had no reports of a stranger entering any of the other rooms."

"She also frequently impersonates a nurse or other allied healthcare personnel, so we should watch for that," Mills said. "If so, maybe she *did* compromise the guard by sending him on what he thought was a legit mission. She's probably become familiar with healthcare staff and their routines. So it's a good possibility that at least one of the staff here has talked to her."

"Since she abducted the baby in the morning," Jared stepped up to the whiteboard, and Hale sat down as they'd planned to switch at this point so the task force heard from both of them. "And did recon earlier in the week, she would've come in the morning and so the morning staff are the most likely group to know her. And it's not surprising that she struck during shift change when chaos can often happen."

Jared slid the door open to reveal the whiteboard where he and the other supervisors had already made team assignments. "We've parsed out the workload so we can take quick action. Some of you will call hospitals and doctors' offices for names of any women who recently lost babies. Others will get infant death records for the past few months and contact these mothers. And some have the task of obtaining warrants to query hospitals and doctors' offices that aren't forthcoming for names of any women who lost babies due to miscarriage, particularly late-term."

Jared paused to run his gaze over the team. "These women will likely be distraught, and we need to be sensitive to that. If you come across anyone who you think we need to talk to or have any questions about the assignments, contact me, Agent Rice or Detectives Hale or Waters."

Hale stood, looked each person in the eye, and then firmed his shoulders. "Let's get after this, people, and bring this baby home alive."

Alive. Wyatt's face appeared in Jared's mind, and he raked his hand through his hair. He suspected Adair might be struggling too as he also had to be thinking of Wyatt and remembering how their team had failed that baby boy. At least Jared's supervisor didn't bring it up or didn't stop him from taking lead here because of it. Maybe Adair thought Jared had learned his lesson. Hopefully he had.

And he wouldn't make the same mistake again. He wouldn't trust anyone, but would verify and investigate anything that made him uncomfortable. And protect the information with his life if needed.

He looked at the team. "Before anyone leaves, you need to get a security pass for the room. No one will be allowed back in here without one."

A few of the team groaned.

Jared got it. They didn't want to waste the time, but Jared knew how important it was to secure the information in this room. He might be overreacting, but his failure with Wyatt told him not to trust even people he'd grown close to. Partnered with. Shared family with. Because they could betray you and people died as a result. He didn't want to go through losing a child due to leaked information. Never again.

~

Network login information from the hospital technology person in hand, Bristol stepped back into the conference room. She hadn't minded stepping away as she was out of place in the group of higher-ranking law enforcement officers. After Jared had defended her family's business to the others, she considered him an ally. But was he protecting her or stating what he actually believed?

She glanced across the room at him, and he waved her over to a folding table in the corner where three agents sat with their laptops open in front of them. She crossed the room, grabbing some sticky notes and a pen on the way so she could assign the passwords to these agents.

A woman with a cute pixie cut sat at the end of the table and cradled a very pregnant belly. Could this be Nick Thorn's wife, Piper? Nick was the Veritas Center's computer expert, and his wife was a cyber agent and due very soon.

The guy in the middle had reddish hair and close-cut beard, and his solid body dwarfed the folding chair. And the man on the end was built and tall like the other agent, but his hair was dark and fuzzy on the top.

She stopped near the woman who held out her hand.

"I'd get up but, well…" She shrugged. "I'm Piper Thorn. I think you know my husband, Nick."

"I do, and nice to meet you." Bristol shook hands. "Congratulations on the baby."

"Just don't have it here." The guy next to her gave her a

gentle elbow jab, then held out a hand to Bristol. "I'm Hunter Lane. Married to Maya also at Veritas."

"The toxicology expert." Bristol shook his hand trying hard not to wince under the firm grip.

"And I'm Colin Graham," the last guy said. "Not married to anyone." His mouth quirked up at the corner.

Bristol had to admit he was one good-looking guy. Not that his smile did a thing for her. But let Jared smile at her, and she was a goner. Something to think about later. Much later. "I'm Multnomah County Deputy, Bristol Steele."

"And the one who can give you access to the security files that you've been nagging me for," Jared said.

"We don't mean to be pushy," Piper said.

"But we are." Colin cocked a smile.

"Not only are we eager to find this child, but I also have a ticking clock." Piper pointed to her belly. "Due in seven days."

"The good news for all of us is you're working in a hospital." Colin smiled again.

Piper rolled her eyes.

Bristol held up her clipboard. "I have the logins and temp passwords here. Give me a second to put them on a sticky note for each of you. Of course, I'll need you to destroy the evidence after you log in."

They laughed at her evidence joke, each of them likely wanting to find a way to relieve stress the same way she was and most officers in tough situations were. Maybe even more so for Piper. In her pregnant state, she had a deeper understanding of the Pratts' suffering.

Bristol remained near the trio until they successfully logged in and set up their own passwords, then collected the sticky notes to shred.

"Thanks for your help." Colin flicked his fingers. "Now go away so we can get to work."

Bristol liked his straightforward personality. She was going to enjoy working with him along with Piper and Hunter.

"One more thing before we go." Jared held out a phone to Piper. "Nurse Johnson's phone for imaging. We'll be asking the parents to surrender their phones and hope one of you can image them too."

"Bring 'em on." Hunter tapped a large plastic case sitting on the floor next to him. "I brought all the equipment we might need."

Colin gave an inquisitive look over his shoulder. "You think the parents might be involved?"

"My gut says they're not," Jared replied. "But we have to consider everyone close to Luna as suspects."

"Roger that." Colin turned back to his work.

Jared looked at Bristol. "I also want to show the woman's photo to the Pratts. You seem to have built a good rapport with the mother, and I'd like you to join me."

"Glad to." She didn't care about the reason, she was stoked to be involved in any capacity and to continue in the investigation.

"Lead the way." He gestured at the door.

She started off, and he stopped next to Reed. Sierra's husband was tall, fit, had near-black hair and wore an equally dark suit with a white shirt that brought out his deep coloring. He was directing task force members in setting up a timeline, but paused to look at Jared.

"We're heading up to the parents' room to show them the suspect's photo," Jared said. "You have my phone number in case you need me, right?"

"I do." Reed smiled at Bristol. "Glad to see we have a Steele on the task force."

She nodded, thankful he didn't mind the potential conflict of interest.

"I'll let you know if anything actionable comes up while you're gone," Reed said.

"Thanks, man." Jared pushed the door open.

Bristol stepped through. In the hallway, she held up her phone. "We should swap numbers too."

Jared got out his phone, and they made the exchange as they walked to the elevator. She pocketed her phone, feeling somehow closer to him by having a way to contact him at all times. So many years had passed since they'd been head over heels. Time when she'd often wondered what he'd done and become. Now, if she chose, she could keep in touch with him after the investigation ended.

Would she choose? Would he even want that? Not likely on either account.

In the elevator, he looked at her. "I'd like you to take lead on this questioning and request the phones."

Wow! He was giving her lead in a crucial interview. Sure, he could jump in if she failed or did a bad job, but still, he was showing that he believed in her skills. A big deal for her. "Glad to."

He took a prepaid cell phone from his pocket. "Colin has set their phones to forward to this device so if the kidnapper calls while we have the parents' phones, they can take the call."

"You think this could be a ransom kidnapping?"

"It's always a possibility, but it's not reading like one. At least not yet." He leaned back against the wall and closed his eyes.

Was he taking a second to recharge or pray? They'd met at a Christian camp, and she supposed he might've turned his back on his faith, but she doubted it. He'd once had a firm handle on his faith and lived it in his life even more than she did at that time. She'd learned a lot from him, and he was instrumental in making her want to be a better Christian. A better person.

Until he bailed.

She couldn't reconcile that behavior with the person she'd thought him to be. Her faith took a nosedive that day. A deep one. She'd struggled hard for years to maintain a Christian worldview. She was too busy trying to will her heart not to fall to pieces. But then Thomas was murdered. Oh, man, that did it. Took her to the edge and her faith plummeted, crashing and burning on impact.

Sure she still believed in God. But she didn't feel His presence in her life like she once had. Like she wanted to. Wouldn't it be something if being with Jared again helped her to regain it?

The elevator doors *whooshed* open, and she stepped out first. She nodded at their company guard at the birthing center door, a woman Bristol didn't know, but her nametag read Sandy. Bristol started to move past her.

Sandy stepped in Bristol's way and planted her feet. "Could I see your ID please?"

Jared snorted.

Bristol gave him the stink eye and held out her badge for Sandy.

"Oh, Ms. Steele." Sandy blushed the same red as the trim on her uniform. "I didn't know. I'm so sorry."

"No worries. I'm glad you asked. Shows that you do your job well." Bristol smiled at Sandy. "And this is Agent Jared Wolfe with the FBI."

"Um, no offense to either of you." Sandy bit her lip. "But sir, can I see your ID too."

"No offense taken." Jared held out his badge.

Sandy's face colored again. "Thanks for understanding."

Bristol used her card to access the birthing center, and

76

they made their way to the new room where the Pratts had been relocated.

The couple looked up, hope burning in their eyes.

Bristol gave a shake of her head, telling them what they needed to know without even speaking, and their crestfallen faces said they understood. She noted the FBI agent standing in the corner. She was there to keep the parents updated, but also to be available should the kidnapper call.

She held out her hand to Bristol. "Agent Toni Byrd."

Bristol shook hands and stepped closer, then lowered her voice. "Which Byrd brother are you married to?"

"Clay." A warm smile crossed Toni's face.

The five Byrd brothers—Sierra Rice's brothers—owned an investigative and protection agency that was also housed in the Veritas Center. Bristol had met them all when they helped Peyton work an investigation about six months ago.

"Clay's a great guy." Bristol smiled at Toni then moved to the bedside to interview the parents. "We have a picture of a potential suspect that we would like you to take a look at. The photo doesn't capture her face, but we hoped you might recognize her clothing or build."

Jared stepped up next to Bristol and displayed the photo for them.

"I haven't a clue." Mrs. Pratt frowned. "I've never seen that jacket, I know that."

"Me, neither," Mr. Pratt said. "Kind of a heavy jacket for this time of year."

Jared stowed his phone but didn't react.

Bristol looked between the pair. "We would like to take both of your phones so we can review the data."

"You what?" Mrs. Pratt shot up in her bed. "Our phones? You think we did this. That we hurt our Luna."

"Do you think she's hurt?" Bristol followed up but hated to do so.

"What? No. I just meant putting her through this could hurt her." Mrs. Pratt shook her head. "This is unbelievable."

"Stop focusing on us and do your job!" Mr. Pratt glared at her.

Bristol took a step closer and let the insult flow off her before speaking. "This *is* our job as much as none of us like it. We have to rule out everyone close to Luna and that includes her family. If you provide the phones, we can quickly get through them and put our resources toward other aspects of the investigation."

Mr. Pratt shoved his hand in her direction, his phone on his palm. "Take it then. And leave us alone until you have something positive to report."

Jared collected the phone, and Mrs. Pratt's too.

"It will take a couple of hours to image the phones." She gave them the prepaid phone. "In the event a kidnapper might call, we've forwarded your phones to this one so you can answer the call."

"If they took Luna for money, we don't have any." Mrs. Pratt wrung her hands together. "We can barely scrape up enough for the hospital bill for Luna let alone anything else."

"We have no reason to believe there will be a ransom demand," Jared said. "But as we said, we have to cover all bases."

Mr. Pratt tilted his head. "I'm sorry for my outburst. Sounds like you're doing your jobs."

Jared gave him a nod. "If you need to talk to either of us, just tell Agent Byrd here, and she'll get in touch."

Bristol headed for the door and smiled at Toni on the way out. When the door fully whisked closed, Jared looked at Bristol. "Good job in there. If you stayed in law enforcement, you'd make a great detective."

"Not a job I want to do at all." The time in that room and forcing the Pratts to answer questions when they were hurting so badly cemented that in her mind. And that was the last thing she wanted to talk with him about right now. Maybe never. "I know your agents will image the phones, but I'd like to get the files to the electronics expert at Veritas for review."

Jared raised an eyebrow as if he figured out she was changing the subject on purpose. "Piper's husband, Nick, right?"

"Right. The Pratts might've discarded files, and he's sure to locate them."

"I'd like to think our team is on the same level as Nick, but I'll be glad to ask them what they want to do."

"Sounds good," she said, but from what she'd heard, no one in the area could compete with Nick's skills and equipment. "I'm going to check in with my family on the way back."

Coglin had given her family access to the staff training room with two tables full of computers and monitors that they were using to review the hospital security video.

"I'll go with you." He rubbed a finger along his nose, a gesture she knew from experience meant he was uneasy about something.

Maybe he believed her family would try to hide or change video files if they came off looking bad. If so, his fear was unfounded. They had read-only access to the files and couldn't make any changes.

She would ask him, but his unease could be due to their past too. She sure didn't want to bring that up. She would keep an eye on him. See if she could pick up the reason for his behavior.

She trusted him. In theory. Or at least she once had. That was years ago. She didn't know him now. He might not be the same man she once knew, and she best remember that.

~

Jared paused in the training room doorway. The large space was filled with people sitting at computers and a hint of burnt coffee snaked through the air. He didn't mean people exactly but the family Bristol loved. He'd never met any of them until today when he'd met Teagan in the security office, but he felt like he knew them. Bristol had spent hours describing each one and talking about their personalities.

Still, when they looked up and locked eyes on him, he knew from the intensity that Bristol hadn't exaggerated it. Had she told them about his past with her?

Could explain the piercing stare of an older man Jared put in his sixties. He still had a full head of deep brown hair and wrinkles near his eyes. Like maybe he liked to smile, but he wasn't smiling now.

Had to be Bristol's father, who was a former detective. The other occupants were women. Teagan and another brunette resembling Bristol, a blonde, and a redhead. Her sisters and cousins, he assumed, though he couldn't tell which were which, nor did he remember all of their names.

"Come on in. They don't bite." Bristol wrinkled her nose.

He knew that expression. She'd once used it as a casual way to transmit her attraction to him in a cute flirting way. He'd taken several body language courses and knew wrinkling your nose could be used in a variety of ways. Distaste or revulsion common. It could also signal attraction. Something he'd rather she not be expressing in front of her very perceptive father.

The older man stood and came around the table,

thrusting out his hand. "Gene Steele and you must be Jared."

Jared nodded and shook hands, trying not to wilt under the punishing grip.

Gene let go and rested his hand on his sidearm concealed under a denim overshirt. "My niece Ryleigh has good things to say about you."

"Ryleigh?" He looked over the women to see if he recognized anyone but Teagan.

"She's not here," Gene said.

"I don't think I've ever met her," Jared said.

"She's an agent at your office," Gene said. "Just transferred there recently. Said she's heard about you. Guess you haven't heard about her."

"No." Jared forced a smile. He would've recognized the name Steele and questioned it if he had. "Have you all located anything in the video to move us forward?"

Teagan stepped toward him and waved a hand over her family. "We've been reviewing the video files, but nothing yet. Dad and I've also been looking into our AWOL guard, Aaron King. My uncle Hugh went to Aaron's house. Place is buttoned up tight. No lights. No sign of him at all."

Interesting. Jared hadn't thought the Steele Guardians had played a role in the kidnapping, but the guard going AWOL could mean Jared's initial assessment was wrong. "Do you think King's totally flaked or might he be inside and not answering?"

"Either one, I suppose." Gene worried his bottom lip between his teeth. "I can't personally vouch for the guy, but our supervisor Zeke keeps assuring me Aaron is one of our best, which is why he got the cherry assignment at the birthing center."

Something really was off. "Maybe he's in trouble and a welfare check's in order."

"My thoughts too." Gene frowned. "Hugh would gladly do the check, but we can't afford to mess anything up here. It needs to be done by someone in law enforcement."

"We want everything to be above board," Teagan added. "If our guy colluded with the kidnapper then we want to know about it as much as you do."

Bristol stepped closer, fire in her eyes. "Text me Aaron's address and phone number, and Jared and I will be all over it."

6

Bristol led the way to Aaron King's bright blue door and radioed in her location as Jared drew his sidearm. She might be on special assignment, but her department needed to know her location for her own protection. Her grandad, who'd been a police officer too, often reminded them of the old cop saying that said, "if dispatch didn't know where you were, then only God could help you." In theory, she knew God could help all the time even if He didn't seem to be present in her life right now, so it was good to have her fellow deputies on her side too.

She knocked on the ground floor door to the condo in a nice suburban area with maple tree lined streets. Jared had decided she could take lead here, not because she was a good deputy, but because he thought if they approached it from a Steele family member asking to speak to Aaron, he would show his face.

Bristol wasn't as sure. If he didn't answer the door for Uncle Hugh, then he wouldn't likely answer the door for her. Still, she pounded again, this time with the side of her fist, the thumps echoing into the air filled only with the sound of chirping birds in a nearby ruby-red Japanese Maple.

"Aaron!" Bristol shouted. "It's Bristol Steele. I need to talk to you."

She listened carefully as a breeze whisked over the stoop.

Nothing.

She knocked harder and pressed her ear against the door, but the solid wood revealed nothing.

Jared moved to the sidelight and cupped his hands around his eyes to peer in. "If he's here, he's not letting on."

"I know others tried calling him. I'll do it too to see if we can hear his phone ring." She pressed his number in the text from her father. Silence.

"It couldn't be that easy, could it." Jared shoved a hand into his hair, reminding her how soft it had been under her fingers when he'd done nothing other than shampoo it. With all the swimming that summer, she'd had to work forever to keep hers soft.

She snapped her mind back and pounded one more time. "We don't really have any reason to bust down this door. No exigent circumstances."

"Not legally, yeah."

"Are you considering ignoring the law?" She watched him, surprised at his attitude.

"A baby's missing."

"We could be charged with breaking and entering."

"Yeah, but we could also find the lead that would break this investigation wide open."

A crash sounded from inside.

She spun toward the door. "Did you hear that?"

"You wanted exigent circumstances." He connected gazes with her. "You got them."

"It's a stretch, but yeah, someone could be in danger."

"Stand back." He backed to the door and slammed a loafer into the wood.

The door groaned. Cracked.

He slammed his foot again. Another crack.

"Where are my tactical boots when I need them?" he asked and reared back to hit the door harder. The wood splintered, and the door went flying in.

Not waiting for him to recover from the force and turn, she drew her sidearm and brushed past him.

She entered a space holding a tiny kitchen with empty pizza box and fast-food bags on the counter and the tangy scent of pizza sauce filling the air. The kitchen adjoined a small living room with black leather furniture and a TV far too large for the space.

"Police," she yelled. "Aaron, are you here?"

A thumping sound came from the direction where a hallway led from the room.

Gun outstretched, Jared rushed past her into the hallway, his footfalls silent on the worn beige carpet. She trailed him.

"Police," he called out too, though neither of them was a police officer. The common term told people how to behave without having to think about it.

He cleared a bathroom that had recently been cleaned if the lingering bleach smell said anything. Or someone cleaned up a crime scene. She preferred to think it was her first thought.

At the end of the hall, Jared spun toward a room with a closed door. He shoved it open, took a quick look and jerked back.

"He's here. Gagged and tied to a chair. On the floor." Jared remained focused on the doorway. "Clear the other bedroom. Then we'll go in together."

She swiveled to the other door, while he remained at the

primary bedroom. Heart pounding, she burst into the space set up as an office and swept her gun in an arc. She moved to the closet. Swung the door open.

"Clear." She let out her breath and returned to the hallway.

Jared held her gaze for a long moment. So many thoughts in his expression.

Take care. Have my back. I'll have yours. Let's do this.

He released his hold and signaled they would go in.

They flooded into the room. She marched to the closet and flung open the door. "Clear!"

Jared dropped to his knees and looked under the bed. "And we're good."

"Release him," Jared said. "I'll cover us at the door where I can see down the hallway."

Just like Jared to want to keep her safe. But then he would likely do the same thing with any officer. The new Jared seemed to be extra cautious instead of fun-loving as he'd once been. But that had been summer. At a camp made for fun.

This was the extreme opposite. A crime scene with a bound and gagged man.

She moved to Aaron and untied his gag.

"Thank God." His words croaked out, sounding like a frog. "I heard your uncle come over but couldn't make enough noise to attract his attention. This stinking chair was wedged between the bed and wall so I couldn't move. Worked for hours on it. Finally got across the room to the table and was able to knock the lamp off before I fell."

She got a pocket knife out and sliced into the duct tape binding him to the chair. "What happened?"

"This is crazy. Just crazy." He shook his head. "I was about to get ready for work and someone knocks on my door. I was in a hurry so opened it without checking through the peephole. He had on a ski mask and forced me back here. Tied me up then stole my uniform. I had it packed up and ready to go for today's job." His gaze clung to Bristol. "Did something bad happen?"

She hated to tell him, but he had to know. "A baby was abducted."

"No, no, no." He scrubbed a hand over his face. "I'm so sorry. If I hadn't opened the door, I—"

"If you hadn't, he would've grabbed you when you walked out to go to work," Jared said. "You can't blame yourself."

Jared's straightforward statement still held suspicion of Aaron that all good law enforcement officers would have at this point. Aaron's captivity could all be a setup to make him look innocent, though her gut didn't tell her that.

Jared continued to focus on Aaron. "How would anyone know you were scheduled to work at Mercy today and specifically guarding the birthing center?"

"Good question. One I've been thinking about this whole time." Aaron stretched his arms. "Best I can figure out is another guard tipped this creep off."

"Why would one of our guards do that?" Bristol asked.

"Money. Why else?"

"Or revenge or both." Jared looked at Bristol. "You fire or discipline anyone lately?"

"We can ask Teagan about that." She ripped the tape from Aaron's ankles. "Can you describe the man? Maybe that can help us figure out if he was an employee."

"No can do. He wore a ski mask. But I can tell you he was around six feet tall and built the same as me. Wore jeans and a plain gray T-shirt. No tats or other marks."

"You're sure on that?" Jared asked.

"Believe me. I looked hard at him as he wrapped me in that stinkin' tape. He had hazel eyes, and he used a falsetto voice when he talked. I can't even ID his voice if it came to that." Aaron rubbed his wrists again. "I can't believe I let him get the jump on me."

Bristol faced Jared. "I'll call this in and get an officer over here to secure the scene and escort Aaron in for a more thorough debrief. Then I'll get Teagan on looking into disgruntled employees or ex-employees."

Jared frowned, remaining in place without speaking for a moment. He jerked his head at the hallway and stepped out.

"Be right back," she told Aaron and joined Jared.

"Go ahead and make those calls, but I can't have you in King's interview." He widened his stance as if expecting her to fight.

"No worries. I figured that would be the case, but can you share what Aaron has to say?"

"Sure," he said right away, but paused, and his gaze lingered on her. "That is if I don't think it will conflict with your interest in Steele Guardians."

Ah, yes, that conflict. It was starting to get in her way, but there wasn't a thing she could do about it so no point in wasting time thinking about it.

She leaned down to her mic and called dispatch. As she waited for them to confirm an officer would be assigned, her grandad's repeated warning flashed into her mind. He told them over and over to make sure someone bent on harming her couldn't use the cord running from the mic to the radio on her duty belt to strangle her. She always threaded the cord inside her shirt as her grandad instructed, and of course, every time her grandad saw her in uniform, he had to find a way to make a fishing reference to drive home the point.

Dispatch came on and confirmed the officer was already en route.

"Roger that." She released her mic and called Teagan to share the information about Aaron. "Did you fire anyone lately?"

"We let a guy go for coming to work under the influence a few days ago," Teagan said. "A Nelson Osborne. We think he was high on pot. But still, how would anyone outside of our team know to approach him?"

"Where was he assigned the day he came to work stoned?"

"First Savings Credit Union. Zeke got a call from the branch manager telling him about the guard. Zeke assigned another guard and told Osborne he would drive him to the lab for a blood test. Osborne refused, so Zeke fired him."

"Maybe our kidnapper has a connection to the credit union." Bristol made a mental note to watch for that. "Get me Osborne's address pronto."

"Will do."

Bristol hung up and returned to the room. "Officer en route." She shared about Osborne.

Aaron frowned. "I know him. Worked a few jobs with him in the past."

"Would he have known about your placement at the hospital?" Bristol asked.

Aaron narrowed his eyes. "There was a lot of talk among the guards about the new hospital contract and our assignments. I got razzed about making sure I knew how to birth a baby, so it's possible."

"Could he be the guy who tied you up?" Jared asked.

Aaron tilted his head. "He fits the build, so maybe."

Jared looked at Bristol. "As soon as you get his address, we need to bring him in for questioning."

She nodded.

"I won't be able to stay here, will I?" Aaron asked.

She wished they didn't have to displace him, but it

couldn't be helped. "You'll be out of your apartment for at least a few days while it's cordoned off and forensics processes it for leads."

Aaron rubbed a hand over his face. "Am I free to pack some things?"

"After the officer takes your statement." Jared stepped closer. "And under our supervision. Then you'll be taken in for a more detailed interview."

Aaron clamped his hands on his knees. "Glad to help in any way I can, but I don't know what else I can tell you."

Jared opened his mouth as if to answer, but his phone rang, and he looked at it. "Excuse me."

"Sir," he said and stepped into the hall.

Okay. What did Bristol do with Aaron while Jared talked on his phone? She didn't want to babysit him. She wanted to listen to Jared's conversation.

"I'm not in trouble, am I?" Aaron asked. "I mean, I won't lose my job, right? I love working for your family."

"I'm glad to hear that," she replied, resisting the urge to step into the hall and eavesdrop on Jared's conversation. "If you've done nothing wrong, you won't be in trouble, but you'll remain a person of interest until we can clear you."

"Yeah, I figured that." He cursed under his breath. "Sorry. That was unprofessional and goes against my faith, but come on, this is seriously freaky."

She nodded but an officer announcing himself at the front door made her ease closer to the door.

"Back here," Jared called out. His phone still to his ear, he waved the officer to move past him.

Bristol didn't know the young officer but brought him up to speed on the situation and shared her and Jared's contact information. He started questioning Aaron.

"How many times am I going to have to tell this story?" Aaron asked.

"As many times as you're asked." She used her deputy voice and eyed him. "There's a baby missing, and even the smallest of details could help."

"Sorry," he said. "Of course I'll do whatever I can to help. I mean a baby. That's hard to wrap your head around for sure."

Jared charged into the room. "We set here so we can leave?"

Bristol looked at the officer. "We good to go?"

"Go ahead. I have your contact info."

Jared looked at Aaron. "Hang tight. I'll send someone to assist you in packing and pick you up."

Aaron gave a sad nod.

Jared turned to Bristol. "Let's move."

He bolted for the door.

She raced after him. "Where are we going?"

He turned, his expression tight and filled with anguish. "Luna's blanket was found in a hospital parking structure, and it's saturated with blood."

The stark cement in the parking structure seemed to bear down on Jared as he walked toward the cordoned off scene and caught sight of the blanket. The yellow tape surrounding Luna's blanket selected by her parents with love fluttered in the soft breeze. The pink fabric with big yellow bunnies a stark contrast to the harsh concrete.

Thoughts of Wyatt froze Jared's feet, and he couldn't take another step. He drew in a long breath of the air tainted with a gasoline leak, but it did no good.

Bristol stopped next to him. "What's wrong?"

"I just need a moment." He curled his hands into fists and forced himself to look her in the eyes. "We had a kidnapping case a few years ago. A newborn boy. Wyatt. Taken from his crib at home. He didn't make it. Found him in a car in a parking structure downtown."

"Oh, Jared, I'm so sorry. That must've been—is—so hard."

He took a moment to breathe before he could speak again. "It's definitely one of those investigations that sticks with you for life, and you keep reworking it to make the outcome change, but it never does. The same ending cuts you to the bone every time." He took in a ragged breath. "Especially when you're the one who screwed up along the way."

"That's got to be even harder." She touched his hand with the back of hers. Subtly. Barely there so none of the officers and techs saw it. But he felt it clear to his core, and the icy aftereffect from losing Wyatt thawed a bit.

She didn't ask what he'd done wrong. He had to give her credit for her ability to wait for him to share it. He dragged his focus back to the scene. "Not sure why I told you. I've never told anyone."

"You needed to get it out. Especially since they found blood on Luna's blanket. We have to expect the worst in a situation like that."

"Yeah, I guess." He shrugged. "If I hadn't trusted others on the task force not to leak certain information, the boy might've lived. Sure, we might not have gotten him back either way, but the kidnappers wouldn't have panicked."

"What happened?"

"It was a ransom case. The kidnappers set a meet in the parking structure. They planned to turn Wyatt over when the money was paid. So they brought him with them. But one of the officers owed a reporter a favor. The guy had done a story on prostitution, and the officer was caught with a prostitute. The reporter told the officer he wouldn't publish his name if he agreed to give him info on future investigations."

"And the kidnapping investigation was a big one," she said, sounding thoroughly disgusted.

"You got it. So he told the reporter that we planned to meet with the kidnappers but not pay any ransom and then storm them to free the baby. He asked the reporter to keep it quiet until after the meet. The reporter saw a huge scoop so he leaked it instead. The story hit the radio as the kidnappers were sitting in the garage. They barreled toward the exit in their car and crashed. They didn't have Wyatt in a car seat, and he died."

She brushed his hand again. "I'm so sorry, Jared."

"I've learned my lesson. That's why I need to keep the command center so secure. Why I handpicked the agents who are working with us."

"And you trusted me too?"

He glanced at her. "I trust you more than others."

"But not totally." The pain in her tone reminded him of the day they parted ways.

He didn't want to hurt her more, but he wasn't going to lie to her. "I want to say I do, but no. I trust no one totally."

"Not even God?"

"Not even Him, I'm sorry to say. If I did, I would be able to trust you too." He took a deep breath and let it out. "We're wasting time. Let's get to it."

He strode ahead, seeing the congealed blood on Luna's blanket even from a distance. The large red splotch wouldn't be life-threatening for an adult, but if it came from a baby?

No. Don't think about that.

Reed stood near the tape, talking to his wife. Sierra held a tackle box shaped case, her expression serious and intense. Reed reached his hand out and squeezed her shoulder as she squatted by the blanket and opened her case.

Nice. A couple who could support each other in a time like this. Just like Bristol's brief touches. Jared honestly could admit he felt some relief from her support. The FBI had offered counseling at the time of Wyatt's death. He didn't go. Was too proud. Maybe arrogant. Or maybe just blind to how much it still impacted him.

He sucked in some air and approached Reed. "What do we have?"

"Blanket was found by a security guard who was patrolling the lots."

He swiveled to look at Bristol. "Why'd it take them so long to do this?"

"We have a routine schedule the guards follow," Bristol said. "These auxiliary lots are rarely used and aren't patrolled as often. Then today we redirected the focus to the most likely areas near where the woman was caught on video and worked the perimeter outward."

Standard policing procedure in a search, but Jared wasn't happy with her answer because it hadn't worked in finding this key piece of evidence early on. He wished they'd found the person who dropped the blanket, not just the blanket. He looked around the area. "No video out here."

"No," Reed said. "I spoke to Coglin. Their budget doesn't stretch to these infrequently used lots. In fact, he said this structure is scheduled for demolition. They plan to build a new cancer center."

"Is the blanket all we have?" Jared asked.

"At this point." Reed looked at his wife. "If there's anything else, Sierra will find it."

Jared liked the man's confidence in his wife. If what Jared had heard about her trace evidence skills were true, the confidence was well placed.

Sierra bagged the blanket in a paper bag used for wet evidence. "I'll get this to the lab, and we'll type the blood right away. We know Luna's blood type. If it's not a match, we know it's not her blood. But her abductor could have the same blood type, so even if it matches, the results won't prove it's her blood. We'll need DNA for that."

Jared gritted his teeth to keep from saying what he really was thinking and fired off a text to Coglin. "I'm requesting the parents' blood types. Though the quantity of blood isn't from a nick or scrape, and they didn't mention any injuries."

"The dad already remains a person of interest, though," Bristol said. "And this could sway our action in one direction or another."

"We'll have the father scanned for injuries." Jared looked at Reed. "I want to hear about the blood results the moment you have them. All actionable evidence actually."

Reed nodded. "Unrelated to this, we've learned the father is scheduled to testify in a gang shooting next week."

"Why didn't he say anything?" Bristol planted her hands onto her duty belt. "The baby could've been taken to stop him from testifying."

Jared swallowed hard. A gang with Luna? The ending was looking grim if that were the case. "If so, we should get a demand call from the abductor."

"Toni says no calls have been received," Reed said.

"We need to talk to Pratt again," Bristol said.

"Agreed," Jared said and was eager to question the man. "But we'll wait for the blood results as that could be telling."

Bristol nodded and shifted her focus to Reed. "What do we know about the gang?"

"They're called the Hoovers. Local gang known for being hard-core. No one has tied down the leader's ID. They go off on their own. Police and street folks, even other gangs, consider them more ruthless. Usually gangs have a culture and code. Hoovers defy it all. They have zero respect."

"Not a good idea to testify against one of their members then," Bristol said. "You have to respect Pratt for being willing to do it."

"But also you have to figure they would take a baby to stop him." Jared swallowed away images of Wyatt dancing on the fringe of his brain. Wyatt hadn't been abducted by a gang but by a ruthless couple who'd once worked for his family and saw a way to make a sizable amount of cash.

But a baby with such a hostile gang? Unthinkable.

"I've looped in the Metro Safe Streets Task Force," Reed said. "We'll see if they can discover a lead."

"The FBI led group?" Jared asked.

Reed nodded. "Various local agencies along with ATF make up the group, and the local officers are federally deputized for speedy action. They'll interface with local gang units, and we should have enough boots on the ground to hopefully get actionable information."

"But it'll take time," Jared said. "Time we don't have."

"It's still the best route," Reed said. "Far better than any of us trying to take on gangs we don't understand."

"Agreed, but I want immediate action." Jared gritted his teeth.

"We all do," Bristol said. "So let's focus on the parents. Maybe Pratt can tell us something that will help us or the gang units to move faster."

"Then let's head back to the command center and prepare our questions," he said, but he looked at Reed. "Don't forget. I want to hear about the blood type the minute you get the results."

"I'll text you both at the same time," Sierra said. "I should have the fingerprint from the Pratts' suite analyzed by then too."

Jared nodded his thanks and looked at Bristol. "Let's go."

He stormed toward his vehicle. He really was thankful for the Veritas Center's quick turnaround of results but nothing could be done fast enough for him now. Fast enough for saving baby Luna's life.

7

Bristol wished she could wipe the distress from Jared's face as they stepped toward the Pratts' room. But in addition to holding the blood results from both parents and Luna's blanket in his hands, they'd also had to waste time locating an entrance not plagued with reporters on their return to the hospital. And now, Bristol and Jared were about to share the blood details with the Pratts. Telling them about the blood-soaked blanket was a task Bristol didn't relish. But Jared had the added strain of having failed a baby in the past.

How did he live with that? True, from the sound of it, she didn't think it was his fault, but she understood how he would take the blame. The only people at fault were the people who took the baby. But if the task force didn't find Luna for whatever reason, Bristol would live with guilt on her back for the rest of her life.

No. Stop. Don't think that way. She wouldn't fail Luna, and while looking for the child, Bristol would do her best to try to help Jared let go of his guilt and the inability to trust.

Listen to her. She didn't trust many people either, except for her family. Surely not God right now. Was that why God put her together with Jared again? Both of them with issues to fix and they could help each other figure them out. After all, it was easier to see other people's problems and tell them how to fix them, than it was to see the same thing in yourself and affect change.

Jared pressed his free hand on the door but turned to look at Bristol before pushing it open. "I want you to take lead again."

She was honored for the job. Of course she was. But he wasn't offering it to her due to her skills. She had a connection with the mom, and they were about to share bad news. That connection could ease their pain.

Bristol drew her shoulders back and slipped past Jared to push the door open.

Mrs. Pratt shot up in her bed. "Oh, no. No. Your face says it's bad news. Is Luna..."

"We haven't located your daughter yet." Bristol remained calm and eased up to the bed. "But we did find her blanket in a parking structure."

"Makes sense that they'd ditch it," Mr. Pratt said. "They knew it could give away her identity."

"Likely." Bristol met his gaze. "But you need to know the blanket was saturated with a large quantity of blood."

"Blood?" Mrs. Pratt clutched her chest.

Mr. Pratt took his wife's hand. "But you don't know if it's Luna's blood, right?"

"We've had the blood typed. It's O positive."

Mrs. Pratt shuddered. "Luna's blood type."

"We can't say it's hers," Bristol said. "O positive is a common blood type so it could belong to her abductor."

"It's my blood type," Mr. Pratt added. "But I assume you know that since they took our blood an hour or so ago." He released his wife's hand and held out his arms. "Go ahead and search me. You won't find any fresh cuts."

"We'll have a nurse do that once we finish talking," Jared said.

Mr. Pratt shook his head. "You're wasting time again. As you said, O positive is common. Could be from any number of people. Do you have anything at all that will help find her?"

Bristol hated to do this but... "You didn't mention that you were scheduled to testify in a gang trial."

"What's that..." Mr. Pratt shoved his hand in his hair. "For the love of God! You don't think they have something to do with this? I mean, if they do. No...she's...they'd." He swallowed and gripped his wife's hand. "They're brutal."

Mrs. Pratt looked up at her husband. "I told you not to testify. Now they have Luna. Those monsters have her."

"Hold on, Mrs. Pratt," Bristol said, making sure to keep her cool when her insides were churning with anguish for this family. "A special gang task force is looking into the connection, but we have no evidence that the gang is involved."

"And you don't have any evidence that they're not, right?" Mrs. Pratt panted for air.

"Right, but jumping to conclusions won't help find Luna." Bristol kept her tone firm to try to help the parents calm down. "We have to work every lead, one at a time. Right now, we need you, Mr. Pratt, to tell us about your upcoming testimony."

He rested on the side of the bed. "There's nothing much to it, really. I was at the wrong place at the wrong time. Getting off MAX in Chinatown for an appointment. I'm an electrician, and I work for a developer who's restoring a building there." He released his wife's hand and shoved both hands into his pockets. "I saw this Hoovers gang member try to mug an older woman. She fought back. The guy pops off a gun and takes her down.

For some reason I can't understand, I took a picture instead of running. The shooter made eye contact with me, and I thought he'd take me out, but sirens sounded down the street, and he bolted. Cops weren't on their way to the shooting but another crime in the area. Saved my life."

"And you shared the picture with the police?" Bristol asked.

"First I called 911 and checked on the lady. She was still alive. Died with me holding her hand. She was something special. Not upset or bitter. Just glad to be going to heaven and thankful that I was holding her hand so she didn't have to be alone. She died before the ambulance or cops got there. I wanted justice for her so I never questioned if I would testify. But if they..." His voice broke, and he covered his face with his hands.

Bristol had considered him a potential suspect until this moment. Here was a man who cared about people and loved his daughter. She couldn't imagine him hurting his baby. Still, Bristol had to keep an open mind and consider any evidence they might locate.

"Have you received any threats?" Jared asked.

Mr. Pratt shook his head. "Which honestly surprised me. I thought they might try to retaliate. I read online that they always use force in the form of retaliation. They go by the gang acronym EBK."

"Every Body Killer," Bristol said. "No one's safe with them. They're more than willing to kill anyone."

Mr. Pratt grimaced. "We've been keeping our eyes open at home and work, but I didn't expect they would come here."

"I don't know why you didn't," Jared said. "They engage in violence for the sake of violence. So why not here?"

Mr. Pratt's eyes glistened with unshed tears. "I'm going to

call the DA right now and tell him I won't testify. Then if the Hoovers have Luna, they'll give her back."

"But if they don't have her, you'll be letting a terrible man get away with murder and walk the streets to kill others," Bristol said.

"I don't care," he said. "I want my baby back safe and alive, and that's all I can think about right now."

Bristol understood his decision, but the blood-soaked blanket said he could already be too late.

The day moved on far too quickly, each moment without a lead weighing heavy on Bristol. Teagan had provided Osborne's address, but the guy hadn't been located yet, and they had a team watching his apartment. She'd interviewed nurses while Jared questioned guards, and the others on the team called women who'd recently lost their babies. They also interviewed the Pratts' parents, not learning anything to help.

The distress of the situation and failure to locate Osborne ate at Bristol, and she needed a break. She was jonesing for some caffeine to help her stay awake, but the team had decimated the coffee pod supply. Maybe she could find a coffee shop open.

She headed toward the door and hoped she wouldn't find any rogue reporters. Thankfully, Coglin had banished the press to the outside of the building so the task force wasn't bombarded with questions every time they left the room, which for Piper was often as she needed frequent bathroom breaks.

Jared came up beside Bristol. "You look fried."

"Gee thanks." She wrinkled her nose at him but quickly

stopped. She already looked younger than thirty and that didn't help make her look like an experienced deputy.

He averted his gaze. "I didn't mean it like that. It was just small talk really."

"You were right, though," she said, trying to mend fences. "I'm tired and heading out in search of caffeine."

He took a slight step back. "Do you mind if I join you? I could use some coffee too."

Did she mind?

She did, but not in the way he meant it. She minded the way he'd crept into her brain each time during the day she'd taken a moment to clear her head. When she'd gone for a walk around the hospital to stretch her legs, being strategic to avoid reporters. Even when she'd checked in with her family, hoping for good news of any kind, but not hearing any.

So, yeah, she minded all right, but... "No problem."

He charged for the door as if he expected her to change her mind and held it open for her.

"Our best bet is the cafeteria." She eased past him, working hard not to touch him. "It's a hike but I think it's open twenty-four/seven."

They started down the hall.

He looked at her. "We should talk about our past."

Ah. Just the reason she didn't want him to come along, but maybe if they cleared the air, he would stop troubling her in such an intense way. Still, she wanted to first give him an out in case he didn't really want to have this conversation. "We don't have to. At least not for me. It's firmly in my past and no need to resurrect it."

"Honestly?" He arched an eyebrow. "You've been giving me some looks since we've reconnected that say otherwise."

Dang. She didn't hide her emotions as well as she'd

thought. "I didn't mean to look at you in any way. In fact, not looking at you is preferable."

"See, that tells me that we need to talk."

She shot him a terse look. "Am I still angry at how you bailed? You bet I am. But I've forgiven you."

"Forgiven me." He slowed and looked at her. "Sounds like even after all this time you don't think I made the right decision?"

She planted her hands on her hips. "Seriously? How could I approve of you encouraging me to fall for you only to decide one day out of the blue that your career was more important?"

"It wasn't such an easy and out-of-the-blue decision." His tone turned dark and heavy with emotion. "From day one I told you I'd enlisted and would report for duty the day after camp ended."

"Yeah, sure." She picked up speed as if walking faster would rid the emotions swirling in her gut. "You told me that, but you didn't *ever* say it meant we would go our separate ways."

"But I never mentioned a future or planned for one with you."

"It was implied."

"Not on my part. I never wanted to lead you on and hurt you."

She came to a stop and looked up at him. "Then you thought the whole time we were together that it was just a summer romance that would go nowhere?"

"Yes. I mean no." He clamped his hand on the back of his neck. "It started out that way, but then I fell in love with you, and I had to work hard to walk away."

She kept her focus pinned on him. "Then why did you?"

"Because the way I felt about you was all-consuming, and I was heading into a career where my every action counted. I was going into the Navy as an officer and men counted on me to do the right thing at all times. I'd never had a role like that, and I had to be sure I could fulfill it."

"I actually understand that. It would be like joining the police force as a sergeant or lieutenant without knowing the jobs of those who report to you. I would want to focus too. But if I was in love with someone, I would take a break at most. Not bail."

"Yeah." He shoved his hands in his pockets and started walking again. "In hindsight that might've been the thing to do, but I couldn't risk failing at marriage. If we continued down the same path, that was the way we were headed. My parents proved how detrimental failing at love can be, and I'm a married-for-life kind of guy. I don't believe in divorce or do-overs, so if I ever get married, I have to get it right."

If he was hoping she would understand, he might get his wish. His motives were clear, and as she walked, they sunk in and even made sense. But still, her heart stung over his betrayal. What soothed it just a bit was his declaration of the all-consuming feelings. She'd burned with the same feelings at the time, and it was good to know he hadn't been faking those.

They reached the cafeteria and paid for their coffees, which they pumped out of large pots at an island coffee bar, the nutty aroma snaking up. He automatically handed her two creamers and a sugar, and she took them. Memories flooded her of having coffee breaks together at camp, the middle schoolers making kissing noises and laughing at them, all the while pointing jealous glances their way when they thought no one was looking.

In many ways, her romance with Jared was like a middle school romance. Fast, furious, and over in a blink of an eye. But unlike middle schoolers, it was a mature love that could've lasted. In fact, they could've still been together.

If she let go of the hurt, could they rekindle that romance, or had it run its course? She honestly wanted to erase the ache in her heart to find out, but the pain was still too big to even contemplate washing it away.

His phone rang, and he dug it from his pocket. "It's Sierra." He quickly answered and led them to a secluded alcove. "Okay if I put you on speaker so Bristol can hear?"

Sierra must have said yes as he tapped the button. "Go ahead."

"First," Sierra said. "We located four DNA samples on the blanket in addition to the blood. Emory Jenkins—our DNA expert—put a rush on the samples and got them all running by four o'clock. DNA takes twenty-four hours minimum which means you won't have results before tomorrow around four."

Jared gripped his phone until his fingers turned white. "We have no choice but to wait."

"I wish we could speed it up, but we can't," Sierra said. "Rest assured it was processed as fast as possible while still using the utmost care, and you'll get results faster than any local agency could've given you."

"Sorry," Jared said. "I didn't mean to imply it's your fault. I appreciate how fast you're handling everything."

"And speaking of speed, I finished processing and running all the fingerprints. None returned a match in AFIS. Sorry."

"None?" Bristol asked, still hoping she didn't hear right. "Including the one on the bassinet?"

"None," Sierra said firmly. "We lifted and processed over two hundred prints in the room and stairwell."

"You work fast," Jared said.

"I called in all of my team and put everyone on this investigation."

"Thanks for that," Jared said. "Any other forensics that might help?"

"Not yet." Sierra might have been giving bad news, but she didn't sound down. She seemed to be an optimistic person for working in such an often-disappointing field. "No blood on Mr. Pratt's backpack, but Emory is running touch DNA from the bag. I also recovered a partial footprint near the blanket. It's small, and I'm trying to match the shoe, but with a partial it's harder to do. There was also enough soil deposited on the concrete that we're running it for soil composition."

"What will that tell you?" Bristol asked.

"If the composition is unique enough, we might be able to place the location where the suspect recently walked. It's a long shot and could take some time so don't count on it being the lead to pin your investigation on."

Bristol shared a disappointed look with Jared. All day they had been counting on the forensics to give them a suspect's name and address. But now Luna had been missing for ten hours and each hour that passed could be the hour that she wasn't fed when needed and her blood sugar caused serious health issues or even death.

8

In the command center, Jared and Bristol joined Hunter, Colin, and Piper. Jared's stomach was full and content from the dinner catered by the hospital—chicken something— the spicy scent lingering in the air, but Piper's face suddenly creased and made him wish he hadn't eaten. She'd just come back from returning the Pratts' phones then resting in a bed arranged by Coglin and was once again sitting behind her computer. She looked more refreshed than anyone in their command center, including Bristol. The stress of the search lingered in Bristol's tight expression.

"You won't believe this." Piper leaned back in her chair and looked up at Jared. "Mrs. Pratt made twenty-one calls about ten months ago to an attorney who handles private adoptions."

"An attorney our agency is already investigating for performing illegal adoptions," Colin said.

"The guy's information is right here." Piper pointed at her screen that held a website for Everett Holloway, Attorney at Law.

"Mrs. Pratt called this guy before she became pregnant with Luna," Bristol said.

Piper nodded.

"They didn't even mention adoption to us," Jared said. "And to find out it's an attorney we're investigating? What if this attorney is somehow involved in Luna's kidnapping?"

"It would be a stretch, right?" Bristol locked gazes with him. "I know illegal adoption rings get babies under false pretenses, but I haven't heard of them stealing babies from a hospital."

"I've never heard of that either," Jared said. "Seems too risky, but abducting from poorer neighborhoods isn't unheard of."

"In this instance," Colin said. "Our investigative team says Holloway has allegedly set up as a baby farmer."

"What in the world does that mean?" Bristol asked.

"Just what it sounds like." Colin frowned in disgust. "He's brought unmarried mothers-to-be from foreign countries to live at his home. Likely women who fear social stigma or are from impoverished families. He pays these women a nominal fee then sells the baby for a huge profit. He's even allegedly registered them as US citizens and welfare paid for all the costs associated with the births. Our team hasn't been able to prove the illegal adoption aspect yet, and the welfare fraud might just be where they'll get him."

Bristol grimaced. "How does he find these mothers?"

"Baby recruiters that he pays a finder's fee," Colin said. "It's an age-old scheme. The most famous investigation involved a woman who adopted out five thousand children and five hundred children died under her care. That agency closed down in 1950. You would think this scheme wouldn't still work in this day and age, but it does."

Piper rested her hands on her belly. "I can't even imagine giving up my baby. This man is exploiting those women, and he has to pay."

"Unfortunately, without any proof we can't bring charges," Hunter, the ever practical one of the group, said.

Jared gritted his teeth and wanted to pound the table. "I don't think their connection to the Pratts is a coincidence. We need to dig deeper."

"I could go undercover," Piper said. "Offer to sell my child."

"No!" Bristol held up her hands. "We can't risk anything happening to you or the baby."

"Well, someone needs to do it." Piper narrowed her eyes. "Either as a woman offering to sell her child or as parents wanting to adopt."

"You and Bristol could do it," Colin suggested. "As parents. We can set up fake IDs for both of you by morning that will hold up under any scrutiny."

"Have either of you been caught on camera by reporters?" Hunter asked. "Because if you have, Holloway might recognize you."

Jared shook his head. "We've been using the back entrance to avoid them so no worries there."

Bristol tilted her head, her eyes narrowing. Jared expected her to object to going undercover with him.

"Even if they have Luna," she said. "With all the public attention around the AMBER Alert, they can't very well offer her to us."

"But you might be able to learn enough about the guy to bring him down," Colin said. "And if he has Luna, we can track her or cut some sort of deal with the creep."

Jared wanted to point out that if this attorney had Luna, he might never be able to place her, and that didn't bode well for the baby. Which meant Jared had to do everything he could to find out if Holloway arranged to have Luna taken.

"Go ahead," Jared said. "Get the undercover process

started. If we haven't located Luna by morning, and you have solid IDs created, we'll go through with it."

The door opened, and Reed stepped in. He waved at Jared, his motions urgent. Jared crossed the room and Bristol followed, all eyes on them.

"Osborne finally came home," Reed said. "He hasn't said a word, but we have him in the interview room."

Jared looked at Bristol. "Conflict of interest. You'll have to wait here."

"No worries," she said, but the frustration in her eyes belied her words.

"Let's go," Jared said to Reed.

In the hallway, Jared looked at Reed. "Did Osborne come along willingly?"

"Not at first, but I persuaded him." Reed grinned.

Jared didn't ask for details. He was likely better off not knowing. "You get a feel for the guy?"

Reed shook his head. "Guy baffles me. His apartment smelled like weed, but he had a gym set up in his living room, and he's built. So either he respects his body or he doesn't."

"Maybe the pot is a new thing."

"You mean like he had something bad happen that took him off track?"

"Yeah."

"Could be." Reed picked up his pace. "We have any information on his finances yet?"

"Not yet, but Hunter's working on it."

They reached the room where a member of the task force stood guard outside. Jared nodded at him and swiped his card for the lock.

Osborne jumped to his feet. He wore a uniform of black pants and white shirt boasting a patch for another local security guard firm. "I have nothing to say to you so you're wasting your time."

Holding out his ID, Jared introduced himself. "Why don't we sit and just clarify some facts that we already know?"

Jared tried to sound laid back, but with Osborne's grimace, he wasn't sure he accomplished it.

Jared turned a chair around and straddled it to look even more relaxed. "So you worked for Steele Guardians?"

"For a year."

"And then you had a problem. Showed up high at work."

Osborne crossed his arms. "No one ever proved it."

"Because you refused to have a blood test." Reed sat and leaned his elbows on the table.

Osborne jutted out his chin. "They couldn't make me do that."

"But if you weren't high and took the test, you wouldn't have lost your job," Jared said.

"No skin off my nose. Plenty of jobs out there." He tugged at the patch on his shirt. "Got one in a day."

Most likely because they didn't know you were high. "But you really didn't need to go to work that fast, right?" Jared asked. "I mean after your big payoff to reveal who was guarding the birthing suite, why work?"

A flash of recognition lit Osborne's eyes, but it was just that—a flash and it disappeared. "Don't know what you're talking about."

"We're talking about a kidnapped baby made possible by subduing the guard from Steele Guardians," Reed said. "And you covering so the woman could take the baby and exit the stairwell."

Osborne smirked. "If you're so sure about what I did, show me something that proves it."

Unfortunately, Jared had nothing.

Osborne's smug smile said he knew it and was smart enough to keep his mouth shut. Jared looked at Reed, and he gave a nod of acknowledgment.

They both knew this man was guilty and time sitting in a holding cell just might convince him to talk.

∼

Jared hadn't given much information to Bristol on his interview with Osborne. He'd just said he believed Osborne was the guy who tied Aaron up. Reed was taking lead on getting proof of Osborne's involvement, including looking at the women in Osborne's life in the event one of them took Luna. Then Jared invited her to join him in talking with the Pratts again. This time to find out why they called Holloway. Not just once, but so very many times.

Bristol peered at the couple and tried to keep her tone neutral, but she had to take a few cleansing breaths to manage it before she continued. Not even their faces that had grown so tired and worried seemed to make it easier not to judge them for contacting a man like Holloway. Jared seemed to be having the same problem. Who wouldn't when it looked like these people had planned to be involved with illegally buying a baby, but just stopped when they had their own child?

Mrs. Pratt crossed her arms. "We didn't need to use Holloway after all."

"But if you hadn't gotten pregnant," Jared stated. "You were prepared to buy a baby from him."

"Not me." Mr. Pratt crossed his arms. "I shut it down before we knew Sonya was pregnant."

"Or so you think you did," Bristol said. "Your wife was still communicating with them when she was three months pregnant."

Mr. Pratt fired a shocked look at his wife. "You were?"

"We didn't know about Luna yet." She tightened her arms.

"But you were still talking to that man?" Mr. Pratt gaped at her. "I thought we decided that we couldn't get a child from someone when he might steal a child from its parents."

"I wanted a baby." She clasped her hands in her lap.

"When were you going to tell me about it? The day the baby arrived on our doorstep?"

"I don't know." She started to cry. "I just know I was desperate to be a mom."

Mr. Pratt's forehead furrowed. "And now you are, but maybe the guy you insisted on talking to took our child from us."

"Let's not jump to conclusions," Jared said. "We don't have any proof Holloway's involved any more than we can prove the Hoovers gang is."

"But you're going to talk to Holloway, right?" Mrs. Pratt asked.

"Yes," Bristol said. "How did you learn about him?"

"I made friends with a woman—Felicity Wetzel. She was in an online group for couples struggling to become parents. I had several rounds of IVF that didn't work. I'd lost all hope, and she told me about him."

"This is exactly the kind of information we need to know." Jared fisted his hands.

"But why?" Mrs. Pratt cried out. "I doubt anyone in the group even knows about Luna. When I got pregnant, I lost touch with everyone but Felicity. And Holloway arranged an adoption for her so she had no reason to take Luna." Mrs. Pratt sat forward. "You're not going to take their son away, are you?"

"We'll be talking to them for sure," Bristol said, hoping

she wouldn't have to destroy another family unit. "What happens after that, I can't say."

Mrs. Pratt shook her head. "Please don't. Please fight to keep them together. I can't be responsible for another woman losing her child."

Bristol opened her mouth to point out that Felicity might have already done that by going through with an illegal adoption, but there was no point in torturing Mrs. Pratt more. "We'll need Felicity's contact details."

Mrs. Pratt picked up her phone and tapped the screen, but took her time as if stalling might stop them from finding this woman.

"Is Felicity married?" Bristol asked.

Mrs. Pratt nodded and shared the woman's contact information.

"Is there anything else about Holloway that you can tell us that might help in our investigation?" Jared asked.

"Yeah," Mr. Pratt said. "One of the reasons I didn't want to proceed with him is the man is a ruthless money-grubber. So be careful. I don't think he would hesitate to turn violent to save himself."

On that very negative note, Bristol started for the door, and Jared followed her out of the room. In the hallway, he called Reed and explained that he and Bristol were going to conduct a surprise interview with the Wetzels.

"Call if anything comes up." He started down the hallway at a quick clip.

Bristol kept up with him. "Do you think the Wetzels are in danger of losing their son?"

"I suppose it'll depend on how Holloway got the child. If he has legit consent from the parents, then nothing will happen. If not, and the parents can be found, then yes. I think it's a good possibility that they will lose the boy."

"Bad possibility, you mean," she said as they took the elevator to the ground floor.

"Bad for them, yes, but if the birth family didn't consent to the adoption, then getting their son back will be positive for them."

"I hate having to upset the Wetzels, but we have to do everything we can to find Luna."

Jared nodded and strode out of the back of the building, his head down. The current day Jared was far more intense than camp Jared. She liked this guy even more. Sure, she'd loved camp Jared, but as she'd gotten older, she'd found men with purpose far more attractive. He'd always known where he was going in life, but wasn't quite this driven.

Inside Jared's car, she took note of the setting sun in the balmy August night. A night that would remind her of the many nights under the stars at camp if she let herself think about it.

"I was hoping for something else on Nurse Johnson or the Pratts' phones, but this is a good lead," Bristol said once Jared got his vehicle on the road. "And I'm glad the team agreed to send the files to Nick too. Just in case."

Jared glanced at her. "Shows that the team won't put their egos in front of finding Luna where I'm afraid some people might."

"Do I detect a hint of your trust issue there?" she asked.

"Probably. "

"I don't have a kidnapping investigation in my past, but losing Thomas so violently left me reeling. Maybe irrevocably damaged my faith in God." She took a long breath. "Where was He when Thomas was brutally murdered? Where is He now?"

"I honestly don't know. My only answer for that is what my pastor told me when Wyatt died. He said sometimes going through a tough season in life often means losing everything around us. Everything we know. At that time, we have nothing but to turn to God or turn away from Him. If we choose to turn to Him despite our circumstances, to hope that He is real and in control—that He's there fighting on your behalf, then your hope is restored."

"Sounds simple, but it's harder than you can know."

"You're probably right. I've had issues in life, but nothing like losing a sibling. Especially in such a horrific way." He rested a hand on her arm. "I'm praying you can find that hope again."

Could she? Would she? Was coming together with Jared the way to do it?

She sat back, closed her eyes, and had a long talk with God that had been missing in her life for so long. Told Him everything she was feeling. Had felt. Didn't want to keep feeling. The car slowed, and she opened her eyes, surprised to see they'd arrived at the Wetzel's house.

The large two-story home was located in an exclusive neighborhood in Clackamas, a suburb of Portland. Up lights lit the façade and landscape, chasing away the nightfall. The couple would need to have money if they were able to buy a child and their home fit an affluent family.

"I wonder what they paid for their son." Bristol climbed out of the vehicle.

"We'll likely find out if we go undercover." Jared got out after her.

"Or we can just ask." She strode up the stone walkway to a mahogany front door, a brisk breeze blowing over her and hinting at cooler night temps. She rang the bell and the chimes sounded into the quiet evening.

Footfalls soon thumped closer, and the door cracked open. Bristol displayed her ID and identified herself and Jared. "Are you Mrs. Wetzel?"

"Yes."

"Can we come in and talk to you?"

"This isn't about Ian, is it?" Mrs. Wetzel clutched her white cotton blouse with one hand then flung long blond hair over her shoulder. "Nothing's happened to him?"

"No," Bristol said. "We have some questions about an investigation we're working on."

"Okay, fine." Mrs. Wetzel opened the door and started through a large foyer to enter the first room on the right.

Bristol followed the woman into a formal living area decorated in warm reds and oranges. Mrs. Wetzel dropped onto a gray sofa in front of a wall with orange and white patterned wallpaper. She pointed at armchairs with orange cushions.

Bristol sat, but Jared remained standing.

"What's this about?" Mrs. Wetzel worried her hands together in her lap.

"We're here to talk about Mr. Holloway and your son's adoption," Jared said.

Mrs. Wetzel gasped, and her gaze darted around the room. "I think I'd like my husband to be here for this discussion."

"We can appreciate that," Bristol said. "But we're looking for a missing baby and Holloway could be involved. We don't have time to waste for your husband to get home."

Mrs. Wetzel's face paled. "I'm sorry but I can't afford to say the wrong thing and lose my son."

"We have no interest in taking your son from you," Jared said. "Unless his birth parents didn't legally relinquish him."

"They did. We have copies of the papers."

They could've been forged, but Bristol wouldn't point that out as she wanted the woman to be forthcoming. "Then you should have nothing to worry about."

"Can I at least put my husband on a video call?"

"Go ahead," Jared said.

She dug her phone from her jeans' pocket and dialed. She frantically explained the situation then turned the phone to face Bristol and Jared.

Jared introduced them again. "We'd like details of your son's adoption."

"What do you want to know?" The guy on-screen had graying temples in sleek black hair.

"Did you pay Mr. Holloway for your son?" Jared asked bluntly.

Mrs. Wetzel gasped again, but if her husband was upset his expression didn't show it. "We did. Which is not uncommon in a private adoption. We paid for all of the birth mother's expenses and legal costs."

"Did Holloway tell you how he located babies for adoption?" Bristol asked.

"He said he was known to doctors, nurses, and hospitals in the area," Mrs. Wetzel replied. "So if a woman came to them wanting to give up their child for adoption, they referred them to him."

"Did you know that Holloway's methods of obtaining the babies were often illegal?" Jared asked.

"I'm not going to answer that question, and Felicity, don't answer either." Mr. Wetzel clamped his lips closed.

"Let's assume the reason you aren't answering is that the answer is yes." Jared leaned closer to the phone. "Didn't you question where the babies came from?"

"No," Mr. Wetzel said. "And there's no point in speculating now. We have our son and have documents on file to show he was relinquished by his parents."

"Tell us the process you went through and how the financial transaction was handled," Jared said.

"Simple. We applied. A home study was conducted. We were approved. We gave our preference for a boy and were told a woman was due in four months with a boy, and he could be ours. We put down twenty grand and then began making monthly payments of five grand until we picked up our boy. Then we paid another twenty grand."

"All told you paid sixty-thousand dollars for your son," Bristol clarified.

"And I would've paid double that, if need be," Mr. Wetzel said. "A few cash payments and we're the family we always wanted to be."

"You paid in cash?" Bristol asked. "Didn't you find that odd?"

"Not after he explained."

"Explained?" Jared asked.

"He said in the past he had issues when government overwatch got involved and delayed adoptions for months just to do all of their paperwork." Mr. Wetzel frowned. "We didn't want that to happen so we withdrew cash according to his guidelines and paid it to him."

"What kind of guidelines did he have?" Bristol asked.

"Nothing much." Mrs. Wetzels' hands tightened. "He just said to keep our withdrawals under ten grand so the bank didn't have to report them to the feds. He said that could trigger inquiries that would slow things down."

"And you never considered the fact that cash made your transactions untraceable, and he needed that because he wasn't performing legal adoptions?" Jared asked.

"The thought might've crossed our minds," Mr. Wetzel admitted. "But there was no evidence of any wrongdoing. As I said, we have the papers to prove our son is ours."

"Let's hope what you're saying is true," Jared said. "Now I have to impose on you. First, don't tell Holloway about our conversation. If you do, you will be charged with an accessory to any crimes he's charged with. Do you understand that?"

"Yes," Mr. Wetzel said, and his wife nodded.

"Next, Deputy Steele and I might be going undercover to gain additional information on Holloway. If we do, we will use your names as the couple referring us. If he calls you to confirm that detail, we will need you to confirm it."

"And if we don't?" Mr. Wetzel stuck out his chin. "Will you threaten to take our son away?"

"Of course not," Jared said, looking offended. "The only thing that could happen—and it's a big thing—is you could be putting our lives and the life of a helpless baby in danger."

Bristol couldn't have said it better but might've added that the clock was ticking down and even a second could matter in saving baby Luna.

9

Jared got up and paced across the conference room a few times to burn off his frustration. Didn't help. He needed to get out of this space holding the evidence of their failed leads. Every single one had fallen through, and he couldn't remain in the place where the walls shouted his failure. Nor could he let the team see his mood. He was the team leader, and he was failing them. He couldn't—wouldn't—bring them down with him.

Maybe a walk. Or he could check in with Tim and Deb again, who were going home in the morning. He'd stopped in after dinner, but it was too hard to see their happiness while the Pratts suffered. He would have to settle for text updates from them until after Luna was found.

Maybe Bristol had a good idea. She'd gone to check in with her family in the training room where they were still diligently reviewing video. Sure, they'd been looking at the monitors all day and had come up empty too. Could be just as frustrating in that room, but he wanted to be with Bristol.

He could no longer deny that he still had feelings for her. Wasn't sure if he wanted to deny it.

He headed for the door and stopped next to Reed, who

was still working on finding anything actionable on Nelson Osborne. "I'm headed to the training room. See if the Steeles found anything."

Reed nodded. "If anyone will find a lead, it's the Steele family." Reed stretched his arms overhead. "I've always thought the family name was appropriate. Or maybe it's the other way around. They're like steel because of their name. They're all forged in steel. You know, strong under pressure."

"I'm beginning to see that."

"Bristol might be the youngest in her family, but she's as much of a force to be reckoned with as the others." Reed cocked his head. "You two still have a thing?"

"Not sure about that."

"Trust me. You both do. It's obvious."

"Maybe," was all Jared would admit. "Call me if something comes up." He turned away to leave.

"Running away from it won't solve anything," Reed said. "I oughta know. Did it for years."

Jared looked back to find Reed's sincere look. "If you want to talk about it after this is all over let me know."

Jared gave a firm nod and strode out the door and down the hallway. He'd never been one to talk about his feelings. Not since he was a kid and his parents ignored them. They only acknowledged things that had to do with living their lifestyle. But his questions about God and sacrificial living had been ignored. He would never forget when he'd told his parents he wasn't going into law like they wanted, but joined Navy ROTC at Oregon State. At first they'd refused to pay for his college and ROTC only covered the last two years. Surprisingly, before his dream was ended, they had a change of heart and decided even if they believed he was on the wrong career path, he needed to have a college degree.

He pushed open the door to the training room and

everyone looked up and locked onto him. Bristol stood near her cousin Teagan who'd continued to manage the guards and made sure the Pratts remained safe. She'd also led the family in reviewing the video in a logical fashion, and Jared could easily imagine her leading the family business.

Jared appreciated her intensity, which seemed to be her normal MO, but he thought it might be taxing over the long haul. She wasn't married. He had no idea why, but maybe her job leading Steele Guardians took up all of her time. Or maybe she just didn't want to get married. Jared didn't think he would ever do so. Why couldn't that be true of Teagan too?

He crossed the room to Bristol, all gazes tracking him. She'd probably finally told them that he was the guy who'd bolted on her that summer at camp. But maybe not. Their expressions didn't show hatred or anger, just curiosity. If she hadn't told them in all these years, why would she now? He was but a blip on the radar of her life at this point. A storm on her horizon. As soon as they located Luna, he would be gone again. Likely banished by her this time.

He didn't like that thought. Didn't like it at all.

He snapped out of his own head and ignored their attention to cross the room. He stopped near the first row of computers, where Bristol looked over Teagan's shoulder.

"Please tell me you've located something to help," he said, not liking how desperate he sounded.

Teagan frowned. "We've located something, but not sure it will help. Take a look at this."

He circled around the computer, coming nearly hip to hip with Bristol. He willed her with his mind to touch his hand again, but she didn't. Maybe he was hiding his mood better than he thought, or maybe she didn't want to touch him in front of her family.

Teagan started a video playing. "We think this is the suspect checking out the birthing center last week."

A woman dressed in jeans and hoodie and keeping her face away from the cameras, strolled across the lobby and entered the elevator.

"She could be any one of many women," Jared said, not impressed. "Other than height, why do you think it's her?"

"We pick her up again here." Teagan clicked another video open on the computer.

The woman appeared approaching the birthing center. She kept her head down and stood outside watching. She was shifty and nervous, moving like a wounded cat looking for help.

"This goes on for about thirty minutes until she talks to one of the nurses." Teagan advanced the video ahead, then hit play.

A nurse exited the birthing center, and the suspect approached her. Her back was to the camera but the nurse's face showed clearly.

"We need to find out who this nurse is and interview her," Jared said.

"Way ahead of you," Teagan said. "Coglin identified her as Mary Raney."

"She's on duty," Bristol said. "Teagan sent the video to my phone, and I was just about to come get you so we could talk to Raney."

"Then let's go." The lead was too good to waste even a second, so he bolted for the door and to the elevator.

The thump of Bristol's solid footsteps followed him. He liked the combat boots hitting tiles over the clicking of high heels. Made him remember the Bristol he'd once known and loved. She'd loved sneakers, especially Converse low tops in bright colors and had told him she wouldn't wear heels unless forced.

In the elevator, he looked at her. "Your family's help is very much appreciated. If we'd had to assign staff to review the video, we wouldn't be nearly as far in this investigation. Not that we're really anywhere, but we've eliminated so many possibilities."

"They like to help—their faith in action. It's really what motivates all of us."

He smiled at her. "I always liked that about you at camp. If there was work to be done you were usually the first to volunteer."

"It just comes natural. Like breathing. As kids, we saw it in action all the time. And if we got into a teenage mood, we were reminded that it was expected of us." She gave a tight smile. "That could be often in high school. We weren't as keen on helping. But then once we got going there was no better feeling than helping someone in need."

"Agreed. It's why I served and why I do this job." Luna's image flashed into his mind. "I need to do more here. Have to do more. Every minute that ticks by and we don't find Luna, makes the odds less of bringing her home alive."

Bristol gave a solemn nod. "Maybe Nurse Raney will give us what we need."

"Hopefully." He offered a prayer to that effect.

The elevator doors opened, and he stood back to wait for Bristol to exit. He followed her to the birthing center where the nurse they needed sat behind the front desk. She looked up at them, and brushed back her short curly blond hair.

Jared introduced them, and they held out their IDs. Mary leaned back in her chair and raised a hand to cover her mouth.

Bristol smiled, likely to help relieve the nurse's fear. "Can you step outside with us for a minute?"

Mary's large blue eyes narrowed. "Did I do something wrong?"

"Not at all." Bristol widened her smile. "But we think you might be able to help us."

"Oh, okay." She let out a relieved breath. "Let me get someone to staff the desk." She dug a cell phone from her flowery uniform pocket and called in reinforcements before standing.

Jared resisted tapping his foot as they waited for another nurse to spell Mary. He didn't want to agitate the woman more, and he didn't want to amp up his own frustrations. The replacement arrived, and Jared hurried out the door and turned to wait for Bristol and Mary.

Bristol already had her phone out and tapped the screen then looked at the nurse. "We located a video from last week where a woman approached you outside the birthing center. She spoke to you for some time. I'd like to show you the video to see if you remember her."

"Sure," Mary said. "But you should know. We get lots of questions from expectant mothers, and don't remember all of them. I'm not sure if I can help."

"Let's try." Bristol smiled and held out her phone.

Mary stared at the screen. "Oh, yeah, I remember her because she wasn't pregnant. At least not visibly."

"What did she ask you?" Jared asked.

Mary looked up. "She said she was trying to get pregnant and wanted to start researching hospitals. I thought it was odd to be looking so soon, but we're trained in customer service. Even evaluated on it. So I didn't want to be rude. I gave her a department overview. Then she asked a bunch of questions."

"What in particular did she want to know?" Jared asked.

"She was really interested in staff scheduling. Said she wanted to be sure we had enough nurses on duty to meet all her and her baby's needs. She also wanted to know about our rooming-in policy and security. Especially the security."

Mary shook her head. "She was going on and on and I was on my break. She'd taken up half of it and just kept badgering me with questions. I told her we did tours for expectant mothers and the rest of her questions could be answered there and I bolted."

"Was there anything off about the woman?" Bristol asked.

"Off?" Mary tapped her chin. "I remember thinking it odd that she was doing this research before getting pregnant, but then I figured she was just concerned about having a baby."

"Can you describe her to us?" Bristol asked.

"No. Not with the hoodie she was wearing. And she looked down a lot. I think she had hazel or maybe greenish eyes. A large nose. Thin lips that she kept pressing together."

"You didn't think the hoodie was odd?" Bristol asked. "Or that she kept looking down?"

"Lots of people wear them, and I thought she was just nervous or shy." Mary clutched her hands together. "Do you think she's the woman who took Luna?"

"Do you remember her well enough that you could give a sketch artist a description?" Jared asked, ignoring her question.

Mary bit her lip and gnawed off more of her pink lipstick that was almost gone. "Maybe. I can try anyway."

"We'll get someone here and arrange for you to have the time to do it, okay?" Bristol asked.

"Sure." She cast a nervous glance at Jared. "If I can help find Luna, I'll do whatever you need."

"You're free to go back to work." Jared forced a smile for the nurse. "We'll contact you as soon as we have a sketch artist."

A tight smile crossed Mary's face and then she spun, her soft-soled shoes squealing as she pivoted.

Bristol looked at Jared. "We don't have a sketch artist on staff. We use the state if one is needed, but they usually have to send someone from Salem."

Jared considered the possibilities. "We have a guy who does electronic sketches, but we should have a professional for this."

"I've heard Kelsey Dunbar, the forensic anthropologist at Veritas, is quite good. She recently had her second child. I know she'll want to help if she can."

"Then get on the phone to her and let's get this sketch made."

Bristol didn't know Kelsey Dunbar very well, but Bristol *did* know the woman was kind and generous and had a heart of gold. She was super feminine. Bristol's opposite. She usually wore dresses like the flowery one she had on now and sky-high heels. She looked nothing like Bristol would expect a woman who dug in dirt to recover skeletonized bodies would look.

She set her tool kit on the small conference table and sat across from Nurse Raney. She smiled but it faded fast.

"Can I get you something to drink?" Kelsey asked.

"Drink?" Mary repeated back. "Please. I missed my break, and I'd kill for a Diet Coke."

"You got it." Kelsey got up and crossed over to Bristol. "Can we get a Diet Coke for the nurse?"

"Sure," Bristol said but didn't understand why this was a priority for starting the session.

"She's jittery and giving her something to do with her hands will help calm her down." Kelsey lowered her voice, as if she could read the question in Bristol's mind. More likely she saw it on Bristol's face.

"I'll get one delivered." Bristol didn't want to leave in case Mary said something important that she'd failed to mention in the interview, so Bristol texted Teagan and asked her to bring the soda from the refreshment stash in the command center.

Kelsey sat and seemed to take her time getting out a drawing board and pencils, setting them just so on the table. Then she leaned back in her chair and crossed her legs, looking relaxed and casual. "I know you didn't spend much time with the suspect. If you can't remember anything as we work just tell me, and I'll move on."

"Oh, good." Mary let out a relieved breath. "I hoped you'd understand."

Kelsey smiled and brushed her fingers over black curly hair that she'd pulled back in a clip. "Just relax. Maybe close your eyes. Form a vision of the woman's face and tell me whatever you see first."

Mary leaned back and closed her eyes. "Her face is round. Not fat but round. And her skin was pale. I remember thinking she didn't get much sun or maybe wore a hat all the time outside. I dunno. Something like that."

Kelsey got out a catalog, flipped through the pages, then handed it to Mary. "This is a facial identification catalog with pictures of basic features. Can you look at the round faces and point to any that remind you of the suspect?"

Mary studied the pages. Her eyes widened, and she pointed at a photo. "This one."

Kelsey took the catalog back. "Good. Good. What else comes to mind about this suspect? Maybe her eye shape or nose."

"She had a huge nose that had like a blob on the end."

Mary smiled. "I almost laughed as it reminded me of Nanny McPhee."

"That movie was great." Kelsey grinned and flipped through her catalog again.

Bristol had seen the movie where the nanny arrived at the children's house with a bulbous nose, a facial mole, and a snaggletooth. Each time the children learned their lessons the features disappeared, and Nanny McPhee took on a more normal appearance.

Kelsey held out the catalog. "While I sketch the basic shape of her face, go ahead and look at noses."

They worked together, Kelsey's pencil whisking over the page, until the door opened. Bristol reached for her sidearm and spun. Teagan stepped in carrying the Diet Coke. Bristol relaxed, took the icy cold can from her cousin, and handed it to Mary.

She rested the catalog on her knees and eagerly clutched the soda. "Thank you. A boost of caffeine is exactly what I need."

She popped the top, the fizz sputtering into the air, and slurped the drink. "I found the right nose when you're ready for it."

"Ready now," Kelsey said.

Bristol didn't want to bother them and risk slowing their progress. She quietly stepped across the room to Teagan.

"How's it going?" Teagan whispered.

"Good, I think." Bristol made sure to keep her voice down too.

Teagan studied Bristol as if she were looking at a suspect in an investigation.

"What?" Bristol tried to swallow down the discomfort of her older cousin's study.

"You didn't tell us Jared is *the* guy." Teagan cocked her head. "The one who got away."

This was the last thing Bristol needed to deal with right now. "Did he tell you that?"

Teagan shook her head. "When I got the Coke, I overheard Reed and Jared talking about you going undercover with him and that you had a past."

Bristol should've known it would get back to her family and should've preemptively told them, but she didn't want them to look down on Jared when he was leading the team. She didn't want it to distract anyone. "There's nothing to even think about."

Teagan moved closer. "The looks you guys shared say something else."

"It's nothing. Really." Bristol clutched her cousin's arm for emphasis. "So don't go blabbing it to the family. I don't want any distractions when we're looking for a baby."

"If you say so." Teagan mocked zipping her lips.

Bristol had no idea if her cousin would comply. The family wild card, she was completely unpredictable. She often did whatever she pleased, no matter the consequences. Sometimes her impulsive behavior hurt others. She didn't plan to hurt them. She loved everyone deeply, but she was a leap-before-looking woman.

Bristol crossed her arms. "If you value us getting Luna back, then you'll keep quiet."

Teagan's expression sobered. "On that note, I'll head back to the dungeon and the videos."

"You all going to work through the night?"

She nodded. "As you said, a baby is missing. None of us will sleep if we can help find her."

Bristol gave her cousin an impromptu hug.

Teagan gripped Bristol tightly and then let go. "What was that for?"

"This is a hard one, and I needed a little comfort."

"I'll stay away then and force you to seek the comfort

from a certain man who's still into you." Teagan grinned and slipped out of the room with a flourish.

Vowing not to need hugs from Jared, Bristol turned back to Kelsey. She'd moved on from the nose to the mouth and was turning the drawing around to show Mary. "How's this?"

Mary sighed and slumped back in her chair. "That's her. That's the woman."

"Thank you for all of your hard work." Kelsey stood. "I'm sure this will be most helpful."

Mary drained the last of her Diet Coke and set down the can. "Let me know if there's anything else I can do."

Bristol wanted to get the sketch out to law enforcement, and the sooner, the better. She crossed over to them to get Mary moving.

"We appreciate your help," Bristol said as she herded Mary toward the door.

The moment the door closed, Bristol turned to Kelsey. "Do you really think the sketch will help?"

"We got a good drawing." She held out her sketch pad. "I'll shoot a few pictures of it, and you can distribute it."

Bristol took the pad and stared at the woman's unique face. Kelsey was right. If they widely distributed the sketch, they might have success in actually finding this suspect. A huge win for the team. But one big question remained.

Was this the woman who took Luna?

10

The unrelenting pounding on the conference room door as the team was starting to settle down for their morning update meeting had Jared racing across the room. Had to be a reporter and Jared was going to send them packing.

He pushed the door open to find an older couple, a large three-tier cart loaded with food between them. The air carried savory scents that had his mouth watering.

The man with gray hair and thick glasses shot out his hand. "Artie Steele and this is my wife, Eloise. Grandparents to Deputy Bristol Steele." He shook Jared's hand then released it, looked around Jared, and lifted the hand to wave. "Morning, Granddaughter."

Bristol gave a slight wave in return, but grimaced and searched the space as if she wanted to melt under the conference room table. Their undercover assignment would begin after the update meeting ended, and she'd dressed the part. She had on a very feminine dress with frilly sleeves, and her hair hung around her shoulders instead of being pulled back. She sure didn't look like a deputy, and maybe that made her more self-conscious today.

"We've brought breakfast for the team," Eloise said.

Jared turned back to the woman who he put in her late seventies. She had short curly gray hair, but her ruby red glasses really caught his attention. She might be older, but there was nothing old-fashioned about her.

"I'm a former detective," Artie said. "And I know you might not want to allow us in the room, but I promise if you do, you'll be glad to have my wife's home cooking. None better than what my Eloise makes." He flashed a loving smile at his wife.

Okay. This was a new one for Jared. What did he do? Send them on their way? That would be rude after they'd gone to a lot of trouble to bring a meal here. Their kindness meant a lot to him, but what about information security? Could they protect it?

"We'll just set up the food then leave and let you get down to work," Artie said. "No intentions of trying to snoop or learn anything. Even if my old detective juices are flowing at the thought of it." He chuckled, a pleasant laugh filled with joy.

Jared had an odd desire to trust this man and his wife. He'd heard so much about them from Bristol, he felt like he knew them, and he knew for certain that they were honest, God-fearing people.

"Let me check with the team," he said before letting this couple sway him to comply without further thought. He let the door close softly. After it clicked into place, he turned to the group and explained. "The whiteboard closes, and we can cover the vital case information. We'll just have to delay any conversations for the few minutes it takes for them to set up. What do you say?"

Bristol didn't move. In fact, she looked like she was holding her breath. Maybe she was expecting one of them to say something to embarrass her. Or maybe she already was embarrassed. But why? Bringing a meal was a kind and loving gesture on her grandparents' part.

"Looks like we're in for a long day," Adair said. "Fueling up would be good."

Curious. Not the answer Jared expected at all from his straight-laced boss.

The others quickly voiced their agreement.

Bristol jumped to her feet. "I'll close the whiteboards."

She rushed to the boards as if she needed to do something to keep busy. She'd never really liked public attention. Maybe that was the reason for her unease.

Jared went to the door. "We very much appreciate your kindness and would welcome the meal."

Eloise smiled, and Jared saw Bristol in the older woman's smile, giving him a hint at what she might look like if he knew her in her seventies.

"Come on, Artie," she said. "Get that cart rolling before the food gets colder."

"Give a fella a chance," he grumbled good-naturedly and started the cart rolling on squeaky wheels through the door.

Jared helped direct it toward the back wall that once held refreshments long ago annihilated by the team.

Bristol finished closing the doors and crossed the room to join them.

Her grandmother quickly squeezed Bristol's hand. "I made all of your favorites. Raspberry scones. Hash brown casserole. Rosemary quiche."

"Thanks, Gran. It all sounds great." Bristol's tone lacked the enthusiasm of her words. "But I wish you'd called me before coming."

Artie raised an eyebrow behind his glasses. "You would've said not to come, and we had to do our part to help bring this little baby home."

A family who believed in service. That's what Bristol had

said last night, and it had come through in the many stories she'd told about her family. That had always stuck with him, as did the fact that her grandfather loved to fish and share tall tales.

"We need to get to our morning report," Jared said. "Let's get the food served."

"I've brought everything you need for a buffet," Eloise said.

"She's right." Artie grinned. "I'm pretty sure I loaded up the kitchen sink too."

Eloise swatted a hand at him. "We'll set it up and be out of your hair in a flash."

Bristol looked at Jared. "You can go back to the others, and I'll help with the food."

"Thanks again for feeding us," he said. "I'd heard a lot about you all from Bristol, and you seem just like she described."

Eloise's eyebrow rose over her red glasses. "Heard about us?"

"When we worked as camp counselors together," he said.

That brought a frown from the older woman. "Ah-ha! *You're* the one."

"The one?" Was she referring to the fact that he bailed on her granddaughter?

"Never mind." Bristol made shooing motions with her hands. "We've got this."

He wanted to explore the situation more, but she was right. He needed to get back to the table and get his notes organized for the meeting.

He turned.

"So we finally know the mystery man's identity," her grandmother said loudly enough for Jared to hear. "And you have to work with him. What are the odds of that?"

"God works in mysterious ways," Artie said. "Like why do some fish like one bait and other gamefish like another."

Jared continued on to his seat, but he felt the couple's eyes on his back. Seemed as if Bristol had told them about a guy she fell for at camp who bailed on her, but not his identity. He'd like a chance to explain himself, but now wasn't the time. Now was the time to get this group moving forward in finding a baby who'd been missing for nearly twenty-four hours. Each hour that passed reduced the odds of finding her alive.

~

Bristol usually savored her gran's cooking, but today the food prepared with love and attention all tasted like sawdust. Even the savory scent of rosemary filling the room didn't fire off Bristol's tastebuds like usual. Not so for her fellow teammates. Continued exclamations of joy for their breakfast sounded around the table as the group reviewed the upcoming undercover operation and took long looks at Bristol and Jared. She was proud of her grandparents' kind gesture. She just didn't want to stand out in a meeting where she was already the topic of discussion.

Wearing khaki pants, a blue FBI polo, and shoulder holster, Piper lumbered to center stage and scribbled notes regarding their undercover plan on the whiteboard, her marker squeaking with her hasty strokes. Late last night, she'd questioned Jared and Bristol about their pasts, interests, and hobbies and used the information to create a married, but childless couple named Christine and Shawn Young.

Piper snapped the cap on the marker and turned to look at the group. "Christine is a human resource manager, and Shawn a logistics expert. They met as counselors at a middle school camp. They broke up when Shawn was entering the Navy right after camp got out and didn't think a long-distance relationship would work."

Adair set down his scone, his focus pinned on Piper. "Good job on the backstory, Thorne, but I don't buy the breakup. Seems contrived."

Piper set the marker on the tray below the board. "Might seem that way, but the whole camp story is true."

Adair swung his gaze to Jared. "Is that right?"

"Yes, sir," Jared said, his face coloring. "Bristol and I met at camp before I left for my naval officer training."

Bristol had wanted to sink under the table when her grandparents had shown up, but as all eyes swung to her now, she wished she could melt. Literally into a puddle. Instead, she rubbed her hands over the pleats on her skirt and lifted her shoulders. "We lived the story. Means we can sell it well and use it to our advantage with Holloway. The fewer things we have to make up, the less likely we'll screw up."

Adair gave a sharp nod, his dark eyes imposing. "Then we'll go with the story. Just be sure if you have to share it with Holloway that you *do* sell it. Try to recall how you felt about each other back then and play it up."

"We can do that," Jared said.

Bristol wasn't as certain and wished Jared would look at her so she could transmit her unease, but he kept his focus on his boss.

"Let's get through the updates," Adair said. "Then you two can head off to meet with Holloway." Adair shifted his attention to Detective Hale. "You're up next."

Piper dropped into a chair with a contented *oomph* and picked up one of Gran's scones. She bit into it and groaned then covered her mouth as if embarrassed. Bristol really liked Piper. She was direct and sharp, but also kind and supportive.

Hale took the spot in front of the boards in quick, short strides and clicked a remote to project a map of the area on the screen. "We've located two eyewitnesses who saw the woman captured in the video, but they couldn't give us any additional physical details. Their statements place her on foot near these crossroads."

He tapped the map in two locations showing the suspect moving at the east end of the hospital's property. "I have officers hunting down security video from businesses in the area. We haven't located any footage of the woman at this point."

"What about calls to the tip line?" Adair asked.

Hale ran a hand over his shiny bald head. "We've had a total of two hundred-seventeen calls. Of those, we prioritized ten tips and tracked them down. We've ruled out all but one of these tips and are still looking for the reported woman. She fits the suspect's build, and she's gone AWOL." He turned to the board, wrote her name down, and pointed a remote at the screen to display a woman's picture. "This is Claudia Doyle, and we have an APB out on her."

"What do we know about her?" Jared asked.

Hale set down the remote and widened his stance. "She lost a child in childbirth nearly two months ago. She's been erratic and unpredictable since then. The tip came in saying another woman feared she was going to take her child at a nearby park. There was a police report taken confirming Doyle's behavior. Upon investigation, the detective learned Doyle was clinically depressed and seeking treatment."

"What else do we know about her?" Adair asked.

"She's widowed," Hale continued. "From what her neighbors said, her pregnancy was a late-in-life miracle child using the last egg she'd stored to have her deceased husband's child. So the loss hit hard. No one has any idea where she is. There haven't been any recent charges to her bank or credit card accounts. She basically vanished."

No one vanished. Bristol knew they could find her. "Did she previously withdraw large amounts of cash that she could be living on?"

Hale shook his head. "But she did stop depositing her paychecks right after the miscarriage and cashed them at her bank. She hasn't been to work for fifteen days. Never called in or emailed. Just stopped showing up."

"Sounds like she might've gone off the deep end and could mean she took Luna," Jared said.

Hale nodded. "We're still running down viable leads, and I've got as much manpower as possible on locating the woman."

"Keep us in the loop at all times." Adair gave Hale a dismissive nod and faced Jared. "Update us on forensics."

Jared stood but didn't move to the head of the table. "Not much to go on yet. Our trace evidence expert recovered four sources of DNA from Luna's blanket found in the parking garage. Sierra processed the blood type and it matches Luna and the father, but he hasn't sustained any injuries. They've rushed the DNA process, but as you know, DNA takes at least twenty-four hours to run. We'll have results late this afternoon."

"And other forensics?" Adair asked, making Bristol think the guy was an impatient man.

"The father's backpack is clear for any blood, and Emory is running touch DNA from the bag. Sierra also located an unidentified fingerprint on the bassinet, but it didn't return any matches in AFIS. They recovered soil in a partial footprint near the blanket and are running it for composition to see if they can place the location where the suspect might've recently walked. They warned that's a long shot and will take time. The size of the print is consistent with the woman's size on video."

"And of course we have the suspect's sketch circulating," Reed said.

"That's probably our best lead until the DNA comes in," Jared said. "The phones have all been processed, and we've learned that Mr. Pratt is scheduled to testify against a notorious gang member."

"That's not good news." Adair frowned. "Let's all hope this gang isn't part of the kidnapping."

A murmur of agreement traveled around the table.

"I've tasked Agent Lane with coordinating with the Metro Safe Streets Task Force," Reed said. "Hopefully they can determine if the gang's involved."

Adair shot a dark look at Hunter. "Keep me in the loop on this."

Hunter nodded.

"Where do we stand on this Osborne fellow?" Adair asked.

Reed sat forward. "We've vetted all of the women in his life. No living female relatives but we located three women he recently dated. None of them fit the build of the woman on video, but we're still bringing them in for questioning this morning. And on Osborne, we're still waiting on his financial records to see if he's in debt and if he's recently made any large deposits."

"I would expect Holloway to pay in cash," Bristol said. "Even if there isn't money in Osborne's account, doesn't mean he wasn't paid off."

Reed nodded. "We're also questioning friends who might've seen him suddenly flashing money around too."

"Keep me updated on that as well," Adair said.

"Will do." Reed sat back.

"Lastly," Jared said. "The undercover operation with

Holloway begins with an appointment to see him at nine. You can be assured we'll do our very best to pass his examination and find a way to infiltrate his network."

~

Bristol sat back as Jared drove toward Everett Holloway's office in posh Lake Oswego. She nearly preened like a cat in the warm sun pouring through the windows. Sunny days were rare most of the year, so she loved summer days that were most often sunny and dry. She wished she could relax and enjoy it more today, but their upcoming meeting had her gut tight with worry.

She twisted the three-carat wedding ring on her finger, the diamond catching in the light and glittering around the vehicle's interior. In the real world, she wouldn't want such an ostentatious ring. This fit the wealthy couple they were trying to play. A married couple. Her and Jared married. *Oof.*

She let her undercover name play in her mind.

Christine Young. Mrs. Shawn Young.

A fine name. One she could remember. But the second version sent her head spinning. After spending time with Jared again, she wanted to forget how he'd hurt her and ask if he might want to try dating after they'd found Luna and returned her to her parents.

Fool. You don't need to get burned a second time. Be careful. Ignore these feelings. Don't get caught up in pretending.

And don't bail. Even if Bristol had second thoughts about this undercover operation, she would continue. She would do anything she could to find Luna and bring her home. If that meant playing house with Jared, she would give her very best performance.

She crossed her legs and pressed out the pleats in her skirt. She dangled one of the infernal heels she'd borrowed from Londyn. Piper had given Christine and Shawn Young ample bank accounts to stop Holloway from questioning their ability to buy a child. Bristol had to dress the part. Of course she couldn't wear her uniform, and her basic wardrobe of jeans and T's didn't quite cut it. Londyn was a detective, but she embraced her feminine side at work to put people off guard around her and filled her closet with professional clothing.

Jared already looked the part in his tailored suits. She glanced at the gray one he wore today, tailored to his toned physique. He'd paired it with another white shirt and red and black striped tie.

What did he wear in his downtime? He used to be a jeans and T kind of guy too, but then that was for camp, not the business world. Or the world of undercover stings.

"You're fidgeting," he said.

"Not used to dressing this way or wearing such an expensive piece of jewelry." She released her ring. "I'm still more comfortable in my jeans and kicks."

"Me too, but it's not appreciated at my office." He laughed. "Maybe we should've decided to go casual so you'd be more relaxed."

"I don't know," she said. "It might not be bad to be a bit jittery when we're trying to do something illegal."

"Or it might put Holloway off."

"Yeah, it might." She scrubbed her hands on the rich fabric of her skirt again. "Then I need to get rid of these nerves."

"Just keep thinking about our past, and you'll get it," he said, clearly oblivious to the fact that thinking of their past was even harder. "I'm glad Piper at least built our identities on our history so we don't need to make that up."

Sure. Maybe. At least it hadn't been uncomfortable sharing the details with Piper. Not that Piper had been judgmental. She just took the facts and created a bio. Unlike the task force leaders. Adair had to question that one point, right?

She peered out the window at skies that had darkened into a heavy gray veil and a fine mist now coated the roads.

"How do you like the occupation Piper assigned to you?" he asked.

"It's interesting. I've never considered being a human resource manager but my patrol experience has given me skills in reading and helping people. Skills in diffusing situations too." She swiveled to look at him. "Come to think of it, being a part of such a big extended family did the same thing."

"I was glad to meet your family," he said. "I always wanted to. Especially your parents."

She grabbed onto the door handle not to turn and gape at him. She'd once thought about taking him home to meet her family, but when he ended things, she was so glad she'd chickened out.

"I can almost hear your thoughts. Bringing a guy home to mom and dad is a big deal." He chuckled. "I didn't mean it that way. I just wanted to meet them. From everything you once told me, I can tell they're great people. You have the kind of family I always wanted. Your grandparents showing up this morning with that feast proves it."

And she'd wanted to melt into a puddle instead of being proud of them. Talk about being ungrateful and putting her priorities in the wrong place. "You're right. They're the best. So are the rest of my family. I take them for granted, but I know I shouldn't." Her thoughts traveled to her brother, and her heart creased with grief nearly as fresh as the day he died.

Jared stopped at a light and watched her. "What's wrong?"

"Thinking about Thomas." She blinked back a wash of tears. "I don't know if I'll ever get over losing him."

Jared shook his head. "I'm not close to my brother and sister. But I know losing either of them would be hard."

"You're still not close?" she asked, glad to change the focus to him.

"Nothing's really changed. They're both set on becoming super rich like our parents and living a lavish lifestyle. That's not me. Not in the least. They don't understand me, and honestly, I don't understand them."

"You fit better with the Steele family," she said without thinking. "We're all about service."

"I once thought the same thing." The light turned green, and he started through the intersection.

What would it be like to take him to one of the family Sunday dinners at her grandparents' house? They were so very perceptive, and they already knew there was something going on between her and Jared. Teagan had confirmed that she knew too. And by now, her grandparents could've told others. She'd asked them not to, but her grandad wasn't as sharp as he used to be, and he would slip up. If not today, tomorrow, or the next day.

Would they think less of Jared? Maybe they would understand his need to immerse himself in the Navy. Maybe they would think more highly of him because he didn't try to succeed at both things and potentially fail at one.

Still, he'd hurt her. That alone would be a huge strike against him.

She looked down, her eyes on the ring again.

"You seem uncomfortable wearing a wedding ring," Jared said. "Is it because it's supposedly the ring uniting us?"

"Maybe," she said. "I'm honestly not sure."

"Are you dating someone and it feels like a betrayal?"

"No." She resisted sighing. "I pretty much gave up on

dating. Demands of my patrol job and all." She slipped her hand under her thigh to keep from looking at the ring. "Then there's the fact that it's hard to find a guy who understands the immense mental strain of a law enforcement job. The only ones who understand are other law enforcement officers."

He took a long look at her. "And you don't want to date someone in the field?"

"Absolutely not!" Oh, wow. She'd basically just told him he was off-limits. *Good.* That should help protect her from his charms.

"And why's that?" Disappointment had crept into his tone.

"The job takes a toll on officers, sure, but not only them. Their spouses too. I'm sure you've seen the high rate of divorce in the field. I've seen it challenge my family at times too. That's one of the reasons I'm leaving the job." She crossed her arms and eyed him. "I don't want anything to do with it or have it in my life except with my family members who choose to remain in law enforcement."

"Wow." He shook his head. "You really are adamant about it."

"I am," she said, but had she just gone on autopilot in her response? Spouted what she'd believed for years? Maybe using it to put up a wall to keep Jared at arm's length? After reconnecting with Jared, she had to admit to feeling a little less sure of her decision.

"I'm not ready to settle down either," she added, clearly feeling the need to add to her prior comments in case he could refute them. "My family didn't want to add another position to the company right now, but I promised to pay for myself by signing big contracts."

"Like the hospital?"

"Yeah. Like the hospital." She didn't want to talk about

that either. Besides, she'd missed an opportunity to discover if he was dating. "What about you? In a relationship?"

"Not currently." He kept his attention pinned to the road. "As you say, the demands of a law enforcement job have been tough on my dating life. Foiled two relationships already. So I'm taking a break. Maybe permanently."

She nodded. She got it. Completely. Was even living her life the same way.

But it was sad to see another person struggling with the same issue. If she was willing to admit it, which was questionable right now, even sadder that it put an end to her fantasies of rekindling her relationship with this fine man.

11

Jared took a seat next to Bristol and across the rich walnut desk from Everett Holloway. The man wasn't exactly what Jared had expected. He'd figured Holloway would be a smarmy guy with a trashy office. At least that was what Jared had thought a baby stealer and seller would look like.

Holloway was the direct opposite. He had a stylish hair-cut, his silvery hair messy with gel. He wore a tailored suit and crisp white shirt and sat behind a massive desk in a large office with floor-to-ceiling windows. His wall held his law diploma, and his photo with several local officials.

No hint of his nefarious work. Not one single hint.

Holloway linked his hands together on the desk and gave a toothy smile, revealing perfectly aligned white teeth. "I appreciate the Wetzels referring you. How are they doing with their son?"

"Hard not to be doing okay when your dreams have come true." Bristol smiled, crossed her legs, and sat back as if visiting a friend.

Perfect. She was pulling this off with ease despite her misgivings. She didn't lie about talking to the Wetzels, and she made it sound like she was desperate for her own child.

"Which is why we're here." She rested her hand over Jared's then clutched it tightly. "We want a family too."

Now that could be considered a lie, but in fact, she thought they both wanted a family. Maybe not today. Maybe not with each other. Maybe would never have one. But still, they wanted children.

Holloway steepled his fingers, his nails manicured. "I assume you've exhausted all other avenues like most of my clients."

"Of course," Jared said. "Or we wouldn't be here."

"Then let's get started with the process." Holloway lifted the lid on his laptop. "A background check will be in order. Any issues with that?"

Jared shook his head and hoped the history Piper created would stand up under Holloway's scrutiny. Not that he was likely looking to see if they would be good parents. His first priority would be to confirm that they had enough money to pay for the baby. Then he would probably check for any red flags that said he couldn't trust them to be discreet.

Holloway poised his hands over his keyboard. "Let's start with your address."

Bristol rattled off the address for the house that Piper rented under their name. The house where they would spend time together for as many nights as needed to determine if this man was involved in abducting Luna. Or until they located Luna from another lead.

"Employers and job titles?" Holloway asked.

Jared went first, listing a bogus startup company with a phone number that would ring to a phone line set up to confirm both his and Bristol's employment if needed.

"Logistics, huh?" Holloway looked up. "That's a demanding job."

"But worth it," Jared said. "No better feeling than when

you get every item you're moving to the right location and your customers are satisfied."

Holloway seemed to buy the answer. He looked at Bristol. "And you?"

"Human resources," she said and listed her bogus company. "My sweetie, here, moves things around, I move people."

She chuckled, and Jared loved that her natural sense of humor could come through even in a tense situation like this one. She'd always been able to make him laugh, and he loved that about her too. He was by nature a serious guy, and he needed to lighten up. She'd made his life so much better when they'd been together. Almost as if God had made her to complete him.

Oh. Wow. Wow. What a thing to think about when Jared needed to focus and not screw up.

Holloway cracked a smile as his fingers flew over the keyboard. He looked up, his jaw now rigid. "Boy or girl?"

"Pardon?" Bristol asked.

"Do you want a boy or girl?" Holloway pressed his hands on the desk. "I should warn you, boys are harder to come by."

Holloway was treating babies like commodities, and Jared's stomach revolted.

"A girl," Bristol said not missing a beat "And I always imagined a little dark-haired girl like my sweetie."

She patted his knee, and her touch sizzled all the way to his heart. He nearly forgot who he was and where they were and tugged her into his arms.

Nearly.

"I want a girl too." Her touch lit his imagination, and he gave in, taking her hand in his. "A mini-Christine." He made sure to include her bogus name and make it sound natural.

"I'm not sure I want a mini-me." Bristol wrinkled her

nose at him. "But I do think a girl will be easier for our first child. Or at least I've read that they can be easier until they reach their teen years. I mean, if our daughter is like I was." She shuddered.

"I didn't think you were so bad back then." Jared smiled at her. "I fell for you after all."

"But see, my parents were trying to protect me from older guys like you." She laughed.

He laughed with her.

"Then you've known each other that long?" Holloway sounded intrigued.

Jared nodded. "We worked together as camp counselors one summer, and the rest is history."

Holloway leaned back. "I've got all I need for today. Any questions?"

Bristol swung her gaze to the man. "How do you manage to arrange adoptions so quickly when agencies take forever?"

Holloway's eyes narrowed, and Jared finally saw the hard, unfeeling man who stole children from their mothers for money.

"I have many sources who help me rescue expectant mothers who can't fulfill their roles, and we find loving homes for the children." He gave a tight smile. "I don't mean to brag, but our reputation of successful placements has made us the premier adoption firm in the area."

Bristol looked like she wanted to snap at him, but curled her free hand into a fist. "Can we expedite this? We've waited so long, and when the Wetzels told us about how quickly you helped them, we knew it was meant to be."

"I'll work as fast as I can and be in touch." He stood.

"Please make it fast." Jared gripped Bristol's hand. "I failed to give this woman everything she's dreamed of, but you can."

Jared made strong eye contact with her to share his sincerity. He failed to commit to this woman he once loved and spoiled her dream of a future together. Now he sincerely wanted to correct that if he could. If she would let him.

"I'll rush it, but I have to do my due diligence too." Holloway escorted them to the door.

Jared continued to hold Bristol's hand and followed, his brain filled with the pain of what could have been with the amazing woman at his side.

What would it be like to really be married and failing to have a child? So many very deserving couples went through the struggle every day, and he had no idea why. He only knew he hadn't lied to Holloway when he'd said he would like to have a mini-Bristol in his life. And that scared him more than he thought possible.

~

Outside where the sun had returned and Bristol enjoyed the warmth on her body, she looked up at Jared. "You can let go of my hand now."

"Holloway could be watching out the window." Jared drew her closer. "In fact, we might want to cement our standing as a married couple in his eyes."

He slid his hands around her waist then he pulled her closer. Memories of kissing him flashed before her eyes, and her heart fluttered.

"Not sure I'm into a PDA," she got out when she could barely think straight with his hands on her.

"Then we'll make it quick." He lowered his head.

He was going to kiss her. Really kiss her. Here in the parking lot in public. And she wasn't going to stop him. Not even consider stopping him. She was going to encourage him. She lifted her arms and curled her hands around the back of his neck to draw his head down faster.

Her heart thumped loudly in anticipation. Their lips met. An explosion of warmth spread through her body. Nothing had changed. The depth of her feelings for this man remained.

She clung to him. His touch. His lips. His urgency. All drove her to deepen the kiss. He met her emotions with his own. He consumed her thoughts. She forgot the time. The place. The investigation. The past hurt.

Only remembered the love they'd once shared. The way they'd been so perfect for each other.

A car backfired in the lot. She jumped back like a child caught misbehaving.

She pressed her fingers against her lips and stared at him.

He closed the distance back to her and circled his arm around her shoulders. "Holloway might not have heard the car, and we can't have him thinking you're afraid of me."

She *was* afraid of him. Or more aptly—afraid of her feelings for him. But Luna came first. So she pushed aside every emotion swimming in her gut, leaned into him, and even circled her arm around his trim waist.

He started for his vehicle, and she moved in sync with him. Step for step, breathing deep on each one and clearing her brain to move it back to the investigation where it belonged. She noticed the FBI's surveillance car sitting across the lot. Hopefully, Holloway wouldn't make the couple in the car as agents.

At Jared's vehicle, he turned her to face him. He planted a sweet kiss on her forehead and opened her door. She slid in before he tried another passionate kiss. She couldn't survive it without having time to think about what had happened and how she so readily gave in to her feelings. For now, she had to keep her focus—their focus—on the investigation.

He slid in and looked at her.

No. Meeting his gaze was not a good idea. She buckled her seatbelt. "The meeting with Holloway went faster than I thought, but I'm not sure we accomplished anything."

Jared shoved the key into the ignition. "We established ourselves as clients, but other than that, we have nothing to go on."

She gave in and shifted to face him. "Now what?"

He gave her a long look before his expression tightened. "I wouldn't be surprised if Holloway puts us under surveillance. Not immediately. He'll have to get it arranged, but we'll have to stay at the house tonight in case he has someone watching it."

Her mouth fell open, but she quickly snapped it closed. She knew she had to play the part of Jared's wife, but hadn't let herself think about what that involved. She didn't want to think about what it meant. Now she knew. If they didn't find Luna soon, Bristol would have to spend the night as Christine Young, wife to Shawn Young. Not share a bed or anything like that, but still. A house with just the two of them seemed very intimate at the moment.

Something Jared didn't seem hesitant to embrace at all. That worried her all the more.

Jared started the vehicle and looked over the seat to back out. Maybe once they returned to the command center, Bristol could let go of the upcoming night. She peered out the window, her gaze landing on a very pregnant woman sitting on the curb. She cried, her whole body shaking.

"Hold up." She grabbed Jared's arm.

"What's wrong?" He shoved the car into park.

She pointed at the woman. "You think she might be one of Holloway's women upset about giving up her child?"

"Could be, I suppose." Jared frowned.

"I should go talk to her. If she's connected to Holloway maybe we can get her to turn on him." Bristol continued to look at the woman with coffee-colored skin and black shoulder-length hair who was clutching her belly as if trying to protect her unborn child. "And even if she's not connected to Holloway, I can't leave without trying to help her."

"Holloway could see you."

Bristol looked around. "She's hidden from view by the trees. We can move the car over there, and he won't see us either."

"You need to be careful of what you say," Jared said. "You can't come out and accuse Holloway of illegal activity without blowing our cover."

"I'll approach her as Christine. I think that will work best."

Jared started the vehicle and moved to a parking space in the shade of the trees. Bristol dug tissues from her purse and bolted from the car.

Nearing the woman, Bristol held out the tissues. "You look like you could use these."

Her head popped up, fear lighting in her eyes.

"I didn't mean to scare you." Bristol held the tissues closer. "I saw you crying from my car." She jerked a thumb at Jared's vehicle. "My name's Christine."

The lie felt awful. A betrayal to this upset mother-to-be.

Concentrate on helping her even if you have to lie to do it.

"I'm Amelia Gasper." She spoke clear English, but Bristol couldn't place her accent.

"Is there anything I can help with?" Bristol gave the woman a closer look, noting she didn't wear a wedding ring. Perhaps her culture didn't wear them, or she had swollen fingers from the pregnancy. Or she couldn't afford one or even was unmarried, which would fit one of Holloway's victims.

Amelia watched carefully, seeming torn between seeking help and clamming up.

Bristol sat on the curb a few feet from her. "Is everything okay with your baby?"

"Okay? Yes. Baby is good." She beamed with a sudden bright smile.

"That's great." Bristol returned her smile. "When are you due?"

"In a month."

"That must be exciting."

Amelia's eyes widened, and a sob tore from her throat.

Bristol scooted closer. "What is it?"

Amelia stabbed her eyes with the tissues. "I cannot say."

"It's fine. I get it. I'm a stranger, but maybe I can help."

"Why?"

She asked a good question that Bristol hadn't prepared an answer for. She would wing it. "My faith is an active faith, and it compels me to help others. Do you believe in God?"

"I do." She frowned. "But He has forsaken my country and my people."

"Your country. Where is that?"

"The Republic of the Marshall Islands."

Where? "I'm not familiar with your home. Tell me about it."

She flashed a brief smile again. "The islands are beautiful. God's beauty everywhere. Except with the people. No jobs. Almost half of my people do not work. So they move to the United States for jobs. We don't want to leave our home but must feed our families."

"That must be hard," Bristol said, trying to put herself in this woman's shoes.

"It is sad, but some come for medical care too. We have a

157

special status here. We are not citizens, but we also do not have to apply for citizenship. We can live here because of an agreement from many years past when your country's military used our islands." She frowned.

Something else Bristol knew nothing about. "I take it that wasn't a good thing."

"No. Not at all." Amelia waved a hand and pursed her lips. "Nuclear testing was done and ruined one of the islands. No one can live there now."

"I'm sorry to hear that." Now Bristol was very interested. "Where are your islands located?"

"In the Pacific Ocean near the equator." A full smile crossed her face. "Midway between Hawaii and Australia."

Sounded tropical to Bristol. "Our weather here must seem foreign to you."

"We get much rain like here, but it is more humid and warmer." She rested her hands on her belly. "I am cold so often, but this little one keeps me warm."

Time for Bristol to get more details about the woman. "Did you come here for work too?"

Amelia shook her head and bit her lip, but didn't speak.

"For medical care for your baby?" Bristol pressed harder.

Amelia looked down and gave another shake of her head.

"You don't have to answer this question, but are you here because of Mr. Everett Holloway?"

Her head popped up. "You know of this man?"

"My husband and I just met with him to talk about adoption." Bristol pointed at Jared who watched them intently from the vehicle. He gave a little wave and such a sweet smile that Bristol wished she really was married to him. Not a couple that was having a problem with becoming parents like Shawn and Christine, but a couple thinking about starting a family.

The simple thought sent terror to her heart.

"This troubles you," Amelia said.

Bristol must be transmitting her unease. "Yes."

"I am troubled too. For the other reason." Amelia took a deep breath and glanced around. "I am giving my baby up for adoption."

Bristol didn't think about it but took Amelia's hand. Her skin was smooth and soft but cold.

Bristol looked her in the eye. "That must be very hard."

"Hard? Yes, but I must do it. My parents are still on the island. They are struggling. Mr. Holloway will pay me much money. It will feed my family for a long time."

Bristol squeezed the woman's hand. "You are so brave."

"I am also ashamed. I became with child before marriage. I cannot tell my family. The shame. So I must do this. Money or not. At least the money is more than I could make working." She sighed.

"What did Mr. Holloway promise you?" Bristol asked.

Amelia raised an eyebrow. "Why do you want to know?"

"You're making such a huge sacrifice for some lucky couple, and I want to make sure you're not being taken advantage of."

"That is kind of you." She smiled. "He is paying all my medical expenses that the state does not cover, and he is also letting me live at his house until the baby is born. After I sign over my rights, he will pay me ten thousand dollars."

So that was the going rate for a baby these days. Sickening. "What happens if you were to change your mind and go home?"

"No. No. This cannot happen." She jerked her hand free. "I cannot go home until Mr. Holloway gives me back my passport."

"He's holding your passport?"

She nodded. "He says he is investing in me, and I need to remain here to make his investment worthwhile."

Everything Holloway was doing made financial sense for him and was on the surface good for the woman and for the couple receiving the baby. But—and this but was huge—selling babies and manipulating mothers was illegal. Even if he didn't arrange to have Luna taken, he was breaking the law and needed to be stopped.

Maybe Bristol could start by helping Amelia. "What about your baby's father?"

"He wants nothing to do with the baby. A mouth to feed that he can't afford." She gripped her hands together. "This is not true of the others."

"Others?" Bristol asked gently as to not scare her off when it looked like Bristol was finally getting somewhere.

"Mr. Holloway has had many women living at his house. He has told the married women to lie about their baby's father. Or to say they aren't married or that the father does not want anything to do with the baby."

"But these women are all there of their own free will?"

"Free will?" She looked up at the sky, a puzzled expression on her face. "Yes. God gives us that, doesn't He? And sometimes we have to use it to do the wrong thing to make the right thing happen for the people we love." A destitute look tightened her pretty features.

A wave of sadness washed over Bristol, and she wanted to take this woman home with her to live so she could keep her own baby. Not a practical thought at all. But what could Bristol do? Try to find a way for her to keep her baby and still support her family back home. Ten thousand dollars would be hard to replace, but Bristol had many resources at her disposal. Maybe she could find a way.

For now, she needed to try to gain information to find

Luna. "Do you know if Holloway places babies that are already born?"

Amelia's eyebrow went up again. "Why do you want to know this?"

"We're so eager for a child." She cast what she thought was a loving look at Jared. "We don't want to wait."

"I can see the love you have for your husband." She gave a sad smile. "If only I could find the same thing."

"I'm sure you will," Bristol said, when she wasn't at all sure of such a thing.

"A few times, I saw a woman bring a baby to the house," Amelia said. "She stays for one night with the baby and then is gone with the child in the morning."

Bristol's heart rate kicked up at the news. "Did you ask about her?"

Amelia shook her head hard. "Mr. Holloway is not a man you ask questions of, but I heard him talking to her one time."

"What did they say?" Bristol held her breath.

Amelia fidgeted with her hands. "The woman said no one saw her, and the baby was clear. That was all I heard before they closed the door."

"What does this woman look like?" Bristol asked.

"She is short like me, but that is all that resembles me. She has really white skin like she doesn't go outside."

Nurse Raney had mentioned the suspect she'd spoken to had pale skin as well, and Claudia Doyle was also fair-skinned.

On a hunch, Bristol pulled up the photo of Claudia Doyle that Hale had used for her alert. Sure, the woman wasn't likely stealing children for Holloway, but Bristol would lose nothing by asking. "Is this the woman?"

Amelia raised a hand over her eyes, blocking the sun. "It

could be, but I'm not sure. I didn't see her for long, and it was her skin that I noticed most."

"But it could be her?"

"I think it could be her, but maybe not. I'm just not sure."

"Have you seen her lately?" Disappointed, Bristol stowed her phone.

Amelia shook her head. "Maybe not for a month or so, but I answered the phone when she called Mr. Holloway yesterday. She sounded upset. He told her to wait, and he would come to her."

"That's all you heard?"

"Yes."

"What would you think about telling a police officer about what you heard and saw?"

"No. No." She swung her head side-to-side. "Mr. Holloway will not like that, and I will not get my money. He might even hurt me."

Bristol could feel Amelia clamming up, and Bristol needed to think of something to get Amelia to keep talking. "What if I could find a way for you to have your money and still keep your child?"

Amelia's eyes flashed open. "You could do this?"

"I can try. Do you have a phone?"

"Not my own. Just one that I share with the others when we have to leave the house. Mr. Holloway monitors the calls."

Of course he does. "How can I reach you if I find a solution where you can keep your baby?"

"You cannot come to the house. He has security cameras and knows who comes and goes." Amelia glanced around then moved closer. "I do have a phone. One that another woman bought in secret and gave to me. Don't tell Mr. Holloway. He will punish me."

Punish how, was what Bristol wanted to ask but didn't want to get off-topic. "I won't say a word."

"I do not keep the ringer on and must hide the phone so I will not answer right away. Then I must find a time to hide and return the call. Please leave a message and be patient." Amelia shared her number.

Bristol tapped it into her phone. "I'll give you all the time you need, and here's my phone number in case you need to call in an emergency." Bristol held out her phone to display her number for Amelia. "I promise I'll help with whatever you need."

She added Bristol's number to her phone. "God has smiled on me today. You are my angel. But I must go now. I will be late for Mr. Holloway. He will be suspicious, and I could get into trouble."

Bristol helped Amelia to her feet, feeling like a fraud and someone who might fail this woman.

God, please. I know I've been AWOL for a while but please hear me again and let me be the angel Amelia desperately needs.

12

Still in his vehicle, Jared stared open-mouthed as Bristol described her conversation with the woman named Amelia Gasper. The woman's story was shocking, but the fact that Bristol had gotten her to open up? Just as surprising.

"And you think she's legit?" Jared asked.

"Yes."

"Let's make sure she really is who she says she is." Jared quickly texted Piper to do a deep dive on the woman.

"Have you ever heard of the Marshall Islands?" she asked.

He nodded and finished his text. "I came to learn about the Marshallese people on a human trafficking investigation. We have a large community of Marshallese in Salem. I'd heard many of the adult workers have moved here, not only because there are no jobs, but due to climate change. Apparently, the warming, rising tides are causing the islands to sink, and they could even disappear."

"That's sad." Bristol clasped her hands on her skirt. "I could tell Amelia was homesick for her country."

"Which means she could be vulnerable." Jared's stomach knotted. "I'd hate to prey on that, but do you think if you spent more time alone with her that you can turn her to our side?"

"If I keep remembering that we're helping her, then I think there's a chance I can do it." Bristol took a long breath. "One problem though. Holloway placed security cameras in the house and is watching the women. I don't know when we could talk to her again. If we can't arrange something soon, we'll have to move on. Luna can't wait."

"Then let's pressure Holloway to come through for us." Jared got out his prepaid phone assigned to his undercover identity and dialed Holloway's office. His assistant put Jared through.

"Mr. Holloway." Jared made sure he came across as cheerful. "Sorry to trouble you. I know we just left, but I wondered if there was any additional information you might need to speed up our application."

"It would be highly irregular to short-cut things," Holloway said.

But he didn't say impossible so Jared went for the kill. "My wife was so encouraged by our meeting that I had such hope. Unfortunately, she started wondering if you'll accept us as clients and how long it might take and her good mood disappeared. I want to give her everything her heart desires and can't stand to fail. Perhaps if we pay a finder's fee for a timely resolution to our issue you could expedite our case."

"You're very eager, Mr. Young." An accusing tone had crept into Holloway's voice.

"That's a kind way of putting it. More often I'm called pushy." Jared chuckled. "I'm used to succeeding at whatever I put my mind to. To be honest, this has thrown me for a loop."

"Let me see what I can do for you," Holloway said. "But you have to understand that I need to do my due diligence. We can't place a child with just anyone."

"Of course not." Jared didn't have to work hard to sound outraged at the prospect as he was sick to his stomach after hearing about the women at Holloway's house. "But still, I'm sure you must have a way to expedite things."

"I do." Holloway let that linger in the air. "What kind of finder's fee did you have in mind?"

"How does a fifty percent bonus sound to you?" Jared sweetened the pot so much the man couldn't refuse.

"That could persuade me to reassign my workers. Would you be available for a home visit in the morning? Say nine o'clock?"

"What about this afternoon?"

"Hah!" Holloway said. "Don't push it, man. It's nine a.m. tomorrow or nothing."

"Then nine it is. My wife and I will be at home waiting." Jared hung up and looked at Bristol. "Looks like we need to perfect our skills in the marriage department by the morning."

Eyes narrowed, Bristol opened her mouth, but Jared's ringing phone stopped her from saying anything.

He looked at the screen. "It's Sierra."

He tapped the button to accept the call. "Putting you on speaker."

"Good," she said. "I'm glad you answered."

"Sounds like you have something important for us." Jared leaned closer to his phone.

"I do." She drew in a long breath. "The blood and touch DNA on the blanket returned a match in CODIS. Your suspect doesn't have a criminal past, but I have her identity. If you're not sitting down, you should be."

～

Two hours later, Jared trailed the black SWAT van toward Reya Isaacs's house just three blocks from the hospital. Bristol watched out the front window, her face still holding the shock of this woman's identity, and his likely did too.

"How could a woman who lost her own newborn put another mother through this?" Bristol asked. "That was rhetorical. I know the answer. She's likely lost touch with reality. It's just hard to think about. Especially after watching all the news stories about her missing daughter for the past six years."

"Seeing her hope to have her newborn returned only to go six years before the baby's remains were found?" Jared let the stories play in his mind. "The pain she must've felt is really unfathomable."

"And yet the investigators still don't know who kidnapped the baby."

"It was nothing like Luna that I remember. They believed the family was targeted after a birth announcement went in the paper, and they put a sign on their lawn announcing the baby's arrival."

Bristol shook her head. "The family was just so happy they had to share."

"And investigators think it brought a stranger to their home, which is very rare."

Bristol turned to Jared. "What if Sonya Pratt's public Facebook announcement did the same thing?"

"Could be, and that will make finding Luna much harder." He gripped the steering wheel. "I get so mad when I learn that people still share things to the general public on Facebook when they can easily restrict their settings."

"In this case, let's just hope that her post isn't the reason for the kidnapping." Bristol leaned forward, her hands on the dash as if she could speed up the SWAT van to arrive at Reya's house faster.

"The Pratts are likely questioning that too. Mrs. Pratt will never forgive herself if it had anything to do with losing Luna."

They fell silent, but Jared assumed Bristol was thinking the same thing as he was. It was going to be hard to not only question Reya Isaacs, but arrest her if she had Luna. Sure, she would've committed a heinous crime, but was likely not in her right mind.

"Think about the six years Reya Isaacs experienced," Bristol said. "What must that time have been like for her? Like for her now? I keep wondering if knowing her daughter died is better than being in limbo."

"If she's responsible for taking Luna, I would say not. Finding her daughter's remains could've triggered her." Jared pulled to the curb behind the SWAT van.

"Hopefully we'll find her and Luna here, and Reya can explain her reasoning." Bristol got out of the car.

Jared joined her, and they waited for the team to get into formation, the lead guy hefting a battering ram. Jared and Bristol marched with the team to the walkway. Half the guys split off toward the back. The others strode to the small bungalow with a neatly manicured lawn and freshly painted exterior, Bristol and Jared following.

On the porch, the SWAT commander gave the signal to hold, allowing the remainder of the team time to move to the back door to prevent anyone from bailing out that way. Reya and her husband had separated two years ago, leaving only Reya living at this address.

A loud commercial for mattress sales playing on the TV inside caught Jared's attention.

"She's here," he mouthed to Bristol.

She gave an eager nod.

Jared's heart pounded like a conga drum and adrenaline pulsed through him. Everything seemed magnified. Time.

The cool breeze. The heat of the sun. The intensity of his fellow officers.

His feet itched to move, but he held fast.

Counting.

One-one-thousand. Two-one-thousand. Three-one-thousand. Four-one-thousand.

On and on until the commander's hand dropped, and the officer with the battering ram plunged it into the door, breaking it open in one shot.

He stepped to the side, and the four SWAT members burst inside. They raced through the empty family room, Jared and Bristol following, guns raised. He wished he could've been the first through the door, but SWAT had better skills for such a raid.

Two men went right. Two left. Jared chose right. Bristol left.

Jared marched down the hallway. The SWAT team cleared a bedroom set up as an office with news clippings regarding Reya's daughter plastered on the walls along with additional information from the National Center for Missing and Exploited Children.

They cleared the second bedroom, a nursery. A white crib sat empty in the corner, just waiting for a baby to occupy it. A mobile of baby animals hung above and the bedding had cuddly little bears. Jared could imagine Reya standing over it, day after day for six years waiting for her baby to come home. *Man.* That would be so rough. Excruciating. But that still didn't give Reya the right to take Luna. No matter the reason, she'd caused untold suffering for another family.

He dragged his gaze down the hallway to where the commander popped back out of the primary bedroom.

The guy shook his head and held up his hand. "We have a body."

Jared's heart dropped.

"Adult with a stab wound," the commander said. "Looks like Reya Isaacs."

"Reya's dead, really? But Luna." Jared started to push past the men.

"No baby in the room." The commander stepped into the doorway, blocking Jared's way. "And no entry in this room without shoe covers. We have a crime scene now, and we need to treat it as such."

Jared knew that, but he'd let his emotions get to him. "Someone needs to check the closets and under the beds."

The commander looked past Jared. "Radar, get a box of booties from the vehicle."

The younger officer spun and hurried back down the hallway.

The commander lifted his mic. "We have the woman. Any sign of the child?"

He didn't move for a long moment then looked up. "Place is a bust. My team confirms no one in the kitchen or dining area."

"I want the attic searched too," Jared said. "If Reya did indeed take Luna—which the forensics bear out—it's likely the person who killed Reya took Luna. But we have to consider that Luna didn't survive either, and we need to change our focus on this property to a recovery effort until proven otherwise."

Bristol came back to join them. She gasped before her eyes hardened into a look of resolve. "Looks like Reya might've used the blanket to stem her bleeding, but makes no sense to leave the blanket in the lot. Unless she wanted us to find it because she took the baby for someone else, and they stabbed her to take control of Luna."

Jared gave her comment some thought. "Could be, I suppose, but she sure isn't working for Holloway. At least, I can't imagine her taking children from their mothers on a regular basis."

"But she could be desperate for a child of her own and didn't have the cash," Bristol said. "I know before she got divorced, the couple spent everything they had to find their daughter and filed for bankruptcy. The only way they could keep the house was when people donated to a crowd-funding campaign. So she wouldn't have any money to pay for an adoption. And with the murder unsolved, she wouldn't likely qualify for traditional adoption either."

Jared wasn't surprised Bristol knew so much about the family as her agency handled the search for the baby. "It doesn't explain why she was murdered, and if she did actually have Luna. Maybe she just found Luna's blanket."

"That would be odd, though, right? That she happened to be bleeding in the hospital lot and just happened to find this blanket."

"Yeah, you're right. If we don't find Luna on the property, we have to assume Reya's killer took her."

Bristol nodded. "I noticed security cameras out front. That could help."

"You need to get a computer expert out here to recover her computer and phone before you touch them," the commander said.

"Then we need to act quick." Jared dug out his phone to call Colin. He explained the situation and asked him to head this way. "Hurry. The video could hold the killer's face and even show us if he took Luna."

Bristol donned the paper booties and prepared to see the victim. It wasn't Bristol's first time at a murder scene, if Reya had indeed been murdered. Not even Bristol's second time.

Not with all the gun violence in the Portland Metro area of late. But it would be the first time when she'd been hoping the victim would have a missing baby or could give them information to find the child.

Jared stepped inside, and Bristol followed. Reya lay on her back on the floor, her lips blue, her face pale. Her arms and legs were at odd angles as if she were dumped on the carpet, but her right hand held a knife.

Jared squatted next to Reya. "Not a lot of blood here and no blood spatter."

"She was killed elsewhere and brought here," Bristol said.

Jared nodded. "Finding the blanket with her blood in the parking structure would suggest that too, but why kill her and then bring her home?"

"The knife in her hand could mean they tried to stage a suicide," Bristol said. "Of course for that explanation to work, the person who killed her would have to be clueless about the lack of blood at the scene or that she ditched the blanket and we found it. And knives aren't commonly used in suicides."

Jared glanced around. "No note, but that's not unheard of in a suicide."

"And after all she's been through, it wouldn't be unexpected for her to take her life," Bristol added. "I suppose she could've killed herself after taking Luna, but why?"

"Like you said, maybe the person who took Luna from Reya doesn't know about the blanket left behind and didn't think anyone would come looking for her. So they wouldn't know we can tie Reya to Luna."

"Seems more likely than suicide, but I'm going to check the office for a note." Bristol spun and exited the room. The coppery smell of blood lingered in her nose. Reya might not have bled out in her bedroom, but blood soaked her clothing.

Bristol stepped into the smaller bedroom, and the walls covered with news clippings sank her optimism even more. Her emotions were so far underwater it would take a salvage diver to resurrect them. After five years as a deputy, she'd seen so much crime and horror, and lately, she had to work extra hard to compartmentalize everything to function in the unsettled world.

The uptick and boldness of crimes committed seemed to grow exponentially each day. More and more, stable neighborhood households were becoming the victims. Some areas were so bad, law enforcement could no longer respond in person. Reports were taken on the phone or online. Officers just couldn't keep up. She had to admit to discouragement on the job at times and many of her fellow deputies felt the same way. Thankfully, she could move on to a family business, which she'd expected to be less disappointing.

Boy, had she been wrong.

She forced her eyes from the photos, but couldn't quit wondering if Kelsey had been called in to recover this baby's body. Although the state had a local forensic anthropologist, Kelsey was world-renowned for her skills, so she could've been. How did she mentally survive recovering a child and even worse an infant? Bristol didn't want to think about such a task, much less do it.

She moved to the desk and flipped through papers. A flyer for August third for a missing children's event at the state capital was stashed on the bottom. A few days away, and Reya was scheduled to speak. Another sign that she planned to be alive that day. But maybe she'd agreed to speak before her daughter had been located and everything had changed on that fateful day in June, and now she could no longer go on. Still didn't explain taking Luna or the offsite stabbing.

Hoping for an answer, Bristol made a thorough search of the room, carefully looking at items but not disturbing them for the crime scene photos that the forensic expert would take. And she kept well away from the computer to keep from accidentally waking it up and altering the files. She didn't want to be responsible for messing up such an important investigation.

"Find anything?" Jared asked from the doorway.

She told him about the flyer. "But nothing to suggest that Reya wanted to end her life."

"Yeah, that doesn't add up. No vehicle in the garage or out front, so I put an APB out on it. Maybe if we find her car, we'll get that lead we've been hunting for. I also called in Sierra, and she's already on her way."

"Good," Bristol said. "Reya's phone isn't in here. Is it in her room?"

"I didn't see it, but could be in her back pocket. We'll have to wait for the ME to check. She left when I called and should be here any minute."

"That's fast."

Jared nodded, but his eyes were tight. "With the abduction of a baby, everyone's willing to let us jump to the head of the line."

She wished they hadn't come to the front of the line for that reason, but they were called to a very important task that they seemed to be failing at. "Luna's been gone for more than twenty-four hours now. Exponentially decreases odds of finding her alive."

"Unfortunately, that's true." Jared frowned.

A female voice coming from the front door grabbed her attention.

"Probably the ME."

"Already?"

"You've been in here for thirty minutes or so."

"Really?" She knew she'd gotten lost in thought, but...

"I'll go meet her." Jared pushed off the door jamb and disappeared down the hall only to come back with not one woman but two trailing behind.

He pointed at the office. "Sierra will start with printing and swabbing the computer so when Colin gets here, he can begin the images."

Bristol nodded and stepped out of Sierra's way.

Bristol greeted the other woman she recognized as Dr. Albertson, the long-term local medical examiner. She was slim and wearing white protective coveralls like Sierra's. Several pathologists worked under her, but she was the top dog in their department, and they were fortunate to have her on their team today.

"Nice to see you again, Bristol." Dr. Albertson continued down the hall, not stopping to talk.

One of the great things about this woman was that she remembered the names of most officers she interacted with at a murder scene. How she did it, Bristol didn't know, but the doctor had a lot of respect for law enforcement, and the officers knew she valued them.

Bristol followed them into Reya's bedroom.

The ME was already kneeling next to Reya and moving her limbs. "Rigor is still present but passing. Stab wound. One, from a large knife that I can see at this point." She inserted a thermometer through Reya's skin, likely accessing her liver, and left it to examine Reya's fingers. "No obvious skin cells under her nails. Doesn't look like there was a struggle, but I'll scrape the nails once I have her on the table."

She glanced at the thermometer, her eyebrows raised below her short salt and pepper hair. "My assistant will have to check the ambient temperature here, but I noticed on the way in that the hallway thermostat was set at sixty-eight degrees. Victim's reached that temperature. Means she's been dead for at least twenty hours."

"And her temperature tells you that?" Bristol asked as she loved to learn as much as she could while on the job. Her grandad had instilled that thirst for knowledge in all of them.

Dr. Albertson sat back on her haunches and looked up. "On average, a body loses one and a half degrees every hour after death. Of course the surrounding area has a lot to do with that, but if she was left here at her death or shortly after, she's dropped from 98.6 to 69 degrees. That's a drop of almost thirty degrees and divided by the one and half degrees gives me the twenty hours. This is assuming her basic body temp is 98.6, which isn't true of all people."

"Thanks for explaining," Bristol said.

"Happy to educate whenever I can. Just don't go playing armchair quarterback and think you can make a determination with this little information. You add in the state of rigor, which is starting to wane, my preliminary estimate puts her death between twenty and twenty-four hours. Likely closer to the twenty-hour mark."

"How long could she have lived after sustaining such a stab wound?" Jared asked.

"I can tell you more once I do the cut, but death from such a wound is typically from blood loss. It takes many minutes and sometimes hours for someone to exsanguinate —bleed to death—from stab wounds."

"We located a blanket saturated with her blood yesterday at twelve p.m.," Jared said. "Twenty to twenty-four hours would put the time of death between ten and two o'clock yesterday, which could fit our timeline."

Dr. Albertson nodded. "The rigor tells me the max, but

don't hold too fast to the early time as she might not have been brought directly here and was left in a car where her body would have cooled off faster, making the window later. Of course, you already know the lack of blood and spatter means she wasn't stabbed here."

"We figured as much," Jared said.

She took paper bags out of her pocket, slid them on Reya's hands, and rubber-banded them around her wrists to protect any potential forensics on the hands.

"Wolfe," a male's voice sounded from the hallway.

"That'll be Agent Graham for the electronics," Jared said. "Dr. Albertson, can you look for a phone in the victim's pockets?"

"Of course."

"I'll get Colin started while you do," Bristol said. She hurried from the room and found Colin heading down the hallway with long strides and determination in his dark eyes. He carried a black tool kit in one hand and evidence bags in the other. A camera strap was slung around his powerful neck.

"The computer's in the office." She stepped into the room, but got out of his way.

Sierra looked up from the chair behind the desk.

"And you are?" he asked, not sounding at all pleased.

"Sierra Rice. Trace evidence expert. Veritas Center."

"You wake up this machine?" he asked.

"Of course not."

He turned on Bristol. "You touch it?"

"No," she said and refrained from pointing out that she'd been a deputy for five years and wouldn't make such a rookie mistake.

"Good. Good." He set his kit on the floor. "My best chance at unlocking it is finding it in the After-First-Unlock —AFU—hot state."

She nodded, pretending to know what he meant but didn't.

"What about a phone or iPad?" he asked.

"The ME is looking for the phone on the victim now, and I haven't seen an iPad, but I haven't searched the house."

"Give it a quick once over. The computer will work to look at the security files, but it'll take some time to image. So our best hope is finding her phone or tablet. They can be imaged in a matter of minutes."

"I'll check with the ME first and then take a look around," she said. "You said the computer will take time, but how long?"

He looked at Sierra. "You about done here?"

"I am done." She pushed to her feet.

Colin turned back to Bristol. "Then I can get straight to work and it only depends on the size of the hard drive, and the amount of data stored. Most home computers take at least three hours. If there are a large number of reallocated sectors or other physical drive damage, it could take upwards of ten hours."

"Then let's hope for the three hours or that we find a phone or tablet," she said as they couldn't afford to sit for ten hours without getting a look at the security footage that could give them the first good look at Luna's abductor.

13

Jared stood behind Colin Graham in Reya Isaac's office. They hadn't located a phone or tablet, but Jared decided to authorize review of the security footage before the image was taken of the drive. Colin assured Jared that even though a record of accessing the file was kept, it wouldn't change this type of file and the log was in its own file. Could be problematic in court if they apprehended the kidnapper, but finding Luna trumped that potential issue.

Colin started the video from outside Reya's garage. "Reya set it up to alert only when a person was detected. Gives us far fewer files to review. The feed started recording at eleven-sixteen a.m. when this guy exits the driver's seat of her car that he pulled into the driveway."

Jared watched the man get out of a red Honda Civic that the plates confirmed as belonging to Reya. The man wore a black jacket with a hood over a baseball cap, blue jeans, and hiking boots.

"He fits Holloway's build." Jared squinted at the scene. "His hat is pulled pretty low, but also looks like Holloway's jawline."

"Hopefully he'll show his full face," Bristol said.

The guy looked around for some time, his face directed away from the camera, then opened the passenger door. He scooped up an adult body and kicked the door closed. He turned, head still down.

"It's Reya," Bristol said. "He's carrying Reya, and she's alive."

The suspect marched toward the house and out of view of the camera, never revealing his face, while Reya struggled weakly to get free.

Colin stopped the video. "She also has a doorbell alarm, and he triggered that too. That feed is coming up next."

Colin clicked another file and started the video. The suspect stood in front of the door camera, his face down and angled away as he fumbled to turn the key in the lock while holding Reya.

"Look up," Jared said. "Look up. Look up."

The suspect remained head down as he got the door open and entered the house.

Jared slammed a hand into the back of the chair. "He knows the cameras are there."

"Might suggest he's been at Reya's house before," Colin said, thankfully ignoring Jared's pummeling of his chair.

"Could be Reya's former husband," Bristol said.

"I'll send the older files to the team," Colin said. "To see if they can find this guy in an earlier video."

"Good thinking," Bristol said.

"Go back, Colin," Jared demanded. "Play it again."

If Jared's tone troubled Colin, he didn't show it and started the feed again.

"There, stop." Bristol stabbed her finger on Reya's face. "Reya looks right at the camera and says something that the audio doesn't pick up."

"You think she's leaving us a message?" Colin asked.

"I hope so," Bristol said.

"Run it again." Jared leaned closer, but with Reya laying on her back and just barely looking at the camera, he couldn't make out her words. "Can either of you tell what she's saying?"

"Not me," Bristol said. "But ideally she's telling us the guy's name."

"That would be good," Colin said. "But it's not clear to me. I'll work on enhancing the audio, but these doorbell cameras don't have the highest of resolutions and recording."

"Do that," Jared said. "And let's get this file to a forensic lip reader. See if they can make out the words."

"We should be the ones to do the death notification call on Reya's husband," Bristol said. "See how he reacts and what he might know."

Jared looked at Colin. "Before you do anything else, I want you to find the ex's address."

"His first name is Harri with an I," Bristol said. "I remember it from the news because it was an odd spelling."

"It's the Welsh spelling for Harry and should make locating him much easier." Colin opened a law enforcement search database on his laptop, and his fingers flew over the keyboard.

Jared counted to fifty when Colin pointed at the screen. "Bingo. His home address and his employer. A collision repair shop in Tigard."

Jared dialed the shop. "Can I speak to Harri?"

"On a break," the frazzled woman's tone was interrupted by the sound of a rivet gun.

"When will he be back?"

"About an hour. Call back then." The stressed woman hung up.

Jared put the address for the shop into a mapping

program on his phone and looked at Bristol. "I'm assuming you want to come with me to talk to Harri."

She started for the door and called over her shoulder. "Just try to stop me."

~

Harri worked in a small repair shop off Highway 99W in Tigard, a suburb of Portland. Under cloudy skies, Jared rushed toward the building that had seen better days, the rusty orange paint flaking in large slivers of color. A truck honked on the busy road.

Stop. Slow down. Don't lose your situational awareness. Let Bristol catch up.

This man could very well have killed Reya and carried her body into her house. They could be coming to see a distraught ex-husband or a killer, and they both needed to be on high alert.

A tangy beefy aroma saturated the air, mixing with the caustic odor of paint from the body shop. Jared noticed a taco truck in the parking lot with three wooden picnic tables sitting under umbrellas. They'd missed lunch, and Jared's mouth watered.

Maybe they could catch a snack here to tide him over to dinner at the house with Bristol. They would head over there as if coming home from work.

Jared looked at her when she fell into step beside him. "Let's get Isaacs to join us at the taco truck. If he wants to run, he'll have to cross a wide-open space to get to his vehicle."

"Sounds like a plan."

They entered the lobby area of the business, and the strong smell of paint eliminated the delicious taco smell.

"Help you." A woman with frizzy gray hair and a face filled with wrinkles eyed them suspiciously.

"We're here to see Harri." Jared worked hard to keep his tone light.

"You called just a bit ago."

"I did." Jared got out his ID. "Jared Wolfe, FBI. This is Bristol Steele, Multnomah County."

The woman cocked her head. "What's he done?"

"Nothing." Bristol smiled. "We just need to talk to him about a case we're investigating."

The woman slid off the stool, grabbing her back with one hand and opening the shop door with the other. An even bigger whiff of the paint odor drifted into the waiting room.

"Harri," she called out, her tone gruff. "Get yourself in here."

Thankfully she didn't tell him the FBI was here to see him. If Harri were prone to running, the guy would have done so before Jared even got a look at him.

He came into the room, wiping his hands with a paper towel. He took a good look at Jared, a longer one at Bristol, running his eyes from head to toe and back up.

"Harri Isaacs?" Jared asked.

"Yeah." His forehead furrowed. "You cops or something?"

Jared held out his ID and introduced them.

His eyes creased. "This about Darcy? You find the person who killed her?"

"No. Sorry." Jared jerked a thumb over his shoulder. "Could we go sit outside for a minute?"

Harri looked at the woman.

"Go," she said. "But that Explorer isn't gonna paint itself so make it quick."

Jared held the door, and Bristol stepped out. They kept Harri between them as they strolled down to the taco truck.

"Food any good here?" Bristol asked.

"Sure," Harri said. "We eat here a lot."

They reached the tables, and Bristol was the first to sit, facing the parking lot.

"You're not here for the food." Harri dropped onto a bench on the other side and slid his legs under the table. "What do you want?"

Jared perched on the splintery wood table top. "We're here about Reya."

"Reya?" Harri blinked a few times before narrowing his eyes. "What's going on with her?"

"I'm sorry to tell you that she's been found dead," Jared said. "We suspect she was murdered."

"Murdered?" Harri slapped his paint-stained hands on the table and gripped it tightly. "That's impossible."

Unless Harri was an Oscar-worthy actor, he didn't know about the murder.

"When's the last time you talked to her or saw her?" Jared asked.

He dropped his hands from the table, and his shoulders slumped. "The day they found Darcy and then her memorial service."

"And did you see Reya in person or just talk to her?" Bristol asked.

"We talked after we got the news. Had to make arrangements for a funeral. Then I saw her at Darcy's memorial service. Haven't seen or talked to Reya since then." His eyes glistened with tears. "You think the same person who took Darcy killed Reya?"

"We don't know." Jared hated to ask this, but... "Where were you at eleven-sixteen a.m. yesterday?"

He frowned. "You think I killed her. But why would I?

We didn't have anything to do with each other anymore. Anyway, I was here. Working. Wilma, the owner you just talked to, can vouch for me."

"Do you know of anyone who might want to harm her?" Bristol asked.

"Nah, unless it was the person who took Darcy."

"Does Reya have family that we should notify?" Bristol asked.

"It was just her and her dad, but he died right before Darcy was found."

"No siblings."

Harri shook his head. "She was an only child. Adopted."

She was adopted. Could that be important to the investigation?

"What about friends?" Jared asked.

"I don't know these days, but all of our friends slowly ghosted us after Darcy disappeared. Some of them thought we did something to her, and the others just couldn't stand our grief. Was the reason we split. Together we couldn't get past it. Alone I could move on. Not Reya. She got so involved in the missing children website and community. I couldn't work with other people's grief like that. Not and not lose my mind." He shook his head. "She has some friends in that group, but I don't know their names."

"Any other thoughts on who might have harmed her?" Jared asked, wrapping up with that question.

"None." Harri took in a shuddering breath. "S'pose you let me know when her body is released."

Jared nodded.

"We done here?" Harri rubbed a hand over his face.

"I'll walk up to the shop with you."

Harri got up, and Jared looked at Bristol. "Want to order a snack since we missed lunch, and I'll be right back?"

"Sure."

Jared caught up to Harri. Jared needed to verify the guy's alibi and make sure Harri didn't talk to Wilma and tell her how to alibi him out before Jared could.

"Wilma," Jared said the moment they entered the waiting area. "Harri says he was working yesterday around eleven-fifteen in the morning."

"Sure was." Wilma cast Harri a sharp look. "Didn't even leave for lunch. We were swamped, and I had tacos brought in."

"Thanks." Jared held his hand out to Harri. "I know you two divorced, but I'm sorry for your loss."

Harri gave a sad nod and went back to the shop. Jared flashed a quick smile at Wilma and exited the building before she started asking questions. By the time he got back to the taco stand, Bristol had placed two baskets holding a taco, chips, and salsa on the table, along with two drinks in bright blue cups.

Jared's stomach rumbled as he sat.

"Sounds like it's a good thing there was a taco truck in the lot." Bristol grinned, then dipped a chip into chunky red salsa.

"Might not have made it to a drive-through." He laughed and took a bite of the soft taco, then groaned.

"Good," he mumbled around a mouthful.

She bit into hers, the rich sauce dripping into her basket. "Very good. Reminds me of when we had taco night at camp."

He took a long pull on the drink that turned out to be iced tea. "Those really were good days, weren't they? Our biggest worries were if the managers or the kids were going to catch us making out."

"And now here we are looking for a kidnapped baby." She dipped another chip and shoved it into her mouth.

He picked up his taco again, careful to keep the contents inside of the flexible tortilla. "Talk about extremes."

"Back then I never thought I'd reach this age and not be married."

"Me either. I had it all planned out. Do my stint in the Navy. Get out. Choose some sort of law enforcement career. Then get married and have a few kids."

She sat back, chip in hand, eyeing him. "You got the first parts right, though I have to go on record as saying you could've had it all by now if you'd never dumped me."

His appetite fled, and he set the remains of his taco in the basket. "Were you thinking marriage then?"

"Honestly?" She met and held his gaze. "Yeah, I was."

"I can only say how sorry I am that I wasn't. That I didn't... I..." He shook his head. "I wish I could change what I did. You deserved so much better."

"Do you really?"

"I do." He wiped his mouth with a coarse white napkin. "I don't know if we would've gotten married though. I mean, since then I thought I'd found someone to share my life with. Twice. That fell through both times."

She cocked her head. "What happened?"

"Law enforcement, like you said earlier. Seems like women don't want to put up with the constant interruptions and demands of my work." He picked up his drink again. "I don't blame them. I would have a hard time being married to me."

"Yeah. Being married to me would be a challenge too." The sadness in her tone cut right through him.

Could they be together? She was getting out of the law enforcement game and said no to a husband in law enforcement in no uncertain terms. So no point in hoping, right?

His phone rang. Perfect timing for an interruption. He

looked at Detective Hale's name on the screen and accepted the call. "Tell me you have something good."

"We located Reya Isaacs's Civic." Hale's voice was higher than normal.

"Where?"

"About a mile from her house."

"Text me the address, and we're on our way." Jared hung up and relayed the information to Bristol. "Let's move."

He grabbed his basket and drink and ditched them in the trash then bolted for his vehicle. He got the doors open with the remote and had them on the road in no time. He chose not to continue their conversation, but put the pedal down and drove as fast as he could through a residential neighborhood. He merged into a commercial area with cafés, coffee shops, and bars.

Hale stood outside Reya's car which was blocked from traffic by two patrol cars. Jared parked and charged toward the detective, stopping only to show his ID to the officer of record obstructing his access.

"Let them through," Hale called out. "They're clear."

Jared shoved his ID in his pocket and slipped under the crime scene tape then held it up for Bristol.

Jared marched over to Hale. "What do we have?"

Hale let out a long breath. "A large quantity of blood in the front and an infant car seat in the back."

Jared leaned into the back seat and took photos of the car seat. He texted the pictures to Piper along with a request to research the details on the seat and get back to him ASAP with any info she could locate. If they were lucky, which they hadn't been, the seat was an unusual brand that was sold in limited shops and they could track the buyer that way.

Piper replied right away. *Researched enough seats for my*

baby to tell just by looking at it that it's a top-selling older model. More details to come.

"Piper says it's an older model." Jared dropped his phone into his pocket, letting his hope for the car seat panning out drop with it.

"Maybe Reya's seat from her daughter," Bristol suggested.

"Makes sense and whoever took Luna has another seat," Hale said. "Or they didn't care about putting her in one."

Or Luna didn't need a seat because she wasn't alive. Not something Jared would say. Nor would he mention what happened to baby Wyatt when he hadn't been restrained in a seat.

"Either way," Hale continued. "We hope to get prints or DNA from the seat. Already called in your Veritas expert. I want to keep all the forensics under one umbrella. We'll figure out who pays for her later. She's on the way."

Jared nodded, thankful Hale wanted to use Sierra and didn't worry about finances at a time like this.

"If cost is a factor, I know Sierra will do the work pro bono if needed," Bristol said.

"We might need to take her up on that," Hale said.

Jared looked around. "Any cameras in the area?"

"None that we can see, but I've already got deputies canvassing the nearby businesses."

Jared's phone rang, and he dug it out. Caller ID displayed Colin's name.

"What do you have?" Jared asked.

"Heard back from the forensic lip reader," he said.

"And?"

"And she believes Reya is saying, Luna. Car," Colin said. "Sounds like Luna was in the car in the driveway when Reya was dropped off."

Jared took a moment to let that news settle in. "We now know where Luna was at that point and you'd think the car might provide a strong lead. But the vehicle's sitting right in front of me and it doesn't look like it will give us anything else to help us locate Luna."

14

Just before dinner, Bristol joined Jared in the family room of their undercover home. She forced the thought of Luna having been in the car they located but not knowing where she was now into the back of her mind. Bristol couldn't think about Luna right now without losing it. The stress of the investigation was mounting, and if Bristol didn't let it go for a moment, she might start blubbering in front of Jared.

So think of something else. She let her mind wander to what it might be like to be searching for a house to buy with him as her life mate. She wouldn't choose this one. It was too contemporary for her tastes. She was more of a traditional girl. She loved the large Victorian she currently lived in with her sisters and cousins.

Jared joined her. "Let's walk the property so we're comfortable with the layout. That way we can easily head straight to any room the interviewer might ask to see."

"Sounds good." She dredged up a smile and a good mood. "Take me to your kitchen, kind sir."

He chuckled and pivoted to point at the room that was open to the living and dining area they now stood in. "I won't be so easy on you. How about taking me to the mud/laundry room?"

She had no problem leading him to the back of the house that opened to the garage. She'd admired the mudroom on their way in.

"Ta-da." She swept out a hand in the room.

"Great," he said.

"It was easy to remember," she said. "Living with five other women in a house without a mudroom or even front closet makes this room a dream come true. All we have are hooks by the front door, and that does nothing for the many pairs of shoes that go through our house in a day."

He laughed. "Sounds like you have a challenge there."

"We just can't afford to be lazy and leave our shoes out or no one will get through the door."

"I'd like to see this house someday." He locked gazes with her, almost like issuing a challenge.

Emotions swirled in her belly, and she took a moment before answering. She had to come up with something to make light of how she was feeling. "Play your cards right, and I'll show it to you without even charging for admission."

He didn't laugh, but his expression lightened. "You want a room like this in your forever house, then."

She let out a squeaky breath. "Especially if I had kids."

He glanced at her. "I never asked if you wanted to have children? I mean you, Bristol, not Christine."

"We never talked about that back in the day, did we?"

"We were young."

"Not too young, though." She didn't add that she'd thought about having his child, but was never brave enough to bring it up with him. Talking about kids implied a future that they hadn't discussed either. Turned out they didn't have a reason to.

192

"I'd have to find the right guy first and be settled at the company before having kids. How about you?"

"I'd like the chance to raise kids opposite of how my siblings and I were raised." His words were crisp and filled with conviction. "Like you, it would have to be with the right person."

Her mind drifted to imagining their children again. *Stop.* "Since I haven't come to grips with getting married, I don't spend a lot of time talking about it, but I've always liked kids and assumed I would have them."

He kept watching her. "We need to decide how many we want for our make-believe family in case we're asked."

"Three, I think," she answered without giving it any thought. "We both have two siblings so that can make it easier to remember if we're stressed."

He took a breath, then smiled. "Lead me to the bedrooms to be sure we have enough rooms for our make-believe family."

He stepped back, and she marched past, accidentally brushing his shoulder. Their kiss came to mind, and she didn't dismiss the thought. She embraced the tumultuous feelings. She wouldn't mind pausing to kiss him again. Shocking, to be sure.

Just exactly how deep were her feelings for this man? *Have I ever stopped loving him?* Could it be the real reason she'd never found anyone she wanted to get serious with?

She shook her head, hoping the newfound thoughts would exit her brain. They didn't. Just the opposite. Each step she took to the second floor, traits she still liked and respected about him came to mind. As if God was extolling Jared's good qualities to erase the fact that he'd bailed on her.

Was Jared God approved? God recommended? She could see her family liking him, and him fitting in just fine.

Leave it alone. Why trust God all of a sudden? Could that be the whole point of bringing them together?

Upstairs, she willed her mind to the task. She had to. She couldn't risk blowing the undercover operation. She memorized the location and approximate sizes of the four bedrooms. Piper had taken care of making the house look lived in. She'd furnished every room and added food and dishes in the kitchen and clothing in their closets and toiletries in the master bath.

Bristol looked at Jared who'd opened the medicine cabinet. "How in the world did Piper get this done so fast? It seems like we really do live here."

"She's super at her job for one, but I wonder if she's in the nesting phase of her pregnancy and that made it easier."

"Could be."

The oven timer beeped in a shrill tone from below.

Jared held out his hand. "Dinner's ready."

Nervous about sharing a meal alone, she slipped past him and jogged down the walnut stairs. Another thing she wouldn't choose in her own house. She would want light floors. White oak, maybe.

She rushed to the kitchen and silenced the beeper. With big mitts on her hands, she opened the oven and removed the basic meal her gran had taught each of the girls to make. A one-pan meal with chicken thighs, carrots, onion, potatoes, and garlic.

The tangy garlic scent snaked from the pan.

Jared came up behind her and looked over her shoulder. "I didn't know you could cook so well."

She looked at him. "First, you should taste it before saying that, and second, it's the only real meal that I can consistently do well."

"Looks and smells good." He leaned closer. "Unless of course you've changed your perfume to garlic."

They laughed together, but tension weighed heavy in the air. He seemed to be uneasy too, or maybe she was projecting her feelings onto him.

"Go ahead and have a seat. I'll serve." She shooed him away before she gave in to the feelings threatening her common sense and kissed him.

"I'll pour some water." He searched the cabinets, lifting out two glasses and taking them to the water dispenser in the refrigerator. "I guess it'll be good that we had a meal here so we know where the dishes are for the visit tomorrow."

"I could always say you're the kind of husband who avoids the kitchen." She spooned the veggies into a bowl and inhaled the savory aromas.

He glanced at her as he filled the second glass. "That would be sexist, though. I could say the same of you."

"And who cooked dinner?" She carried the bowl to the table and wrinkled her nose at him.

He set down the glasses and took a seat. "You told me to wait until I tasted it."

She swatted at him, and he snagged her hand to tug her into the chair next to him. She'd barely hit the seat when he leaned over and gave her a quick but passion-filled kiss.

She pulled free and caught her breath. "We shouldn't."

He continued to hold her hand, his touch making her want to move closer.

"Someone could be watching the house," he said. "This will make our cover more believable."

"Um, Jared." She extricated her hand and stood. "The window faces the fenced backyard. Pretty sure no one is out there watching."

"Yeah. I know." He grinned. "But figured I had to have a legit reason to kiss you or you might get mad."

"I'm not mad." She stood to get the platter with the

crisply browned chicken thighs. "I just don't think it's a good idea."

She joined him at the table, handing him the platter and taking a seat in the same chair. She shifted it away from him and earned a raised eyebrow for her effort.

He took a thigh and dropped it on her plate then served himself. "Would you ever consider starting again? You and me, I mean. Dating?"

"I don't know." She emptied a spoonful of veggies on her plate.

"Is it because of my job or because you don't trust me?"

"Both, I guess."

"Do you think you can ever trust me not to hurt you again?" He took the veggie bowl from her. "Because I won't."

She paused, fork in hand to look him in the eye. "How do you know that for sure?"

He set down the bowl and held her gaze. "The past few days have shown me how much I still care about you. How much I once cared about you. What a terrible mistake it was to leave you."

"I'll admit I care about you too, but my trust issues extend way beyond you." She sat back. "If I can't trust God who is perfect, how can I ever trust another human with all of their flaws?"

Jared fell back in his chair as if defeated. Yeah, she'd caused him to collapse. Defeat weighed heavy on her too. She wanted to trust him. Trust God.

Help me to trust You again, please.

Jared's phone dinged, and he grabbed it as if it were a lifeline. "It's one of the backup agents staking out our house."

Bristol had forgotten all about the team of agents watching the house in case they should need backup.

Not a good thing to do.

"And?" she asked.

Jared lifted his head, and their gazes connected. "And it looks like we have company."

Jared's first response had been to grab his weapon and check the ammo. He didn't. The last thing he needed to do was add to the worry on Bristol's face while they ate. The strain remained in place through the whole meal and even as she carried dirty dishes to the counter.

He needed to do something to help alleviate it. He put his plate and silverware in the dishwasher, the clanking echoing in the room. "Remember we thought Holloway might send someone to watch the house. To verify we're legit. That's likely all it is."

"Yeah," she said, but didn't sound convinced.

"I'd suggest we go make out in front of the window and put on a show for them," he said, making sure his tone was lighthearted. "But I know that would make you even more nervous, and I definitely don't want that."

She spun to look at him, anguish radiating from her eyes. "How could you leave me back then?"

Her pain cut into his heart, and it mixed with shock at the change in topic. He was responsible for her pain. Not Holloway's men at the road. Him.

So what did he say? What could he say?

"Looking back at it, I don't know," he started, hoping the words would come. "I guess when I was younger, I was much more impacted by trying to be everything my family wasn't."

"And what?" She fired an accusatory look at him. "Being with me somehow was the same as being with your superficial family?"

"No. Not at all. I foolishly thought the relationship just stood in the way of becoming the guy I wanted to be. To serve. To be useful and needed. Not superficial like you said."

She sighed. "I don't pretend that I get that because I grew up living a life of service."

"Trust me when I say without it, life is empty. Even if my family makes it seem like they're happy, they're all still searching for the next great thing when it's right there in front of them." Thoughts of the way they chose to live made him frown. "I continue to work hard to invite them to church and get them involved in something."

"And have you succeeded?" Her anguished expression had seemed to brighten just a bit.

"The best I've done was get them to serve at a soup kitchen. Unfortunately, they just used it as a photo-op for social media and to build up their self-serving status."

She touched his arm. "I'm sorry, Jared. Like I said, I don't know how it feels. I can try to imagine it, and I guess that can help me forgive and forget our past."

Was there hope for them? Could there be hope? He had to know. "So do you forgive me for being an immature jerk?"

"I forgive you for leaving. The rest, I'm not sure about." She winked and put the last plate in the dishwasher. "Why don't you go play your guitar and relax for a while?"

Right. She was trying to lighten a situation that had become very heavy—or maybe even get rid of him. That left his heart heavier than the anchors he'd once dropped on huge Navy ships.

15

The doorbell rang at nine a.m. sharp.

Bristol expected the visitor, but she still jumped up from the couch where she and Jared had been anxiously waiting for the last thirty minutes. She glanced around to be sure they hadn't left anything out that would give away their real identities. They'd locked all of their information for the investigation and computers in his trunk well in advance of the woman's arrival. They had no idea how much she might snoop on Holloway's behalf, and they had to be prepared to maintain their undercover personas.

"Relax." Jared headed for the door. He wore another one of his sharp suits, a deep blue with very subtle stripes. "We'll be fine. If she asks a question we haven't discussed, don't answer, and I will. I'll do the same for you."

Bristol strode behind him to the door. He opened it to a tall, lanky woman with a clipboard in hand. She had obviously dyed black hair, the opposite of what you might find with her fair complexion. Her lips were colored with a vibrant red lipstick.

Could she be Luna's kidnapper? The height didn't fit the woman in the video, but maybe the woman in the video wasn't their kidnapper after all. Bristol had to suspect anyone connected to the case. And that meant she somehow had to take a picture of this woman.

It would also be good to try to transmit her suspicions to Jared. She took his hand and gave it a sharp squeeze. He responded with a very subtle nod.

"I'm Olive Wallace with Multnomah County Social Services." The woman flashed an ID badge but stowed it in her pocket before they could take a close look.

"I'm sorry." Bristol did her best to sound like she really was sorry. "But I didn't see your ID before you put it away. We're very careful who we share our information and home with. That will be even more important when we have children. I'm sure you can understand and wouldn't mind letting me see it again."

Olive frowned but took the ID out and held it long enough for Bristol to view. Looked legit, but anything could be forged these days, and Olive could be their kidnapper. Bristol noted the woman didn't wear a wedding ring. Didn't mean anything. Not all married people wore rings. And she didn't have to be married to want a child. She looked to be in her mid-thirties and too young for her cynical expression. But then, if she worked for Holloway, she could likely be a cynical person.

"Thank you." Jared flashed a very charming smile at the social worker and stepped back. "Please come in."

Olive seemed to thaw at his response but gave Bristol the stink eye.

Bristol hoped she hadn't ruined the interview, but she needed to see if Olive's county ID was a fake. Bristol would check with a friend at Multnomah County after the interview to be sure the social worker was legit.

"I moonlight for Mr. Holloway," she said as if she could read Bristol's mind. "Social workers aren't paid well enough to make ends meet. Especially with the crazy high cost of housing around here."

"I'm sorry to hear that." Jared spoke in a mellow, almost soothing tone. He was probably equally as sorry that this woman was moonlighting for the likes of Holloway.

At least Bristol was. "Where would you like to start?"

"Let's take a tour of the home. I'll check things off as we go." She removed a packet of papers from the clipboard. "Of course you'll want to childproof the house. Not necessary for an infant, but you'll need to do it anyway and get a jump on it. Children grow so quickly."

She handed the packet to Jared. "Directions on how to childproof."

He glanced at it and gave a serious nod. "We'll get right to it."

She took a pen from her pocket and started around the room, clicking the pen when she wasn't writing. "I'll review my findings at the end."

She marched into the dining area and then into the kitchen. "How long have you lived here?"

"Just a month or so," Bristol said quickly as that was a question she could easily answer. "We wanted to move up to a bigger house for the family we hope to have."

Olive nodded and moved on, opening a few cupboards and closing them then checking off more boxes. She stepped to the patio door located behind a round table and chairs. "Can I see the backyard next?"

Bristol and Jared had only gone outside once, and she didn't want to fumble with the lock so she gestured for Olive to go ahead. She got the door open and stepped outside.

Still holding Jared's hand, Bristol held him back before he followed Olive. She leaned close and whispered, "Olive could be our kidnapper. We need to take her picture to show to Nurse Raney to see if she's the one who asked all of the questions."

"You go out with Olive, and I'll try to snap a shot from the doorway without arousing her suspicion." He squeezed Bristol's hand and dropped the packet on the countertop.

She stepped out to another sunny morning and took a moment just to breathe while Olive walked the fence line. Bristol's hands trembled, so she shoved them in her pockets. Good thing Jared was going to take a picture. Bristol's shaking hands would have spoiled a photo.

Bristol had often wondered what it would be like to be undercover. Her clammy hands and the tightness in her stomach said she wasn't cut out for it. She had to ignore her nerves and do the right thing. She couldn't mess up. Just couldn't. Finding Luna was too important to blow this potential lead.

She crossed the yard, her heels sinking into the moist lawn. Londyn would be mad if Bristol ruined the mile-high pumps, but it couldn't be helped.

"Nice piece of equipment and in good condition." Olive patted the upright on the wooden play structure and stared at Bristol. "You do know this is too big for any child under the age of four?"

"It came with the house," Bristol said, trying to come up with a suitable answer. "We're planning to add a toddler swing but will restrict access to the rest of it. And we'll get a smaller more age-appropriate structure too."

Olive nodded and started for the house. "On to the bedrooms."

She brushed past Jared, and Bristol's phone chimed. Jared had texted the photo he'd taken of Olive. He'd added a message. *Texted backup team to make sure they follow her when she leaves.*

Perfect.

Bristol held her phone up to him and nodded. He started after Olive, and Bristol trailed behind for a chance to forward Olive's photo to Teagan and ask her to show it to Nurse Raney.

Teagan replied. *Will head right up there.*

Bristol stowed her phone, hoping they would know if Olive was the woman Nurse Raney talked to before Olive left. If she was at all suspicious of them, she could go underground.

At this point, she seemed more bored than anything, but if a person wanted to work for Holloway they had to be good at hiding their emotions.

Bristol caught up to Olive and Jared in the third bedroom. A small room that Piper had decorated as a nursery with a white crib and rocket ships.

Olive turned to look at Jared. "How many children are you hoping for?"

"At least three." Jared circled an arm around Bristol and drew her close.

She fit perfectly at his side as she had back at camp, and the love she'd once felt for him overwhelmed her common sense. She forgot about Olive. About the undercover sting and smiled up at him, lost in his gaze.

"I've always wanted little Christines running around." Jared's use of the fake name burst Bristol's love bubble. "But I'll be happy to give a good home to as many children as the love of my life here wants."

Bristol expected Olive might gag at the sentiment, but she sighed. Bristol didn't blame her. If it were an honest comment, she would respond the same way. Jared was a dreamy guy, and if Olive was unmarried, she might be more susceptible to the romance in his tone. After all, Bristol was. Completely. Sweep-her-off-her-feet susceptible even when she knew he was playing a part.

"Well, I'm done here." Olive flipped the pages on her form closed. "You passed, but you'll need to do the child-proofing before your baby arrives."

What? Olive didn't want to ask more questions?

Bristol was sure this inspection was a much more super-ficial review than the ones done in legal adoptions. Olive was more likely tasked with checking to see if Jared and Bristol seemed legit and appeared to have the means to pay for this baby. Because after all, it was all about money to Holloway. Not qualifications—just money.

The woman started down the stairs. At the bottom, she turned to hold out the clipboard. "I'll need you both to sign."

Jared took the form and scribbled his fake name. When it came to Bristol's turn, she had to go slower to get it right, but Olive didn't seem to notice. She ripped off pink copies of her forms and handed them to Bristol. The pages had Everett Holloway Attorney at Law on the top and all the little boxes had bright blue checks in the yes column. She'd added a few minor notes about childproofing the house, but that was all.

"What happens now?" Bristol asked.

"I give my report to Mr. Holloway, and he'll be in touch."

"Can you get it to him right away?" Jared took Bristol's hand and kissed it. "I've wanted to make my wife's dreams come true for years and don't want to wait another minute more."

She looked Jared in the eye, that wistful look back on her face. "Of course I can."

"Thank you." Jared tugged on the knot of his tie, which Bristol took as a signal that this meeting was indeed over.

Olive opened the door and looked back. "Good luck on the adoption. If the love you show for each other is lavished on a child, you'll make great parents."

She marched down the walkway.

Jared closed the door, got out his phone, and dialed. Gone was the fake love. Evaporated with the close of the door. And so was the fake desire to do whatever he could for Bristol.

"She's leaving now," he said into his phone and went to the window. "Tail her and *do not* lose her."

Right. Back to the real world where Bristol and Jared were coworkers.

Forget about him holding your hand. Giving you the same look he'd once shared at camp. This is reality.

He turned to face her, all business now. "We need to find out if Olive's who she says she is or if she had a fake ID. By the way, nice follow-up on insisting on getting a closeup of her credentials. Looked real to me, but Holloway has the means to buy a forged ID, and I'm sure none of his clients would make any waves and look into her. They wouldn't do anything to threaten their chances at adoption."

"I have a contact at Multnomah County who can confirm her employment," Bristol said. "I also texted Olive's photo to Teagan and asked her to show it to Nurse Raney. Olive's height is wrong for the woman on the video, but Olive could be the woman who questioned Raney outside the birthing center."

"I thought the same thing." He grabbed a pad of paper and pen and jotted down a license plate number. "Can you run Olive's plates through DMV too? See if the car she's driving comes back registered to her?"

He handed the pad to Bristol, and she stepped in the other room to search for a better connection to make the call to dispatch.

"Vehicle is registered to one Everett Holloway," the dispatcher said. "Did you need his address?"

"Please," Bristol said, in case Holloway had the car registered to a different address from his home or office.

Dispatch shared the address. Holloway's home.

"Look up an Olive Wallace," Bristol said. "I don't have a DOB. Especially look for someone with priors. She's around thirty-five."

Bristol tapped her foot as she waited.

"Search came back with three listings, but none of them have priors and none are that age. All are women fifty and up."

"Thanks." Bristol ended the call and scrolled through the contact list until she found Liddy, a county social worker. Her friend answered on the first ring.

"Liddy? It's Bristol Steele. How are you?" Bristol tried to sound cheerful and casual.

"Good." She paused. "But you really don't want to know that, do you? You want a favor."

Bristol cringed. "Am I that transparent?"

"I can't think of a time you called just to say hi." Liddy chuckled. "But then I do the same thing, and it goes both ways, right? So what do you need?"

Bristol had always appreciated Liddy's straightforward behavior and helpfulness. "I'm checking to see if you have a caseworker named Olive Wallace in your department."

"Name's not familiar, but we have a few new hires so let me check the directory."

Bristol heard Liddy's fingers clicking over her keyboard. Bristol wanted to hurry her up so she tapped her finger on the walnut dining table as she waited.

"Nope," Liddy said. "No one named Olive at all."

Drat. "If I text you a picture, can you tell me if you recognize the woman?"

"Go ahead. I'll wait."

Bristol located the picture from Jared and sent the text.

"Got it," Liddy said. "But no to that too. I've never seen this woman. Did she say she worked here?"

"I could be mistaken," Bristol said, not willing to give away any information on the investigation.

"Ah," Liddy said. "You can't say. Okay. Anything else?"

Was there? Could she mention Holloway? She had to give it a try. "Have you ever heard of an adoption attorney named Everett Holloway?"

"Heard of him, but never had any dealings with him."

"What have you heard?"

"Just that he's a high-priced adoption attorney and places a lot of babies."

"Any concerns about him?" Bristol tried not to lead Liddy but wanted to go deeper.

"I've heard he likes to shortcut the home study." Liddy tsked. "But he meets the minimal requirements, so no charges can be brought against him."

"But he's legit as far as you know?"

"As far as I know, but I assume if you're asking questions that might not be true." She sighed. "I can ask around about him if you want."

"Not necessary." Bristol left it at that. She didn't want anything to get back to Holloway and raise his suspicions. "Thanks for your help, and I'd appreciate it if you'd keep this conversation confidential."

"Will do, as always," Liddy said.

"Have a great day." Bristol hung up before Liddy could ask additional questions.

Bristol's phone chimed a text message from Teagan.

Raney says this could be the woman she spoke to. Couldn't comment on height difference. She said, and I quote, "What I gave the cops was more of a feeling than exact details."

A feeling? Seriously? Bristol thanked Teagan as Jared's raised voice came from the living room. Bristol hurried to the front of the house and entered just in time to see Jared shove a hand into his hair as he cupped his phone against his ear.

"What do you mean you lost her?" he demanded.

They'd lost Olive? Bristol's heart dropped.

"Did you notify the local authorities to get eyes on her?" Jared paced the room and stabbed his thumb into his phone as he looked at her. "An accident with a cement truck cut off the backup team. They didn't call for an alert on Olive's vehicle so I need to do that now."

He tapped his phone a few times and raised it to his face. "Hale. Good. We have a suspect my team was tailing, but they lost her." Jared shared the location of the accident, and Olive's vehicle information. "I need you to put out an alert on this woman and get your officers in the immediate area actively looking for her."

Jared listened, his eyes narrowed. "Good. Let me know if she's spotted."

He hung up and slammed a fist into the wall, breaking the drywall. "Did we have better luck with your calls?"

Bristol didn't want to answer and upset him more, but he needed to know. "Olive's car is registered to Holloway but no records for Olive Wallace in the general age range of the woman we just saw. Nurse Raney thought Olive could be the woman she saw. She couldn't comment on the height, and said it was all about a feeling not exact details."

He looked like he wanted to thrust his fist into the wall again, but maybe his already red knuckles stopped him. "What about Olive being a legit social worker?"

Bristol shook her head. "My contact never heard of or saw her before, and she's not in the department directory."

"Then we can't locate her that way." He paced the room, sharp, crisp steps back and forth his phone still clutched in his hand. "If the locals don't spot her car, there's no way to get to her except through Holloway. So much for that lead."

He stopped and stared at Bristol, his eyes haunted and dark.

"You're thinking about the boy you lost," she said.

He nodded. "This is exactly the same. One careless error and a child died."

"Not a careless error, and we don't know that Luna has died," she said. "The team was doing their job and got cut off. They couldn't go through that cement truck."

"You're right, I guess."

"And you're not to blame for the loss of that boy." She moved closer to him. "I'm the last one to say anything about turning a situation over to God, but I know if you did, you could let it go once and for all. Will you continue to think of it? Sure. Will it cut you in half like it's doing now? No."

"I've tried."

She couldn't very well tell him to try harder when she was in the same situation. She took his hands. "Let's pray together."

She didn't give him a chance to say no, but offered her most sincere prayer for his peace and comfort. When she struggled to find more to say, he took over and prayed for her ability to trust. He squeezed her hands and released them.

He held up his phone. "I need to update Adair. He needs to know we lost Olive."

Bristol took a seat on the couch and checked her email while he continued to pace. His steps were less frantic, but that haunted look remained in his eyes.

What did she think—that one simple prayer would fix him on the spot?

She knew it could happen. Had happened. And she wanted to believe that her plea had just worked for Jared, but she knew deep anguish could take time and countless prayers to recover from. She was a perfect example. But, and it was a big but, she did feel better about her struggle since the prayer. Maybe God really was working in her heart.

Jared ended his call.

"Adair's not happy, huh?" she asked.

"Guess my expression is saying it all." He sat on the end of the sofa.

She was thankful he at least had stopped pacing.

"He didn't miss the chance to remind me not to let this turn into another Wyatt situation. He even threatened to take me off lead if we have any other issues."

She resisted taking his hand. "But you aren't responsible for losing Olive. Adair is just looking for a scapegoat."

"In this situation, I know that. Still not sure with Wyatt, but this and your prayer are opening my eyes to at least thinking I could get rid of this blame." He cracked a tight smile.

Bristol's phone rang. She looked at the screen, and her mouth dropped open. "It's Amelia."

Jared raised an eyebrow. "The woman you met in the lot?"

Bristol nodded and answered on speaker, holding the phone closer to Jared.

"She's here." Amelia's voice whispered quietly through the phone. "The woman who brings babies is here."

"Slow down. Slow down. I can't hear you." Bristol turned up her phone's volume.

"The lady. The one I told you about. She's here looking for Mr. Holloway. Yelling and screaming, 'Where's my money? Where's my money?' She is angry. So very angry. She said he is not at his office or home so he has to be here."

Bristol looked at Jared and cupped her hand over her phone. "How can Holloway be missing when the surveillance teams we have on his office and home are not telling us he's gone?"

"Good question. One I want an answer to." Jared got his phone out again and stepped to the other side of the room.

Had Olive seen through Jared and Bristol's façade and that's why she was so frantic to find Holloway? Maybe figured out they were lying about their identities? Could also be why she went through the study so quickly.

Or maybe she was just afraid that Bristol would check up on her ID since Bristol paid so much attention to it and it freaked Olive out. Maybe it had been a mistake to demand to see it again.

Bristol couldn't waste time thinking about that now. "Give me your address, and I'll come over," she said to Amelia.

Amelia rattled off an address only ten minutes away.

"Try to keep the woman there, but don't use force," Bristol said with emphasis. "Or if she seems dangerous don't try to stop her. If Holloway shows up stay well away from him, and unlock the front door for me."

"Hurry. Please." Amelia's anguish cut through Bristol.

Hopefully the stress wouldn't send Amelia into labor. The last thing they needed was to put another baby in jeopardy.

16

Jared pulled close to the sprawling single story house at the address given by Amelia and pointed out his windshield. "Olive's car is still in the driveway. No other vehicle so Holloway likely never showed up."

"How do you think Holloway got out of his office without our team seeing him?" Bristol asked.

"My best guess is his assistant helped somehow. Maybe let him ride on the floor in the back of her car."

"I guess we won't know until we find him."

"The team is working on that." Jared pulled in behind her car to block it. "Right now we need to focus on Amelia and Olive." And forget that Adair was going to lose his cool when he found out.

The backup team who'd lost Olive parked at the road. Jared shifted into park, and Bristol jumped from the car before he could get the key out of the ignition.

He jerked it free and raced after her. He caught up and rested a hand on her shoulder. She'd taken a few minutes to change into her uniform that she'd stowed in the trunk so she could carry her sidearm and affect an arrest when they arrived.

"Take a beat to calm down," he said.

"I'm good. Been to plenty of tense situations while on patrol." She shifted her Kevlar vest. "Especially domestics."

"This isn't a domestic. Just because Olive's name didn't return any priors, doesn't mean Olive's even her name." His eyes narrowed. "She's broken the law and doesn't want to go to jail. She might indeed have priors and have served time. If she has, she'll likely do just about anything not to go back to prison. She could be armed and very dangerous."

"I understand the risk." Bristol eyed him. "As I said, it's not my first rodeo. Let's move before she has a chance to hurt Amelia or her baby."

Jared wanted to go in before Bristol to minimize the risk to her, but FBI agents didn't often go into such dangerous situations. Patrol deputies lived the life each and every minute of their shift, and Bristol had entered more homes than he had in his career, giving her the greatest experience here.

She tried the knob. It turned under her hand as she'd requested of Amelia. Bristol pushed into the house, her gun in hand.

"Police!" she called out.

Jared trailed her down the tiled hallway, his own gun out and ready.

Olive stood in the living room talking to Amelia, who flinched and tried to back away. Olive grabbed Amelia's hand and jerked it behind her back.

"I knew you two were too good to be true." Olive glared at them. "But I wanted to believe in love. Shame on me for being so gullible. Stay where you are, or I'll hurt her and the baby."

Jared scanned Olive. No sign of a weapon, but he wouldn't charge her. She could still hurt Amelia or the baby. Better to negotiate than risk that.

"You don't want to do that," Bristol said to Olive, obviously thinking the same thing, but still keeping her weapon drawn. "Why don't we sit down and talk about it?"

"Hah." Olive raised her chin. "You lied to me once. Made a fool of me. Why should I believe you now?"

"Because we want to make sure Amelia's okay," Jared stated plainly. "Let her sit down. Rest. You don't want to trigger preterm labor."

"Hah!" Olive said. "Why do I care?"

"You could go down for murder if the baby doesn't make it," Bristol said.

Amelia burst into tears. "Please. Please let me sit."

"Come on, Olive." Jared used that soft tone that seemed to impact women. "Please let Amelia rest."

"Olive." She snickered, but kept hold of Amelia. "Two can play at the fake name game."

"What's your real name then?" Bristol asked.

"Like I'd tell you." She snarled at Bristol. "Put your guns away, and I'll let Amelia sit down."

Jared glanced at Bristol, and she nodded. Since Olive wasn't armed they could afford to holster their weapons, but be ready to draw again.

Olive watched them carefully. Jared hated to comply, but he did and the moment they put their handguns in their holsters, she sat on the sofa and jerked Amelia down next to her.

Perfect. Olive couldn't run now, and without a weapon, she wouldn't seriously hurt Amelia. Still, she could give a swift punch to Amelia's belly, and that could end in disaster.

"Where are the other women?" Bristol asked.

"In the sunroom," Amelia said. "They made me come out to see what Olive or whatever your name is, was shouting about."

Jared smiled at Olive. "Just tell me your first name. Can't ID you from that."

She tilted her head as if considering telling them. "Pam. It's Pam."

Of course it had to be a common name so the odds of locating her details based on the first name were not in their favor. Their only viable option was to get her talking.

"Well, Pam, mind if I sit down across from you?" Bristol asked.

"Stay where you are!"

"Okay. Okay." Bristol held up a hand. "Why don't you tell me what you're doing here, and we can go from there?"

"Looking for Everett Holloway." She spit his name with a burst of anger. "He owes me a big chunk of change, and I can't find him. Thought he might be hiding here to avoid me."

"Why does he owe you?" Jared asked.

"Work I did for him."

"What kind of work?" Bristol asked.

Pam lifted her chin. "None of your business."

"Did you help him find babies for adoption?" Jared asked.

"I'm not telling you anything, so save your breath." She clamped her mouth closed.

"What if we help you find Holloway?" Bristol asked. "Will that help?"

"I'm not an idiot." Pam sneered at Bristol. "You won't help me. You'll arrest me, and I'm not going to prison. So the only thing I want to hear out of your mouth is how I'm going to get out of here."

"Your best bet right now is to tell us about Holloway." Jared used that soothing tone again and took a couple of steps closer. "We can go to the DA for you and tell him how you cooperated. If we bring Holloway down, the DA will surely cut you a deal for your help."

She sat back and tapped her foot.

"Even if you could manage to overpower both of us," Jared said. "With our reinforcements outside, you won't get far. So help yourself by making things easier for you."

She bit her lip. "I don't know."

"At this point, all we have you on is trespassing here and detaining Amelia," Bristol said. "I'm sure if you let Amelia go, she wouldn't press charges."

"I will not. Please." Amelia clutched Pam's hand. "My baby. I must not have her yet. It's too soon."

"Holloway will be too busy with his own issues to charge you with trespassing," Jared added. "Surrendering is your best chance."

Pam shook her head and got up, tugging Amelia to her feet. "We're leaving and you better call off your officers outside. Pull out one of your guns and the baby gets a swift kick."

"Not a good decision, Pam," Jared said. "You don't want a pregnant woman with you. Why not take one of us instead?"

"Because you'd turn on me in a flash." She approached Bristol. "I'll take that gun."

"No," Bristol said. "That's not happening."

"Then the baby—"

Bristol struck, kicking out and sweeping Pam's feet out from under her and reaching to steady Amelia.

No, his mind screamed as he rushed them. *You could get hurt.*

But Pam went down hard, hitting the tile floor with a solid thump. *Perfect.* Bristol succeeded.

Wait! Pam shot out a hand to grab Bristol's ankle, catching her off guard. Jerking her off her feet.

Bristol landed on Pam. The woman grabbed for

anything to clutch onto. Grasping first at Bristol's shirt. Her hair. Failing and flailing out before Jared could get to her.

He wrenched Pam away and subdued her on the floor. He handcuffed her hands behind her back.

"You okay?" he called to Bristol.

"Fine." She got up and went to Amelia. "How are you?"

"Fine, I think." Amelia gave a wobbly smile. "I'll just go lay down if that's okay."

"Of course," Bristol said. "I'll come check on you soon."

She smiled at Amelia but when Bristol turned her gaze on Pam, Bristol's eyes darkened.

Jared helped Pam into a sitting position. "Before we take you in for questioning, suppose you tell us if you had anything to do with the recent kidnapping of the baby from Mercy Hospital."

"Are you nuts?" She blinked her eyes, now wide open. "It's one thing to help Holloway with the interviews for potential parents. Another thing to steal babies."

"But Amelia says she saw you here with babies."

"She's mistaken." Pam sneered up at them.

"If you keep lying to us, we won't be able to speak to the DA on your behalf," Jared said.

A sneer crossed Pam's face. "Fine. I might have brought a few babies to him from drug-crazed moms who weren't taking care of them and didn't want them. They gladly gave them up. What's the crime in giving a baby a better life?"

"Were they sober when they signed them over?" Jared asked. "Or so stoned they didn't know what they were doing?"

Pam shrugged.

"But you didn't take the baby from the hospital?" Bristol clarified.

"No."

"Do you know who did?" Jared asked.

"No."

"Do you know if Holloway was involved in it?" Bristol asked.

"Could be, I suppose." Pam shifted as if trying to get more comfortable. "I know he asked me to do a special job for him. A client specific retrieval. But I told him no. Didn't want to get into something like that. It's okay if I refer women to him or like I said, find those babies who need care, but nothing else."

"Do you know Reya Isaacs?" Jared asked.

"Reya Isaacs? You mean the woman who was in the news lately when her baby was found?" Pam sat forward. "Nah. Is she related to this investigation?"

"What do you do for a living?" Bristol asked.

"I'm a social worker like I told you. Just not for Multnomah County." She cast a superior look their way. "I didn't want people to track me down so had Holloway get the bogus ID. Not that anyone ever asked to see it again. Not until you."

Bristol shook her head. "And you think going outside the system like you're doing is better?"

"Heck, yeah." Pam lifted her chin in defiance. "The system is broken. Those babies would go into foster care until the mom cleaned up her act or relinquished her rights. That could be years and years. This way the baby has a loving home and isn't yanked out of it when the mom sobers up for a while and decides she wants to play mom again."

"Does Holloway have others who do the same thing for him?" Bristol asked.

Pam gave a sharp nod. "A whole big network."

"Can you give us a list of names?" Jared asked.

"Sure, once that deal is in ink." A smug smile claimed her mouth. "But you're never going to shut him down."

That's what you think. Disgusted with this woman and with Holloway, Jared lifted Pam to her feet.

"While you hand her over for processing, I'll go check on Amelia," Bristol said.

Jared nodded and escorted Pam out to the patrol officer waiting to take her down to booking at County.

"We'll be in to talk to you soon," Jared told her as he settled her into the backseat of the squad car.

She eyed him. "You better go to bat for me like you said. The better the deal, the more I tell you. Who knows, I might even give you enough info to find that missing baby."

Bristol met Jared in the entryway as he returned to the home Holloway used to farm babies. Jared looked so tired and disillusioned, and a lock of hair had fallen over his forehead.

She couldn't resist and stroked it back into place. "You look tired."

"Would it be rude if I told you the same thing?" He caught her hand in his, his skin warm and rough.

"No. Just truthful," she said when every bit of her wanted to concentrate on the feel of his skin against hers.

"The few hours we got last night will have to hold us over. We can't stop until we find Luna." He lifted her hand and kissed it.

Oh my. She should object. They were on the job after all, but no one could see them, and she needed something warm and comforting as her fear for Luna's life grew with each lead that didn't pan out.

"How's Amelia?" He released her hand.

Good. Bristol could concentrate now. "Okay, I think.

Maybe in shock. I called her doctor, and he's agreed to do a house call."

Jared curled his hands into fists. "Let's hope she doesn't go into labor."

"I guess one positive is that she realized how much the baby means to her, and she wants to explore ways to keep the child and still make money for her family. Not sure I can come up with anything, but I'm certainly going to try."

"I'll pray you succeed."

She nodded. "We need to get forensics in here to process this place. We could find evidence of Luna having been here."

"Agreed. I also called Adair before I came in, and he's working on an arrest warrant for Holloway and search warrants for Holloway's office and home. I'm out of here the minute they come in."

"I'd like to go with you, but I don't want to leave Amelia until her doctor examines her and declares her fit. Then we need to relocate these women so they can't talk to Holloway if he shows up and so we can keep an eye on their health."

He frowned. "Any suggestions?"

"My grandparents and parents both live in huge farm-houses. The women could stay with them."

He arched an eyebrow. "And your family would agree to that?"

"I'm sure they would."

"Then let's do that." He ran a hand through his hair, dislodging that wayward strand again. "We should also gather all the women together and question them. They might know something about Luna."

"I'll do it. Maybe Amelia will join us and speak to the others on our behalf. Can you call Sierra and then we'll meet in the living room?"

"Glad to." He got out his phone and stepped outside.

Likely to keep the mothers-to-be from hearing about the request for a forensic expert to process their home.

Bristol remained in place and called her grandparents. They agreed to pick up the women to stay with them as she knew they would. Bristol stowed her phone and went straight to Amelia's bedroom. Bristol found the woman seated on the bottom bed in a set of bunk beds. The room held four matching beds. How these pregnant women climbed to the top at the end of their pregnancy, Bristol didn't know, but maybe they were given the lower bunks as they neared their due dates.

Amelia lifted her red-rimmed eyes to peer at Bristol. The woman had been through so much, and her emotions would already be amplified due to her pregnancy.

Bristol had to find a way to comfort her before asking for her help. Bristol sat beside her. "I know you believe in God."

"Yes," Amelia said.

"Then let's choose to look at the positive here. Let's choose to believe that God will work everything out for your good instead of worrying." Bristol spoke with confidence she didn't feel.

Amelia's eyes brightened. "That is a good idea. Thank you."

Bristol squeezed the woman's hand. "I need to talk to all of the women staying here right now. Would you mind helping me gather them together?"

"It will be a good thing to keep my mind occupied." Amelia stood.

Bristol started for the door. "How many women are in the house?"

"Only two others." Amelia led the way down the hallway toward the back of the house. "When I came there were twelve. Now I don't have a roommate. I'm sure we'll find the other two in the sunroom. We miss our more tropical weather and hang out there all the time when it's sunny."

They walked through a large but outdated kitchen into a sunroom that held a strong smell of mold or mildew. Not good for these women to be breathing. But it was far enough away from the living room that they likely didn't even know about Pam's attempt to hurt Amelia.

"This is my friend," Amelia announced. "She is helping me and wants to ask questions of us." Amelia introduced her to the two women. The one with short hair was named Katana, and the other woman named Fae had long hair.

"Holloway won't like that." Katana ran a finger down a long scar on the side of her face.

"Holloway is breaking the law, and we'll soon be arresting him," Bristol said. "He won't be able to hurt you."

"But you can't arrest him," Katana said. "He's helping us."

Bristol hated that they thought giving up their babies for money was considered help. "He's paying for your babies, and that's a crime."

"You're going to ruin this for us." Katana came to her feet and cast a threatening look at Bristol. "I need that money. My family needs that money. I'm sure you can look the other way until after we deliver and get paid."

Fae ran a hand over her sleek black hair tucked behind her ears. "We're both due in a few weeks. Please. We can pay you to look away. Not all of our money but some. This is what is done in our country a lot of the time."

"That would be bribing a law enforcement officer," Jared's voice came from behind. "Something neither of us would condone."

Bristol glanced back at Jared. "Katana and Fae, this is my associate Jared Wolfe. He's an FBI agent. Do you know what the FBI is?"

Katana nodded. "We watch them on the television all the time."

"Then you probably know we investigate kidnappings." Jared stepped closer. "And we're investigating the kidnapping of a baby from Mercy Hospital. Do either of you know anything about that?"

"Why would we?" Katana fixed a combative stare on Jared. "We would never be involved in anything like that."

"What about Olive Wallace?" Bristol asked. "Might she have brought a baby here this week?"

"Not that I saw." Katana sat. "But she has delivered babies here in the past."

"Didn't you wonder about it?" Jared asked.

"Yes, but we keep our questions to ourselves." Katana crossed her arms. "We can't afford to make Mr. Holloway mad, or he'll throw us out, and we won't get our payment. We've seen it happen to others and won't let it happen to us. He must find a home for our babies."

"You sound so matter-of-fact about giving up your child," Bristol said, trying hard not to sound judgmental.

Katana glared at her. "I don't want to be a mother. Ever. So this is the very best solution."

"I do." Fae stroked her belly. "I want this little one, but my family must come first."

"I thought the same thing." Amelia peered at her housemates. "But I have changed my mind. I will find a way to have this baby and support my family."

Katana scoffed. "Good luck with that. See you on the poverty line."

"Do any of you know a Reya Isaacs?" Bristol asked before things got out of hand between the women.

Katana and Fae shook their heads.

"Have you ever heard her name?" Bristol asked.

"On the news," Amelia said. "Her daughter's body was found. That is so sad."

"And that's all you know?" Jared asked.

All three nodded.

Katana sat forward. "What's going to happen to us?"

"You can't stay here now," Jared said. "We'll be relocating you to a safe location. You'll be allowed to pack one bag under our supervision."

"Just what do you think we might be taking that you need to see?" Katana demanded.

Bristol looked at Jared as did the women.

"Let's get to packing," he said, ignoring their question but continuing to stare at Katana. "Deputy Steele will start with you."

Katana lunged to her feet, amazingly agile in her advanced pregnant state. Bristol followed her through the house, and the process of packing began. Bristol hated to have to watch every move these women made, and then thoroughly search their bags and their persons, but she and Jared had to be sure the women didn't try to take anything that could lead to finding Luna.

Bristol felt especially bad about searching Amelia. Not only because Bristol had made a connection with her, but because her expression held such disappointment that Bristol almost backed off.

Almost.

She couldn't. She was a sworn officer of the law, and she had to do her duty.

Finished, she stepped back, and the doorbell rang. "That must be my grandparents. You'll be staying with them on their farm."

"Grandparents? I thought it might be a safe house like you see on American television." Amelia stood. "Are you sure they want the three of us living with them?"

"They have the most generous hearts of anyone I know," Bristol said. "But I warn you. My grandad often tells fishing stories, and you might be begging to leave before long."

Amelia gave a wavering smile. "I can tell him about fishing in my country then. We have the most amazing beaches."

"Thank you for making the best of this situation." Bristol squeezed Amelia's shoulder then picked up her suitcase. "Follow me to the living room, and you're good to go."

Bristol headed down the hallway, Amelia's lumbering steps behind her.

"Will you come visit?" Amelia asked.

"Yes," Bristol replied. "Once our investigation is over."

"I will pray you find this baby."

"Thank you." Bristol set down the suitcase by the couch where the other women sat under the watchful eye of a local patrol officer.

Bristol went to the door and opened it for her grandparents, their gazes solemn, very out of character for how cheerful they usually were. They laid eyes on her and both smiled, their love for her flowing from their expressions.

"Boy, am I glad to see you." Bristol's heart warmed, and she returned their smiles.

"Any strong leads on Luna yet?" her grandad asked.

Bristol shook her head, all the emotions of the past days coming to the surface and tears wetted her eyes. "And I fear we're running out of time for a good outcome." Her tears intensified, and she swiped at her eyes before they started flowing in earnest.

"Come here, sweetie." Her gran scooped her up in a hug and held her tight.

Bristol inhaled her jasmine scent and thanked God for the amazing, beautiful life she'd been given. Especially after seeing these women feeling forced to give up their children to feed their families. How hard was that?

Why God? Why?

No answer came. She knew it wouldn't, and she shouldn't question, but her heart ached with the pain of the situation.

"Come on." Her gran released her and took her hand. "Let's get these women in the car so your grandad and I can get to spoiling them."

"Have I told you both lately how much I respect and love you?" Bristol asked. "Because if I haven't, I need to."

"We're just doing what God called us to do honey," her grandad said. "Be His hands and feet on earth."

"Well, you're doing a fantastic job of it."

A flush of embarrassment rushed over his cheeks. "We should get going."

"One more thing, Grandad." Bristol stopped him with a touch to his arm. "I had a suspect attack me a little bit ago. Thanks to your great teaching, she couldn't get a hold of my radio cord to wrap it around my neck."

He tilted his head. "Wore it inside your shirt, did you?"

She nodded.

"That's my girl." He shifted his stance, as if the thought impacted him more than he'd expected. "Now we have to get out of here. I have to get to passing on some fishing instruction before these ladies move on."

Bristol wrinkled her nose at him. "Amelia says she's going to tell you about fishing in her country. I think you might have a rival for your tall tales."

"We'll see about that." He winked.

Bristol let out a breath of satisfaction. No matter what happened to these women in the future, for now they would be safe, secure, and surrounded by love. As her grandad had said. God's love in action.

Such incredible and life-affirming love from their God above that Bristol had always taken for granted. Well, no more. She'd been in rebellion for too long. Time to have a chat with God, repent of her ways, and restore her trust in Him.

17

"In here!" Jared called out to Bristol from the bedroom Fae and Katana had shared.

Bristol's footsteps clipped down the hallway from the bedroom she'd been searching since a quick lunch. Nearing two o'clock, they'd ordered in lunch and had eaten in Jared's car before beginning the house search. They might not make time to sleep for long, but they had to eat to keep up their strength.

She entered the room, her gaze expectant.

He lifted up the mattress, displaying a cell phone. "Can you take a picture of the location and then grab it while I hold up the mattress?"

She snapped a few shots before reaching with gloved hands between the mattress and box spring to retrieve the device. "We need to get this to Colin to image."

"Agreed." Jared held out an evidence bag. "I'll get Sierra to fingerprint it first so we can see which of the women might have been using it. What do you have left to do in your room?"

"I have a nightstand to search, and then I'm done."

"Good. That shouldn't take you long. I just got the

warrant for Holloway's home and office search and arrest. Our field teams report that he's not at either location, but if we're lucky he'll show up. We'll send a team to breach both his house and office."

"We should go to his office," she said. "It's the most likely place to find him at this time of day. Unless you have a different thought."

"I was thinking the same thing."

"Then I'll finish up and meet you at the door." She nearly bolted from the room.

Clearly she was as eager as Jared was to get a look at the items in Holloway's office. Hopefully, the lawyer had just stepped out to avoid Pam and would return. The team could even have him in custody by the time Jared and Bristol got there. If so, Jared could finally confront the sick creep. When questioned, guys like him either broke down or dug in their heels. Jared wanted Holloway to confess and lead them to Luna. Not likely, but Jared could hope.

He texted Colin. *Need you to meet me at Holloway's office to image two cell phones.*

Be there in 10, Colin replied.

Jared couldn't ask for better support than his fellow agents were giving. His respect for them had grown, especially for Piper. She had to be far more fatigued than the rest of them, and yet, she continued to work as hard as everyone else.

He noted the details of the phone on the bag then went to look for Sierra. He found her in the family room kneeling on the floor next to a glass coffee table.

He held out the evidence bag. "Another cell phone. This one found in the bedroom. Can you process it for prints and DNA so I can take it with me?"

"Sure, but first you'll need to add it to my evidence log."

She handed him a clipboard. "Can I hope you took pictures of the location where you located it?"

Her tone thoroughly chastised him. He should've called her instead of Bristol to retrieve the device, but he wanted to improve Bristol's mood as she seemed to be feeling down. She wouldn't tell him why, but pressure from the investigation was wearing on all of them.

"I had Bristol take pics," he said. "I'll have her forward them to you."

Sierra took the bag. "Our guy can handle the phone imaging for you if you need."

"Thanks, but I have someone who can do it right away."

She frowned.

"The FBI does have qualified agents, you know." He grinned.

"I know. With Reed as my husband and several of our partners married to you feds, I hear about it all the time." She chuckled as she got out a jar of fingerprint powder and set it on the table next to a brush and several vials holding white swabs.

Jared turned his attention to adding the phone details to the log while she swabbed and printed the device.

"Only one set of prints on the phone." She shuffled a stack of cards holding fingerprints that she'd taken from the women. "Belongs to Katana."

Jared nodded. "Figured it might be hers."

"She's the rebellious one of the three." Bristol joined them. "But then Amelia had a phone too, and she's very cooperative."

Jared had taken the phone from Amelia before she'd departed, and Sierra had already processed that device to discover that it held only Amelia's prints.

"Life here must've been very interesting." Sierra flipped the phone. "I wonder how many babies Holloway placed."

"Hopefully he kept records, and the home and office raids will answer that question." Jared tried to look optimistic, but his hope was waning fast. "Will your team be able to process both of those locations if needed or have we maxed you out?"

"It'll all depend on what we find here." Sierra handed the phone back to Jared.

He pocketed it and looked at Bristol. "You ready to go to Holloway's office?"

She nodded. "What about getting the phones imaged first?"

"I've already arranged for Colin to meet us there."

"Thanks for coming again, Sierra." Bristol pivoted toward the door.

Jared trailed her out to the car. He stopped to tell the surveillance team to remain in this location to keep an eye out for Holloway. Okay, tell was a nice way of saying demanded they stay and didn't screw up this time. As he strode to his car, guilt ate at him for being so terse.

Bristol was right. It wasn't their fault that an accident got between them and Pam. And thanks to Amelia, Pam had been located so it wasn't a problem. Unless, of course, she disposed of valuable evidence during the time they were looking for her. Jared would love to search Pam's home, but until they got a last name that wouldn't be possible.

Bristol studied him when he climbed into the car but he didn't say anything. She'd heard his conversation with the agents, and he had nothing to defend his cross behavior. Better to concentrate on getting them on the road for the short drive than to bring her down even more.

She faced him. "Do you think Olive, or should I say Pam, had something to do with taking Luna?"

He shrugged. "If she did, why didn't she bring the baby to Holloway's house like the other ones?"

"Maybe because of the AMBER Alert they worried the women might recognize Luna."

"See that's the thing that's been troubling me in all of this. I know Holloway is a criminal, and we'll make sure we keep digging until charges can be brought against him, but taking a baby from the hospital seems too risky for someone who's been careful all these years."

She frowned. "Unless he had a custom order like Pam mentioned. Maybe he had clients like us who agreed to pay a lot of money for a baby quick. If he did, he could steal the child, and even if the adoptive family figured it out, they wouldn't report it, right?"

"I don't know," he answered honestly. "Maybe not."

"And newborns aren't easy to identify," she continued. "If they were, hospitals wouldn't have to take careful measures to keep the baby from being switched at birth. Even if they are immediately footprinted."

"That's true."

"And if the child is no longer with the woman who we think took her, then that could put an end to the trail and Luna won't be found." She sighed. "I mean look how we're struggling to get a solid lead."

"True, too," he said. "But an age progression study could be done in the future, and the child could be recognized. Especially if the child didn't resemble either parent."

She started to say something, but he held up a hand. "All of what you say is true, which is why we got the warrant for Holloway's home and office. I just wanted to let you know I'm not feeling it."

"Fair enough. Just keep an open mind."

"Trust me, it's so open a Navy destroyer could sail through it."

She chuckled, just the response he wanted, although his mood was anything but fun-loving. As he wound closer to the office, he let his thoughts wander. At this point, was Luna still alive? If Holloway was behind taking her, he could've decided she was too hot to place with anyone—even a custom order—and then what? Could the man kill a baby? Or maybe he would place her out of the country?

Jared couldn't let that happen. He had to do better. Work smarter. Harder. If something happened to Luna, he would lose it. Sure, it wasn't about him. It was about the baby, but he would sustain collateral damage that he didn't know if he could recover from.

The urge to take Bristol's hand and hold tight nearly had him reaching out. The GPS voice told him to turn ahead, interrupting his thoughts, and he turned into Holloway's parking lot. Colin waited for them, leaning against his car. Jared parked, and Colin raced to his door, his hand held out. Jared got out. Bristol too. Jared gave the phones to Colin.

Colin studied the phones through the plastic bags. "If they're not locked, these will be done in a flash."

"And if they are locked?" Bristol asked.

"Could take some time, but don't you worry. I can crack them." He jerked his head at the building. "The others have already gone in. Holloway and his assistant aren't here. Had to get the building manager to open the door."

"Thanks." Bristol's expression tightened.

Holloway not being on-site wasn't unexpected, but it was still disappointing.

Colin went back to his car and slid in, leaving his door open. Jared and Bristol wound through the vehicles in the lot and up to Holloway's office. Even the warm breeze and sun beating down on Jared didn't clear the chill, raising his apprehension. He couldn't shake the thought that finding Luna had already taken too long, and he might've failed her too.

Hunter Lane met them at Holloway's office door. "Holloway cleaned the place out. Back room is filled with garbage bags of shredded documents. Computers are gone. About all we'll get out of this place is whatever forensics might recover."

Jared hadn't expected this response, and it set him back for a moment. There had to be *something* they could do. But what?

He looked around the place, and his gaze landed on the assistant's desk. "What about an employment file for Holloway's assistant? Anything on her?"

"Gone."

"Amelia or the other women might know her name." Bristol's expression continued to hold the hope that Jared was trying to keep. "After Colin images the phones, we can review them and then head out to the farm to talk to the women."

Hunter took a deep breath. "You should also know that the gang task force hasn't heard a thing about the Hoovers being involved in a kidnapping. The members seem to think they would take a much more straightforward approach to retaliation."

"You mean take out Pratt himself."

Hunter nodded. "Or his wife. Or wait until the whole family got home and take out all three."

"Sounds like this isn't a top priority but keep after it until we know for sure." Jared's phone rang. "It's Reed. Maybe he found something actionable at Holloway's house."

Jared answered. "This about Holloway?"

"Partly. He's not home as expected, and he's purged his home office of anything that might help. We will, of course, do forensics."

"And the part that's not about Holloway?" Jared asked, hoping for good news this time, though honestly hearing that the Hoovers might not be involved in the kidnapping was good news. Real good news. If the task force members were right.

"Adair took another run at Osborne. The guy finally admitted to impersonating Aaron King. A woman paid him ten grand to disable the security alarm for the stairwell and pose as the guard. He swears he didn't know a baby would be kidnapped."

Finally. A lead. "And the woman who paid him?"

"Osborne claims he doesn't know her name. She came to his apartment. Paid him five grand in cash and gave him Aaron King's address. Then met him off-site and paid him the final five grand after the woman left the hospital."

Jared resisted slamming a fist into the wall. "Did he describe the woman?"

"He said she's short with curly black hair. That's all he could say."

"Think he'd meet with a sketch artist to do a sketch of this woman?"

"Says he will if he gets a deal. Adair's talking to the DA now, and I'll let you know if we get an ID." Reed ended the call.

Jared shared the details with Bristol.

"You think she could be the woman who took Luna?" Bristol asked.

"Could be." Jared locked gazes with Bristol. "We just have to hope Adair can persuade the DA to give this creep a deal. And then live with the fact that a man who aided in abducting a baby will get a lighter sentence."

~

Bristol's heart warmed as Jared pulled into her grandparents' long driveway leading to their two-story white farmhouse with a neatly painted red barn located down the hill. She needed this good feeling after Reed's call to tell them Holloway had cleaned out his house as well. She was losing hope fast, and it was taking everything she was made of to hide it and try to keep Jared's flagging spirits up.

He glanced at her. "You told me so many stories of growing up on a farm that I have to believe you did. But I honestly can't see you out here with the animals and crops."

"Look across the field, and you'll see it." She grinned at him.

He chuckled, and she loved the sound of it. They hadn't had many opportunities to lighten up since they reconnected. And why should they? A baby was missing. That was serious business and getting more serious with every passing hour. She'd been missing for over thirty-two hours now, and Bristol could feel every one of them in her heart.

Again, she wouldn't show it. Better to keep the conversation light. "I can smell my grandad's grill. Means they'll likely be out on the patio. Just follow the drive, and it'll take you around the back of the house."

He circled slowly down the gravel drive, leaning forward to take everything in. "You really did grow up this way, didn't you?"

"Yep."

"So different from my life."

"I have to say it was a great place to be raised. Running around with my sisters and Thomas and my cousins all day long. Even if I was the youngest and couldn't keep up. One of them looked out for me." She smiled. "But I'm not sure if I would want to live out here now. Maybe if I had kids I would."

He rounded the building where Bristol's grandparents sat with the three women at a long table, mason jars in front of them. If Bristol knew her gran, the jars contained iced tea with lemons.

Jared shifted into park. "Even from a distance, the women look far more relaxed. I hate to ruin that."

Bristol released her seat belt and the buckle slid into the holder with a *whoosh* and *clunk*. "Me too, but finding Luna is all that matters."

She scooted out and jogged up the incline. Her grandad came to his feet and drew her into a hug.

"This is a surprise," he whispered against her ear. "A very nice surprise."

She melted into his hug, and for a second, forgot the reason she was there. Took in the familiar scent of his Old Spice aftershave and let go of the pressure to find a missing baby. Tears fought to release, so she backed away and straightened her duty belt.

"You'll both stay for dinner." Her gran cast a practiced eye over Jared.

Jared smiled, but it was tight and reserved. "Thank you, but we don't mean to intrude."

"You'd be doing me a favor." Her gran smiled. "Artie's grilling enough fish for the whole county to eat. You'll save us from having leftovers for days on end."

"In that case." Jared smiled. "It smells great."

"Trout I caught on a recent trip." Her grandad fixed his gaze on Jared. "You fish, son?"

Bristol groaned. "He hasn't even sat down, Grandad. Give him a chance to have some tea before pouncing."

"Pouncing?" Her grandad clutched his shirt. "I only asked a simple question."

"Feel free to ignore him and take a seat," her gran said. "I'll grab some tea."

"This isn't exactly a social call," Bristol said. "We have some questions for your guests."

"Ah." Her gran's eyes narrowed. "You want us to disappear for a while."

"Would you mind?" Bristol asked.

"Can't leave my fish alone on the grill." Her grandad crossed his arms, and Bristol felt a battle coming.

"It'll be fine." Her gran slipped her arm in his. "Just tell Jared or Bristol what to do."

He grumbled, but his eyes twinkled. "It's good for a few more minutes, then it needs to rest. Just put the grilling baskets on the cookie sheet when the timer rings."

He reluctantly backed into the house as her gran dragged him along. Jared cast Bristol a fun-loving glance. Her grandparents were always guaranteed to bring comic relief. Not that they tried. They just had such joyful spirits and were very content in their shoes.

Bristol took a seat next to Amelia, her mind still on her grandparents. She'd always wondered what they were like when they were young. Adventurous she knew, but if her grandad was in her position right now, would he be intense or try to make things lighter? She just didn't know the answer, but she did know he'd been a top-notch law enforcement officer.

Jared took the chair next to her just as her gran brought out two glasses of tea. She placed them on the table in front of them, gave a lingering but pointed look at Bristol that she couldn't interpret and then headed back into the house.

Jared looked at Katana. "We found your phone and reviewed it. You frequently communicated with Olive Wallace."

Katana crossed her arms. "So what?"

"So what did you talk about?"

Katana leaned back, but her body was rigid. "This is none of your business."

"You don't seem to understand that you could be charged for your participation with Holloway," Bristol said. "But if you cooperate, things can go easier for you."

Katana glared at them, but her body relaxed. "Fine. I'll tell you, okay? She was helping me learn how to recruit mothers-to-be. After I have the baby, I planned to move back home to find other women Holloway could help."

Bristol tried not to let her revulsion show. "And you would be paid for doing this?"

"Yes. Holloway would pay me for each woman who comes here." She tightened her arms and jutted out her chin at Jared. "I would be doing nothing wrong. Just helping these women who want help and make a living to stay in the only home I've ever known."

"From our earlier conversation, you must now realize what you would be doing would aid Holloway to sell these babies, thus breaking the law," Jared said. "Have you referred any women yet?"

She shook her head hard, her gaze darting around.

If Bristol was reading Katana right, fear lingered behind the bravado. "You labeled the phone calls with Olive's name, but they go to a prepaid phone like yours so we can't track her. We know Olive is a fake name, and her first name is Pam. Do you know her real last name?"

"No," Katana said. "I only talked to her on this phone and when she came to the house. She always used the name Olive."

Jared looked at Fae. "Do you know how to find Pam?"

"No." Fae held up her hands. "I have never even talked to her."

"What about Holloway's receptionist?" Bristol asked. "Do any of you know her name?"

"Melissa," Fae said.

"Gibson," Amelia said eagerly. "Melissa Gibson."

"What can you tell us about her?" Jared asked.

"She worked for him for ten years," Fae said. "Respected him and would protect him with her life, I think."

"Do you know how to find her?" Bristol asked.

"I know Holloway paid her well, and she lives in Arlington Heights," Amelia said. "She said it's a really expensive place, but I do not know the address."

"Thank you," Bristol said. "That should be enough information to track her down."

The grill timer dinged, and Bristol got up to place the baskets on the large cookie sheets. Her gran was right about the quantity. Her grandad used any excuse to grill fish so he could go catch more, and he could gladly eat it for breakfast, lunch, and dinner. The rest of the family, not so much.

She returned to the table. Her grandad watched through the patio doors, and she gave him a thumbs up.

"We haven't been able to find Holloway," Jared said. "What can you tell us about him that might help?"

"He likes to golf," Fae said. "He spends a lot of time at his private club."

"Do you know the name of the club?"

"Waverly Country Club," Amelia said. "He was so proud of it, he made sure to mention it all the time."

Katana rolled her eyes. "Not like we even know anything about it or care enough to look it up."

"Anything else you might know?" Jared asked.

"I think he might've had a thing with Melissa," Katana said. "No proof. Just a feeling."

"I agree," Amelia said. That gave the suggestion more credence.

The patio door opened, and Bristol's gran poked her head out. "Can we eat now?"

Bristol looked at Jared, who nodded.

"I'll help bring out the food." Jared got up.

Bristol followed him to the house, her mind split between thinking what a great guy he was to offer to help and how they could use the information they'd learned to find Holloway.

Inside the house, Jared grabbed a bowl of salad but his phone rang so he set it down and gave Bristol a pointed look. He answered, and she shooed her grandparents out of the house.

He put the call on speaker.

"Glad you answered," Reed said. "Osborne got his deal, and he's sitting down with Kelsey Dunbar from Veritas right now to do the sketch."

"I want a picture of it the moment it's finished."

"Will do."

Jared locked gazes with Bristol, and she spotted the excitement in his eyes. "Also, Holloway's a member of the Waverly Country Club. Could be hanging out there. Get over there as fast as you can and call me the minute you know if he's there and have him in custody."

18

Still reeling from Reed striking out at the country club, Jared wanted to be the one to break down Melissa Gibson's front door. But he stood back while the SWAT team rammed the door. If Holloway had barricaded himself inside, he could be armed and dangerous. Jared and Bristol had to let the team trained for such an event take charge.

Amelia had been right. Melissa did indeed live in Arlington Heights, where homes sold in the millions of dollars. Her two-story traditional house was smaller and more modest than other homes on her street, but probably still went for more than a million dollars. But after a short surveillance of the property, they determined she either wasn't home or was hiding out inside and unwilling to answer the door. The warrant Adair obtained while Jared and Bristol ate dinner with her grandparents allowed the team to enter.

"Police," the team leader shouted as he and the team entered then fanned out.

Bristol's hand drifted to her sidearm, and she took a few steps closer to the house then planted her feet. She'd put on a ballistic vest for this raid as had Jared. They couldn't be too careful. When a criminal was cornered, even a white-collar criminal, they could turn dangerous.

"This waiting is hard," Bristol said. "Just when I think we might be making some progress, we strike out."

"It would've been much easier if Holloway had been at his club."

"It's starting to look like he went to ground," she said. "Makes him hard to locate."

"Hard but not impossible." Jared firmed his stance. "Especially with the alert out on his and Melissa's vehicles, and the task force digging into everything they can find about the pair."

"He could've ditched his car and gotten a rental. Or borrowed one." She ran her hands through her hair, but kept her gaze pinned to the house. "I have to admit my hope is waning. I'm trying to remember what you said, how losing everything could bring us to the end of ourselves, and we have to rely on God. Maybe I'm at that point. Maybe I have to turn it all over to Him. Let Him lead my steps and trust Him to do so."

She opened her mouth to continue, but the commander came to the door. "Place is empty. Bedroom dresser and closets are nearly empty. Looks like your suspect has taken off."

"Thanks for your help," Jared said. "Secure the home and put someone on guard detail while we take a look."

"Will do."

Jared looked at Bristol. "Let's get inside."

Bristol climbed the stairs to the long porch then entered the home. Jared remained close to her, sharing his attention between watching her for her attitude and looking at Melissa's property. The home was decorated in gray and teal and the furniture was mid-century modern. The place was spotless, and they quickly went through the great room filled with boxy furniture and holding a dining table. They cleared the small kitchen and the first bedroom down the hall. The next bedroom was set up as an office, and they paused to get a better look at the space.

"She took her computer too," Jared said, noting the empty desktop that held a power cord for a Mac computer.

Bristol strode to the desk and stared at it as if she hoped something would materialize in front of her. "I think we can assume they're together."

Jared pulled out drawers with his gloved hands but found only office supplies. "We need to get a warrant for their bank accounts. See if we can track them that way, but if Holloway is the kind of guy I think he is, he has offshore accounts that we might never find."

"We need alerts at the airport." Bristol turned. "All public transportation for that matter."

Jared got out his phone and crossed the room where a selfie of Holloway and Melissa sat in a silver frame on a credenza. They stood in front of Multnomah Falls, a popular tourist attraction in the area. He had his arm around the woman, and she was smiling up at him.

"I'll text Reed the details to get an alert out for both of them with all public transportation." He sent it along with the request and also asked Reed to obtain the banking warrant.

Jared trailed Bristol down the hallway to Melissa's bedroom and then her bathroom. He opened a medicine cupboard. "Men's grooming products here. No pictures of a guy in the house other than Holloway so likely his things."

"Forensics can confirm that." Bristol looked up from her search of the drawers.

"Then let's get them out here, and go take another run at Pam. She could know something about Luna that's she's not telling us."

Bristol had always thought it odd that the Multnomah County Detention Center was located in downtown Portland. But as part of the Multnomah County Justice Center, transporting inmates to court hearings was much easier.

She and Jared surrendered their sidearms and phones and headed down a long hallway that smelled of orange cleaner toward an interview room where Pam waited. She'd failed to provide her last name to the booking officers, and her prints didn't return a match. Could tell them two things. She likely didn't have a record, and she probably wasn't a social worker as they had to be fingerprinted.

Meant Pam's last name remained a mystery. The task force members had been trying to hunt down the county Pam worked at, but nearing ten o'clock now, just finding someone to talk to was difficult, and they hadn't located any leads.

Bristol's first job was to get Pam to admit her name. "You said you were a social worker. Which county?"

Pam glared at her.

Bristol ignored the attitude. "You can't be a social worker without fingerprinting. Nothing on file matching the prints taken at booking."

Pam sniffed. "Not my fault. Just moved to the area. Maybe they haven't uploaded them yet."

She could be telling the truth or maybe she'd been playing them the whole time. No way to know at this point. They should be able to locate her tomorrow when the offices were open. But tomorrow could be too late for Luna.

"It really is time for you to give us your full name and date of birth," Bristol stated firmly.

Pam leaned back and crossed her arms.

Bristol held her head high and planted her best intimidating stare on the woman. "I'm assuming you've been told that you'll be charged for obstruction along with other charges that we'll bring after we finish our investigation into Holloway."

Pam jutted out her chin. "Good luck in finding anything."

Bristol leaned forward. "Here's the thing. Holloway is a smart guy who will protect himself. If that means throwing you under the bus, he will."

Bristol didn't mention that they hadn't managed to find Holloway yet. Pam didn't need to know.

"Of course you'll sit in jail here until we properly identify you," Jared added. "And while you do, charges and fines will continue to accumulate daily. You're not making friends with anyone by being difficult, and if an opportunity comes up to make a deal, you're jeopardizing that too."

"What kind of fines?" she asked, her façade cracking a bit.

"You can be fined for your maintenance and upkeep. That can include the cost for the staff that needs to babysit you as well as room and board. You sure you want to go down that route?"

Pam continued to glare at them.

"Be that way. Don't tell us your name and rack up the fines," Jared said. "But tell us more about your work with Holloway."

She fired a testy look his way. "If I won't give you my name without a deal, why do you think I'm going to turn on Holloway without one?"

"There's no deal to be had here when you're being uncooperative," he said. "The best we can do if you decide to talk is tell the DA you helped in our investigation into the missing baby."

"Don't play me for a fool," she said. "As a social worker, I saw deals go down all the time when the DA wanted something. A missing baby is something you want help with. So get me that deal."

She sounded convincing, but was she really a social worker?

"If I do," Jared said. "You have information that can help find the child?"

"I have information on Holloway. You'll have to decide if it will help your investigation."

"What kind of woman are you?" Bristol had enough of this woman's behavior and jumped to her feet, planting her hands on the table. "So callous about this baby's life. You're a social worker, for goodness sake. A job that exists to help others."

"Judge me all you want." Pam slunk down in her chair. "Get me a deal or you get no information."

Jared cast the woman a scornful look and went to the door to hold it open for Bristol.

Anger surged through her body, and she marched out. She stopped to look at the deputy on duty. "Take her back to her cell. She's of no use to us."

"Wait," Pam called out.

Bristol turned back to the doorway.

Pam sighed and dropped her arms to her sides. "Fine. It's Pam Vogel." She crossed her arms again and added her birthdate.

Bristol wouldn't show the woman how relieved she was to get this information so she schooled her expression. "Give us a minute."

She and Jared exited the room and left the deputy in charge of Pam. They went to the booking computer to look up Pam's name.

Bristol performed the search and stood back as the computer churned. She started sweating as time was disappearing so rapidly and there was nothing they'd been able to do to help Luna.

"C'mon. C'mon. C'mon." She pounded the top of the monitor, and Pam's record finally populated. "No priors. Lives in an apartment in Vancouver. Her DMV record said she didn't lie about recently moving here."

"I'll call Reed and ask him to get a warrant to search her apartment." Jared grabbed the office phone and made his request. "If you get the warrant before we finish up here, conduct the search the minute it comes in."

They returned to the interview room and took the same seats across from Pam.

She sat up in her chair. "Well? What's going on?"

"We were just confirming you were who you said you were and that you didn't have a prior record." Something Bristol already suspected because her prints hadn't returned a match, but there could always be a glitch in the print database so best to confirm it.

"Of course I don't." She narrowed her eyes. "And I shouldn't be here now. What I did wasn't illegal. I just asked people questions and filled in a form."

"Ah, yes," Bristol said. "But you impersonated a social worker from Multnomah County, and that's a criminal offense."

"But I *am* a social worker." She sat forward and planted her hands on the table.

"Not in Multnomah County," Jared said. "But we'll be glad to speak to the DA on your behalf if you'll give us additional information about Holloway."

"What do you want to know?"

"Everything you know."

"I first met him on a dating app after I moved here." She rolled her eyes. "Cliché, I know. Turns out he was two-timing me with his assistant, but we hit it off as friends so kept in touch. One day he asked if I wanted to make some extra money working for him. All I had to do was assess prospective parents."

"Besides the questionnaire, what did he want to know?" Bristol asked.

"Honestly, I was the one who wanted the questionnaire. He didn't really care if the people I evaluated would be fit parents. Just if they had the ability to pay and keep their mouths shut."

"And that didn't bother you?" Bristol asked, trying hard to hide her attitude that was growing by leaps and bounds on this woman.

"Not when I learned that he was helping unfit mothers find homes for their babies." She flipped her hair over her shoulder with a sharp flick of her hand, and her cuffs jingled. "It meant there would be fewer children in the system needing our intervention and protection. It was a win/win for everyone. Me too as he paid me five grand per couple and ten grand for each child I found."

"Found—or abducted and brought to him?" Bristol asked.

"No comment." She clamped her mouth closed.

"You already admitted to getting parents to sign over their babies and bringing them to his house," Jared said. "And the women staying there saw you."

"Hmm." She tapped her chin. "I don't remember saying anything like that."

"We both heard you, and the women saw you bring in babies." Jared looked like he wanted to growl at the woman.

"Good luck in getting any of them to testify to that fact." She grinned. "They've been beaten down so much by Holloway that they can't think for themselves anymore."

Resisting the urge to reach across the table, grab the woman's shirt, and shake her, Bristol took a calming breath instead. "As you know, Holloway isn't at his usual places. Do you know where he might be?"

"He always talked about a beach house he went to with Melissa. That's his assistant."

"Do you know where?" Bristol asked.

"I think he said Netarts Bay, but I'm not sure. I pretty much zoned him out when he talked about Melissa. It's too hard to see others so happy when you've been striking out in your own love life."

Maybe that's the reason she was so bitter, but no matter what, Bristol still couldn't condone her behavior. "Does one of them own the beach house?"

"Don't know."

"Anything else you can tell us about Holloway's operation or how to find him?" Jared asked.

"Nope. That's it. And it should be enough to share with the DA to go easy on me."

Bristol stood and stared down at Pam. "No deal. No way. You stole babies from their mothers. Sure, you might have gotten them to sign a form, but they likely didn't know what they were doing. For that, you will pay."

Bristol bolted from the room and into the hallway, gulping big breaths of air.

Jared joined her. "She's really something."

"With that personality, I can't see how she ever got into social work." Bristol continued to breathe. "The worst part is, if Holloway destroyed all of his records, we really have no proof of what she did either."

"Our agency will locate adoption records that involved Holloway and launch an investigation," Jared said. "Not sure if charges other than impersonating a county official will be brought, but we can try."

"Either way, she didn't help with finding Luna." Bristol

marched down the hallway and retrieved her phone and sidearm.

Jared was pocketing his phone when it rang. "It's Adair."

He answered and listened. "On my way."

"Good news."

He shook his head. "Adair is frustrated that Holloway is still in the wind and wants an in-person update. I need to head back to the command center for that, and we'll get started on the beach house lead too."

"The last thing I want to do is sit in an update meeting," she said with conviction. "I need to move. To do something."

"But what?"

She let the investigation steps race through her mind. "Since Luna was in the car at Reya Isaacs's house, I think I'll go back to her place to see if we missed anything."

"We didn't," he said.

"You don't know that."

"You're right. I don't." He rocked on his heels. "You should follow your gut."

He didn't hide the fact that he didn't believe her idea held any value, but she didn't care. She would borrow a car from her family and head to Reya's place. Taking action of any kind was better than sitting and doing nothing.

Bristol broke the seal on Reya's door and inserted the key she'd gotten from evidence. She pushed open the door, and a waft of death enveloped her. Not the stench of a body left for a long period of time, but a stale earthy odor mixed with the metallic blood smell. A deep breath would fortify her to enter, but she wouldn't fill her lungs with the smell.

She closed the door behind her. Silently. Why? She didn't know. There was no one in the house to disturb.

What would become of this house that Reya had lived in with her husband and baby, albeit only for a short while? A place where the photos on the walls and table spoke of love and happiness for the few days they'd had Darcy in their lives.

How fast a life could be destroyed. Bristol had seen that all too many times on the job. Life changed in literally the blink of an eye. Sometimes in a good way, like a woman giving birth on her drive to the hospital, but more times than not, Bristol had witnessed the worst days of people's lives.

She flicked on an overhead light. The bare bulb left dark shadows in the empty corners. Bristol aimed her phone's flashlight around the room. Searching, hunting.

What for? Why was she even here?

Because she couldn't stop moving. She had to keep looking for a lead. She couldn't admit they were failing—big time.

"No," she whispered. "Don't think that way."

She took in the pictures on the wall. Family gatherings, many with Reya robust and pregnant. All before the baby was born. Before she went missing. Before she'd died. Before the family had been destroyed.

Had Reya believed in God? If so, how did she reconcile her losses? Did she feel like Job, tempted by the devil to curse God? Or had she already done so?

The closest Bristol could come to understanding was Thomas's brutal death. But losing a child? How horrific to experience such a loss. How must Sonya Pratt be feeling right now?

Tears bit at the back of Bristol's eyes, but she willed them away and moved on. She looked in the end table drawers. Rummaged through shelves and drawers of a TV stand. Finding nothing. She got down on the floor. Looked under the sofa. Dust bunnies lingered around the legs and nothing else. She lifted cushions. Shoved her hand into the creases.

All tasks Sierra and her team had performed.

"What are you doing in my house?" a female voice came from the doorway.

Bristol froze and flashed her gaze to the door. A woman pointed a handgun in Bristol's direction.

Bristol reached for her sidearm.

"Don't even think about it," the woman said.

Bristol's hand stilled over her weapon, and she gaped up at the woman, blinking and looking again. Carefully.

How could what she was seeing be possible?

The woman staring wild-eyed at Bristol was none other than Reya Isaacs come back from the dead.

19

Jared stood with his supervisor in the conference room, their update meeting coming to a close. What a waste of time. He could've been doing something active instead of recapping their failure. He could've at least helped Bristol search Reya's house. Not that he thought they or Sierra had missed anything. They'd turned that place upside down. But sometimes it helped to return to a crime scene to jog something in your mind. To find new avenues to pursue.

He hoped Bristol came back with investigative ideas and plenty of them.

His phone rang, the call from Sierra Rice. He stepped to the corner of the room and answered.

"Glad I caught you," she said. "I just finished processing the prints from Reya Isaacs's house, and there's an anomaly."

"Anomaly?" he asked, hoping this anomaly was in their favor. "What did you find?"

"I think it best if you stop by so we can talk about it in person."

He didn't want to waste time, but he would be glad to get

out of the room where Adair kept looking at him, disappointment on his face.

"I can be there in thirty minutes." Jared headed for the door.

"Good," Sierra said. "I'll tell the night guard to expect you."

He hung up, told Reed about the call, and jogged out the back of the building to his car. He cranked the engine, the sound lifting into the night with only the slight hum of traffic in the distance. Could one of those cars be Bristol heading back to the hospital? Should he call her? Maybe check to see how she was getting along?

He didn't want to seem like he was an overprotective person, and he wasn't worried about her. He just missed having her at his side. He could tell her about the call from Sierra but not knowing what she'd found, he didn't want to tell Bristol about it yet.

He navigated traffic and pulled into the Veritas Center parking lot in twenty-six minutes. Four minutes ahead of the predicted time. Two six-story towers connected by a building on the ground floor and a skybridge on the top were lit from outside as beacons in the night. Many of the interior lights were on too. Quite a posh place for a lab. With the high prices they commanded for their services, they could likely afford such a building.

Nearing midnight, the parking lot was deserted but well-lit by street lights. He parked close to the building and could see the uniformed guard standing right inside the door. Jared stepped up and held his ID out so the guard could see it through the glass door.

The burly but short guy unlocked the door and held out his hand. "Pete Vincent. Welcome, Agent Wolfe."

Jared took Pete's hand, not at all surprised by the man's firm grip.

Pete held the door. "You been here before?"

Jared shook his head and took in the lobby decorated more like a spa than a lab. The only thing that gave away the lab's job of processing evidence was the evidence lockers filling the back wall. Or at least Jared assumed they were evidence lockers.

"Follow me and we'll get you signed in." Pete strode ahead of Jared to a reception desk in the large lobby. Pete tipped his head at an iPad on the counter. "Fill in the visitor's form, and I'll let Sierra know you're here."

Jared tapped the screen to enter his details, impressed so far with the lab's security.

Pete telephoned Sierra to tell her that Jared had arrived. After Pete hung up, he created a security badge that he connected to a blue lanyard. "Wear this at all times, and turn it in when you leave. Also, don't go anywhere in the building without being accompanied by a Veritas staff member."

"Top-notch security," Jared said. Everyone vouched for the place, but it was good to see in person that the evidence Sierra collected was being handled safely.

"Can't be too careful with evidence." Pete firmed his stance. "Also, we've had issues in the past with DNA customers getting violent when they weren't happy with their results. Threatening the staff. Our partners are very special people, and we aim to keep them safe."

Jared liked how much this guy seemed to care for the workers. "You work for the lab then. Not contracted."

Pete puffed up his chest. "Been working here almost since opening day. They didn't have security guards at first, but then like I said, a customer went off on one of our staff, and they didn't waste time in hiring guards."

Jared slipped the lanyard over his neck. "You're former law enforcement."

"You can tell." His face beamed with pride.

"Hard not to spot with the way you carry yourself." Jared didn't mention the guy's buzz cut gave him away too.

Pete gave a sharp nod, and his phone rang. He turned his attention to answering it.

Jared didn't know if Sierra would come down the stairs or out the glass door in the back, so he went to stand at the base of the open staircase, seeming to float above a seating area. The center's logo—Connecting Loved Ones Around the World, in bold red letters circling a black globe—was painted on the wall. Pictures of smiling people filled the wall below. Jared suspected they were private clients the lab helped reunite through DNA testing.

Those clients probably didn't even know about the criminal work handled by the lab. Either way, it was all about finding truth here. The center's name—Veritas—meant truth in Latin. Fitting for sure.

The glass door opened on the far wall, and Sierra waved to him. "This way."

He hurried across the lobby. "So what's this anomaly you found?"

"We'll want to wait until we get to the lab." She led him down a hall to an elevator and summoned the car by using a fingerprint reader mounted on the wall. "Is this your first time here?"

He nodded, wishing she'd skip the small talk and get to the business at hand.

In the car, she selected the fourth floor button. "All the labs are in this tower and most of the partners still live in condos in the other tower. Also my brothers have an investigative agency on the sixth floor—Nighthawk Security—and they live in the condo tower too."

Interesting. "It's quite the building. Not what I expected from a lab."

"Our toxicology expert, Maya Lane, inherited the building from her grandfather, and that's when we started the lab."

"Hunters wife, right?" he asked.

"Right," she said.

The doors opened, and she led him to the back of the floor where hallway windows overlooked a large trace evidence lab filled with state-of-the-art equipment. She unlocked the door using the fingerprint reader and stepped in. He followed.

"Now this is what I was expecting to see here." He turned to take in the large room noting four lab techs working at stainless steel tables. "You work round the clock?"

"We do when a baby is missing." Her urgent tone spoke to her desire to help find this child.

"And we appreciate it."

"It's the least we can do." She crossed the room to a computer sitting on a cabinet on the back wall.

Finally, they were getting to the point of the visit. "So what do I need to see?"

"Prints on Reya Isaacs's phone had been wiped clean. Odd, don't you think? But they didn't do a thorough enough job. I kept at it, and after fuming and other procedures I know, I finally recovered enough of a print to run through AFIS."

"And?" He blinked at her.

"And it returned a match, which is why I called you down here." She rested her hand on the computer mouse. "I don't think Reya Isaacs is your victim."

What in the world? Bristol and most of the law enforcement world vouched for the abilities these Veritas experts possessed, but the lack of sleep must have impacted Sierra.

He eyed her. "That's impossible."

"It's quite possible." She lifted her shoulders and woke up the computer. "Meet Valerie Zupan, the woman I believe is Reya's twin."

"Twin? But..." He stared at the picture on the screen of a woman who lived in Southeast Portland. A woman who was a dead-ringer for Reya Isaacs. "This is wild. They must be identical twins."

Sierra switched websites. "While I waited for you to get here, I researched Reya. With all the press on her daughter's abduction, there's tons of information about her on the internet. I confirmed that she was adopted as an infant. I didn't find anything to suggest she had a twin. But I think it's a good possibility that the baby went to another home."

Jared gritted his teeth and gave the new development some thought. "If this is true, how did we miss it?"

Sierra shrugged. "They must have somehow kept it quiet, but I don't know how with all the investigating surrounding the disappearance of Reya's daughter."

Jared's mind whirled with possibilities and landed on one of them. "Maybe they didn't know about each other. Which again I think would be nearly impossible with all the pictures of Reya on the news."

"I didn't find much national news coverage until after the baby was located. Valerie lived all her life in Arizona and only moved here a few months ago. Could mean she didn't see a picture of Reya until recently."

"Could be," Jared said. "Maybe Valerie doesn't watch the news on a regular basis. More and more people don't these days."

"Do you blame them?"

Jared shook his head, but horrific news or not, he believed people needed to keep up with what was happening in the world. "You think the twin is the one who died?"

"Evidence would suggest that."

"Not the blood on Luna's blanket. That belongs to Reya."

"True, but my gut says the woman is Valerie. I can't be sure unless we fingerprint the victim or we wait for the DNA samples Emory is running." Sierra's shoulders relaxed. "Fingerprinting would be faster for sure."

"Agreed." Jared took a moment to ponder the development. "If this is indeed Reya's twin, why weren't there other prints recovered at Reya's house?"

"I can't answer that other than to say there was no evidence of someone trying to erase prints anywhere else in the house. The only logical answer is Valerie had never been there, or if she had, she wore gloves."

"Wearing gloves would be odd. Not being there is possible, I suppose. Especially if they were trying to keep their relationship out of the news." His mind raced with questions. "I'm assuming you located her prints in AFIS."

Sierra nodded. "She has an old record for bank fraud."

"Interesting. Doesn't seem to be related to our investigation, though. Guess we first need to find out who died. Then we can figure out the print situation, and if the fraud charge is relevant." Jared dug out his phone and dialed Dr. Albertson, praying the woman would answer. He needed to know if Reya Isaacs was still alive, and he needed to know now.

"Calling this late means you need something important or you have a death wish," Dr. Albertson said in way of answering.

Jared explained his need. "Can you take her prints and run them?"

"It'll take me a half-hour to get back to the lab," she said, not at all sounding upset by the request. "We use electronic scanners but it could still take several hours to run the prints."

"Thanks." Jared ended the call, praying that the fingerprints would tell them whose body was found in Reya's home, and what, if anything, Valerie Zupan had to do with Luna's kidnapping.

∼

Bristol remained frozen in place on the floor, staring up at the woman who was a match to Kelsey's sketch. From what she'd learned about Reya in investigating her, the woman didn't own a gun. Could mean she'd recently bought it and didn't know what she was doing. Which could further put Bristol's life in danger.

I know I have no right to ask anything but please don't let her hurt me so I can get Luna away from her, if she has her, and back to her parents.

"Could you put the gun down, and we can talk?" Bristol tried to sound friendly but her voice shook.

Reya narrowed her eyes and left the gun pointed directly at Bristol. "Who are you and why are you here?"

"I could ask you the same thing. You said my house, but the homeowner, Reya Isaacs died. I saw her for myself."

"My twin sister, Valerie," she stated with no emotion.

"You have a twin?"

"Surprise, right?" She scoffed. "We were split up at birth and adopted out to separate families."

"When did you find out about Valerie?"

"Not until recently. When my daughter was found actually." Reya's eyes narrowed. "Valerie lived in Arizona. She'd heard the story about Darcy from people talking at work but didn't watch the news so didn't see my picture. When Darcy's remains were found, the national news exploited it, and they plastered my picture everywhere. When Valerie saw me, she knew we had to be twins. She contacted me and then moved here so we could get to know each other."

Reya smiled. "It was so great. Not only was she a person who didn't judge me, but I changed my hairstyle to match hers so I could pretend to be her and get away from the awful publicity."

"And then you killed her?" Bristol threw out the wild accusation to see how she responded.

Reya's eyes cut around the room. "I didn't mean to."

Bristol stifled her shock at the reply. "But you did."

"She was taking the baby. I couldn't let her give the baby away when I'm alone. I tried to stop her. Give the baby to me. But she didn't listen. So I had to use force. Don't you see? I had to stop her."

"That you did," Bristol said. "But if you stopped her, you must have the baby."

She jerked her head at the door. "She's safe in her seat on the porch."

Luna was outside? Really? This close.

Bristol swallowed and breathed deep to keep from losing it and scaring Reya. "Why leave her outside?"

Reya's nostrils flared. "Because I saw you and didn't want to put her in danger."

"I won't hurt her." Bristol made sure her tone was convincing and soothing. "I'm a deputy. I would never hurt a child. Bring her in."

"Don't you move." She backed to the doorway and bent for the car seat.

Bristol thought to rush Reya, but didn't want the woman to drop the child, and besides, Bristol couldn't get to her feet in time.

"I'm only here for Darcy's supplies, and then we're leaving." She set the seat on the floor.

Luna. It really *was* Luna. Fast asleep and looking plump and healthy.

Bristol had found the child, and she was alive. Rather, the child had found her.

Bristol let out a long breath of satisfaction, but quickly thought of a way to get this woman to turn Luna over to her. "Since I'm here, I could help you."

"No!" Reya bared her teeth. "You'll try to take my daughter from me."

"That's Luna in the seat, not your daughter."

Reya waved the gun, eyes flashing with anger. "Stop it. Stop lying to me."

"Sorry," Bristol said as the woman had lost touch with reality. "I didn't mean to. How can I help you?"

Reya remained standing, her gaze furtive and wild. "Stand up. Slowly."

Bristol did as directed, all the while looking for a way to subdue Reya without Luna getting hurt.

"Take out your phone," Reya said. "Turn it off then smash it."

Bristol hesitated. She would be out of touch for any help. She'd broken a cardinal law enforcement rule. She hadn't given dispatch her location. Sure, Jared knew she was here, but he was busy. If dispatch had known she was here, and they hadn't heard from her, they would try to contact her.

"Do it now!" Reya growled out the words like an angry animal.

Bristol complied, dropping her phone on the floor and stomping on it.

"Harder! Harder!"

Bristol gave it a few more stomps, and her heart seized. Her lifeline was gone.

Except for You. I want to believe You can help me. Help me believe.

"Now come with me," Reya said. "Slowly."

Reya left Luna behind and backed toward the hallway.

Bristol crossed the room and wanted to grab the baby and run, but the risk was too high. She settled for taking a better look at the sleeping infant. She seemed healthy enough, but then as Nurse Johnson had told them, the blood sugar issue might not be visible.

Bristol followed Reya, who backed down the hallway to her daughter's room. Reya moved to the far corner and pointed at the dresser. "In the top drawer are sleepers. Get them out. Darcy needs them."

Bristol complied and looked for a way to overpower Reya, but she'd stepped back out of reach.

"Put it all in the laundry bags in the closet then open the bottom drawer. You'll find baby blankets, bibs, diapers. Add it all to the bag. Hurry before Darcy wakes up."

"Did you know Luna has a problem with her blood sugar and needs to eat every few hours?"

Reya jutted out her chin. "My Darcy doesn't have any health problems. She's perfect."

"How often are you feeding her?"

"Not that it's any of your business, but whenever she wakes up."

"How often does that happen?"

"Don't know. Just happens when it happens."

Reya wasn't really listening, making it even more urgent that Bristol get this child back with her parents and medical professionals. "Where are you taking all of these things?"

"The family cabin."

Cabin? What cabin? "I thought your finances were stretched to the breaking point, and you lost everything except the house."

"Was my dad's place. He recently died and left it to me." She sighed. "I put it in Valerie's name so no one could come after me and take it away. We'll be safe there. I made sure of it."

"Safe?" Bristol asked to clarify. "How did you do that?"

"None of your business."

"Can I come along and help you out?" Bristol smiled.

"No. You'll try to take Darcy."

"I won't."

Reya waved the gun. "Your time ends here."

Panic set in.

God, please. Please. Is this the end? No. No. I'm going to trust that You'll get me out of this. Not because I deserve it. But surely baby Luna does.

Bristol searched for the right reply for Reya and swallowed hard. "You don't want to shoot me. You'll draw the neighbors' attention. And they'll call the cops. Nearby houses have cameras. They'll record you leaving, and then the police will hunt you down and take Darcy back. But if I go with you, no one will even know you were here."

Reya tilted her head. *Good. Good.* She was thinking it over. Bristol didn't speak but stuffed the laundry bags with the items from the drawers to give Reya more time to think.

With two cases nearly filled, she looked up. "I can carry these to the car while you carry Luna."

"I told you it was Darcy. Darcy."

"Right, Darcy. I forgot." She lifted the laundry bags. "Now what?"

"You can come with me. Maybe it will be good to have someone to drive. That way I can tend to Darcy if she wakes up." She nodded at the cases. "Bring them."

Bristol gripped the fabric in her sweaty palms. Should she swing them at Reya? No. A bullet ripped through air much faster than she could swing the cases. "You could've purchased all of this at a store. Why come back here and risk being discovered?"

"Darcy needed her things. Not something from the store. *Hers.* Now move." She waved the gun.

Bristol figured the woman had stared at, maybe handled all of these items for years and in her crazed state justified the risk of returning to collect them. Bristol headed for the door and led the way to the front room where Luna continued to sleep peacefully. Just the sight of the baby brought joy to Bristol's heart. But it evaporated in a flash.

Bristol was so close to bringing this case to a close and yet so far away. At least, she'd persuaded Reya to let her come along with her, but Bristol had to be careful with her moves to free Luna. Seemed like Reya had a complete break with reality and would kill to protect the baby she thought was her daughter, and she wouldn't hesitate to shoot Bristol.

20

Jared paced the lab as he waited for the return call from Dr. Albertson. Sierra and her team continued to work processing forensics from the many scenes, but Jared couldn't sit still. He'd tasked his team with doing additional research on Valerie Zupan, and he hoped they would locate something that would move them quickly forward with this lead.

He got out his phone to text Bristol to tell her what had happened. *No. Stop.* Wait until the deceased's identity was confirmed.

He took a few more steps then caught Sierra's eye, her pointed look telling him to stop. He settled on a stool at an empty lab table to ponder. Everything was starting to make more sense. Reya had likely assumed Valerie's identity and was moving about freely with credit cards and access to a bank account that no one on his team would've checked. And he hadn't put any alerts out on Reya. Why would he when they believed she was dead?

Well, they were checking it all now.

But the really big questions were, did she have something to do with Luna's disappearance, or did they just have a case of a woman being murdered and the team had the wrong ID?

They surely couldn't discount the fact that Reya's blood was on Luna's blanket. The blanket could belong to another child, but the odds were astronomical for such a unique blanket ending up in a parking structure of the facility where Luna had been taken in the same style blanket. Especially since it was purchased from a small internet boutique.

His phone chimed from his pocket. He jumped up to get it out.

Expecting to hear from Dr. Albertson, he was surprised to see the text from Reed with a photo of Kelsey's sketch for the woman Osborne hired. Jared tapped the photo and shot up a hand. "Yes!"

"Did Dr. Albertson have a match?" Sierra asked.

"Sorry, no. It was another lead that finally came through." Jared turned his attention back to his phone and typed. *This woman is Melissa Gibson. Holloway's assistant. Focus the team's effort in hunting her down.*

On it, Reed replied.

Jared's phone rang.

"Dr. Albertson," he answered. "I'm putting you on speaker so Sierra Rice at the Veritas Center can hear."

"I just finished the prints. We have a match. A Valerie Zupan with a record for bank fraud."

"So it's true." Jared cut his gaze to Sierra, who had saved the day when she'd successfully found Valerie's latent print. "We had the wrong ID. Reya Isaacs is still alive."

Sierra frowned when he thought she might be glad for the right ID. "With Reya's blood on the blanket, she likely has Luna."

"No. Oh, no." Jared jumped to his feet. "Bristol went back to Reya's house to look for forensics. I have to warn her that

Reya's alive." Jared tapped Bristol's phone number, though he doubted Reya would return to her house.

The call went straight to voicemail.

"She's not answering." Jared locked gazes with Sierra. "She could be in trouble at Reya's house, and I need to get over there now!"

~

In the pitch dark of the countryside, Bristol turned into the long driveway leading toward Reya's cabin, the tires crunching over gravel and branches scraping against the vehicle's sides. Bristol hadn't found a way to leave behind any kind of clue for Jared, except her smashed phone and that Teagan's car would be in the driveway.

Hopefully when Bristol didn't answer her phone, he would go check on her. Surely, he wouldn't just give up, but then he might as he had no reason to know Reya was still alive and Bristol could be in jeopardy.

Then Bristol also had to hope that Jared would remember Reya's father had passed away recently and track down the cabin in his property records. Or maybe he somehow found out about Valerie and could locate the cabin that way.

All wishful thinking really.

Or not. God could do anything. Everything. Nothing was impossible for Him. She just had to trust Him. He brought her this far. He could take her all the way to the finish line where Luna was reunited with her parents. Where Bristol was reunited with her family again.

And with Jared.

She would tell him that she loved him. Her feelings had become clear on the drive over here. The thought of never seeing him again felt like Reya had indeed shot her. Bristol had to swallow her pride over being dumped, forgive and forget, and give a relationship with him a chance. That was, if he wanted it as well.

And if she lived.

She followed a big curve on the drive and pulled into a clearing that revealed a small A-framed cabin with a bright orange door. A real throwback to the sixties.

"You'll carry everything while I keep my gun on you." Reya waved the weapon in the car, lit only with red dashboard lights. "Now get out and stand by your door. No false moves as I won't hesitate to shoot out here. This is nothing like my house. There's no one for miles around to hear my gunshots."

Jared pulled down the road toward Reya's house and cut off his headlights. Reed leaned forward in the passenger seat, staring ahead.

They neared the house, and Jared had to swallow before he could speak. "Teagan's car is in the driveway."

"Lights are on inside, so Bristol might still be here." Reed leaned closer to the windshield. "Could be as simple as her phone died."

"Could be." Jared swung his car to the curb down the street from the house for a silent approach on foot under cover of darkness.

"But you don't believe it," Reed said.

Jared shook his head. "Bristol is a detail-oriented person. Letting her phone die isn't like her. Or the her I once knew."

"She could be caught up in the task force and not doing the things she normally does." Reed removed his seatbelt. "Looking for a missing baby can mess with your normal routine."

"Yeah." Jared opened his door.

"Or you don't know her anymore." Reed got out.

"But I do. In just the time we've been together, I can see she's basically the same person only we're both more mature. And she's one fine deputy."

Reed started for the door, and Jared fell into step beside his fellow agent. The door stood ajar. Not good. He let go of all thoughts except successfully breaching this property and finding Bristol alive and well. He climbed the stairs, and his gut twisted. He had to force himself to breathe. He drew his weapon as did Reed.

Jared reached the door first and pushed it open. He swung his gaze around the family room. Empty. Almost. No people but a phone lay smashed on the floor. A phone in Bristol's case that held her family photo on the back.

"Bristol's phone," he whispered and led the way into the house. They crept down the hall and cleared each room.

Jared held his breath at the primary bedroom, then swung in. Took a long look. Sagged in relief. The room was empty. Bristol hadn't met the same fate as Valerie.

"Kitchen and dining room," he said and reversed course. They quickly cleared the rooms.

"She's not here," Jared stated the obvious. "Reya could've come home and taken her with her."

"Too bad we took down the WiFi," Reed said. "Means her cameras aren't working."

Jared got out his phone and called Teagan. "Have you heard from Bristol?"

"Not since she asked me to talk to Nurse Raney. Why?"

Jared explained.

"What can we do to help?" Teagan sounded like someone was strangling her.

"Figure out where Reya could've taken Bristol."

"I'll put the family on it, stat." Teagan ended the call.

Jared called Piper and put her on speaker so Reed could listen in. "Bristol's missing, her phone's smashed, but Teagan's car is here at Reya's house. I need to figure out where Reya might've taken Bristol. Information on Valerie Zupan could help. You got anything yet?"

"The home address we found in DMV is legit," Piper said. "Landlord says she occupies the apartment. And Colin has info on her life in Arizona. He's right here, so I'll put you on speaker."

"You're not going to believe this." Colin's excited tone came racing through the phone. "Zupan was arrested for soliciting a woman to give up her child for payment. Charges were dropped when the mother-to-be recanted her story."

"Not a coincidence, I'm sure," Jared said. "She could be the one who took Luna, not Reya."

"Could be, but then who killed Valerie and where are Reya and Luna?" Piper asked.

"And who was the guy in the doorbell video who dumped Valerie's body here?" Reed asked.

"We'll head over to Zupan's place while you keep digging." Jared headed for the door. "Maybe one of them owns property somewhere else."

Jared connected his phone to his car and got them moving toward Valerie's address in the southeast side of the city.

Reed leaned his seat back. "You gonna pursue Bristol after we find Luna?"

How could the guy be so laidback? Be thinking of dating at a time like this?

"Should I take your silence as a yes or none of my business?" Reed asked.

Jared didn't know. Was he planning to ask her out? Not consciously, but if he took a moment to think about the way his gut was tied up as if strangling itself after not finding her at the house, he'd have to admit he was still in love with her.

"If she'll agree to it." Hopefully it would satisfy Reed, and he'd leave it alone.

"You know I struggled too before I married Sierra. But I can say being married and a dad is the best thing that happened to me." Reed crossed an ankle over his knee. "I once thought the job was everything, but I'm here to tell you, it's not. You need balance, even if it does sometimes skew toward the work like now when we have to put all of our focus on an investigation."

"I'm starting to see that," Jared admitted. "But as you said, right now our focus should solely be on finding Luna."

That ended the conversation, and they rode in silence until they reached Valerie's apartment. They went straight to the super's apartment for a key. He didn't like the late-night disturbance, but he unlocked Valerie's door and quickly turned back toward his own place.

Jared and Reed waited for the guy to disappear then drew their guns and entered.

"Police," Jared called out to what appeared to be an empty one-bedroom place with the smell of stinky garbage.

They quickly cleared the few rooms.

"I didn't expect to find Bristol here, but..." Jared shrugged and holstered his weapon.

"Let's take a look around." Reed shoved his pistol into his holster, slipped on gloves, and stepped over to an end table to pull out a drawer.

Jared gloved up too and went to the kitchen. He leafed through mail lying on the counter. All junk mail. He wandered through the kitchen and spotted photos on the fridge of an A-frame cottage where Reya and Valerie had taken selfies outside the place.

"Check this out," Jared said. "Looks like they either rented a cabin or there's one in the family."

"We thoroughly checked Reya's property records," Reed said. "Only property in her name is her house."

"The ex could know something about a cabin." Jared scrolled through his phone until he found Harri's contact info. The call went to voicemail. "It's Agent Wolfe. Call me as soon as you get this message. It's urgent."

He tapped Piper's number. "Look for a cabin. An A-frame. I know Reya doesn't own the property but maybe the sister does."

"Reya's dad died a few months ago too," Piper said. "Maybe he has a house that didn't clear escrow yet and is still in his name."

"Find out like yesterday," Jared demanded. "And get back to me as soon as you know anything."

Bristol grabbed the laundry bags while Reya got Luna out of the car, that infuriating gun still pointed at Bristol. For a woman who seemed to be dancing on the edge of sanity, Reya did a good job of keeping Bristol at bay, not giving her any chance to take Reya down.

Tires crunched over the gravel.

Bristol spun to look.

Headlights off, a truck pulled up behind them.

Bristol stared, trying to figure out the driver. Could it be Jared? If so, why was he in a truck? Or maybe it was Holloway.

Reya set Luna's carrier down and shoved Bristol in front of her. Bristol got it. Reya was putting Bristol in the line of fire in case the driver was armed.

The truck door opened, and a man slid down, his face in

the deep shadows cast by tall maple trees, but he was about the same height as Holloway.

Holloway? Could it really be Holloway?

"You can stop right there," the man said. "You have something that belongs to me."

No. The voice is all wrong. Not Holloway. Bristol might not recognize his deep and commanding voice but sounded like he was used to being obeyed.

"Show yourself," Reya commanded.

He stepped out of the darkness, revealing a full head of blond hair and a full beard to match. Bristol didn't recognize him as anyone they'd encountered in the investigation but knew if he was willing to show his face to them, he didn't plan to let either Bristol or Reya walk away from here alive.

Bristol searched him for a weapon and noted the telltale bulge of a holster under his flannel shirt.

Was he law enforcement?

Dear Lord, please let that be true.

Reya waved her gun at him. "Who are you and what do you want?"

He lifted his hands. "Hold on now. No need to point that thing at me. I just came to collect my daughter, and I'll leave the two of you to what you have going on here."

"Your daughter?" Reya asked as the same question echoed in Bristol's head. "I don't understand."

"Luna." He pointed at the carrier. "Or so her mother called her, but that'll be changing. She's my child, and there's no mistake about it."

"That's impossible," Bristol said. "I met her father at the hospital."

He raised his shoulders. "You met the man that Sonya claims is her baby's father, but I'm the dad."

"How?"

"How do you think?" He laughed. "We work for the

same company, and I was in town for a week. One day she was all upset over failing in vitro again. My wife was having a hard time conceiving too, so I could empathize with her. I took her out after work, and we got drunk together. Ended up in a one-night stand. And now, nine months later, here's our child."

Seemed like quite a reach. "Did Sonya tell you that?"

"Nah. We agreed to never speak again after the fling. No point in breaking up our marriages."

"Then how did you know about Luna?" Bristol asked.

"Social media. Sonya posted a picture of the baby, and her ears gave it away." He reached up to tug on his earlobe. "Connected earlobes just like the baby. Thanks to my genetics class in school, I know with neither Sonya nor her husband having that trait, she has to be mine."

Bristol had read genetic studies in the past, and the facts he claimed were in question, but it was a possibility. "Do you know your blood type?"

"O positive, why?"

Bristol wouldn't confirm that the blood type made it possible for him to be Luna's father. "What's your name?"

"Now *that's* none of your business." He chuckled.

His response didn't surprise Bristol. She knew he was likely planning to kill them. The only question is why he didn't come out firing. Maybe he didn't want to risk hurting Luna.

Bristol had to keep him talking. That was her only hope that he wouldn't kill her and Reya to take the baby. "How did you figure out Reya had Luna?"

"Stupid Holloway, that's who." He clamped his hands on his hips. "You know who he is?"

"Adoption attorney," Bristol said.

"Yeah, well he screwed this up big time. Sonya told us about him when my wife and I couldn't get pregnant. We were going to adopt through him. But then I found out about Luna. Why not have your own kid instead of someone else's?"

"If she really is yours, you could've fought for custody," Bristol said.

"Best we could hope for is part-time custody, if that. We wanted her full-time. Holloway said he had someone who could bring Luna to us." He fired an angry look at Reya. "You were supposed to give her to Holloway, but you took off with her."

"I didn't take her from the hospital," Reya said.

"Her sister did," Bristol clarified. "And Reya killed her sister to get the baby. Still doesn't say how you found us tonight."

"I tried going through Holloway, but he disappeared, and I couldn't get any information on him. So I did the only thing I could think to do. Watch Reya's house. Turns out it was a good idea. Saw you both arrive and Luna too. I knew I didn't want to take on a deputy. Figured I'd follow and see how things played out." He took a step toward them.

"Don't take another step or I'll shoot," Reya said.

"But she's mine."

"No!" Reya's cry rose into the night, echoing in the trees like the call of a wounded animal. "When will you people realize? This is *my* child. My Darcy. I did not take your Luna. Now go away."

"I can't do that." He slowly reached for his gun.

"You were warned." Reya pulled the trigger, firing off four charges.

The man, maybe Luna's father, dropped to the ground and lay unmoving.

Reya turned to Bristol. "We go inside now. This is what can happen to you if you don't listen."

21

"Don't even think about it," Reya said.

"Think about what?" Bristol played innocent though she'd been looking for a way out of the cabin while sitting in the hard oak chair as Reya held a gun on her.

"Escaping." She jabbed a finger at the windows. "I nailed them shut. Added a reinforced lock on the door. And I'm not sleeping. Ever. No one is taking my baby. Not again. Not ever again." Reya was losing even more of her already fragile hold on life as the minutes ticked by.

Bristol wished she were imagining it, but the wild look in Reya's eyes, along with her babbling while she fidgeted in place across the room from Bristol, told her as much. As did the way she'd dispassionately ended the man's life in the driveway.

The sound of the gun discharge. The thud of the body. His eyes wide but unseeing. All of it echoed through Bristol's brain.

Father, please. I'm trusting You. I know I've been lost since Thomas died, but I know Your will will be done here. I can only ask that Luna will live and be returned to her family.

Bristol stared at the pine walls and ceiling. Searching.

Looking. Seeking. The A-frame ceiling sloping to the ground seemed to close in on her. More likely the murder or the gun constantly pointed in her direction was the reason for Bristol's uncertainty.

"What do you plan to do with me?" Bristol really didn't want to hear the answer, but she had to ask.

"You'll stay with me as long as you're useful."

"Useful, how?"

"Maybe the cops will find out where I am, and they'll come for me. I can use you as a hostage."

At least she didn't have plans to kill Bristol right now. But she would soon tire of holding the gun. Maybe when Luna woke up to be fed, Reya would realize she couldn't keep the gun on Bristol and feed the baby too. Maybe she would tie Bristol up then. If Reya did bind Bristol's hands, she would have less of a chance to escape.

Bristol glanced at the wall clock. They'd been at the cabin for nearly two hours. Bristol wanted to make noise to wake the baby up so she could eat.

Reya suddenly shifted toward the window. "Did you hear that?"

"What?"

"Crunching on the gravel. I need better protection." She backed across the open kitchen to the countertop holding a black padded gun case. She opened it, displaying multiple handguns.

"I didn't know you were so into guns," Bristol said.

"I'm not, but Valerie was. She was crazy about guns. Told me this one had the most bullets in it." She lifted out a Springfield XDS 9mm, one of Bristol's most often used guns.

Reya aimed it at Bristol and pretended to shoot it then laughed and flipped off the overhead light. The room was draped in darkness, but a shaft of moonlight flowed through the window over the sink and over Bristol.

"Don't think I can't still see you," Reya said. "I can and my gun is pointed at you."

Bristol wanted to get up and charge Reya. She sat on her hands instead and listened.

"Do you hear anything?" Reya asked.

"No." Which Bristol would continue to say even if she heard a sound outside.

"There. Footsteps. I'm sure I heard them."

Bristol heard the steps too, and her heart leapt. Could it be Jared? Did he find her?

Was he walking into a trap?

Jared lifted his hand telling Reed to stop. His partner eased closer to Jared. They'd both seen the light that had shone from the right window go dark.

"You think they went to bed or made us?" Reed's tone wasn't more than a whisper.

"We have to assume we've been made." Jared hated the thought.

"Then what's the plan?"

"I'd hoped to have the element of surprise on our side so I honestly don't know." He took another look at the building hunkered down in dark shadows. "We could slip in a window."

"None on the sides. We'll have to circle round back."

Jared lamented the A-frame style building. "Then we go to the back. We use hand signals from now on."

Reed nodded, and Jared started down the drive, but came to a sudden stop. He pointed ahead where a male body lay on the ground next to the truck. Jared signaled for Reed to have his back. He stepped closer, his weapon raised.

Jared dropped down to check for a pulse. "Dead, but still warm. Don't recognize him."

"What do you want to do?" Reed asked.

"We keep moving, but be even more careful." Jared prayed for everyone's safety, then eased closer until the front door was flung open, the moon coming out from behind clouds and bathing the area.

Jared jerked his rifle in that direction.

Bristol stepped onto the porch, Reya Isaacs's arm slung around Bristol's neck and a handgun to her head.

Jared had to stifle a gasp, and it took all his effort to keep his gun raised when his arms suddenly felt like gelatin.

"If you've come to try to steal my daughter, go away," Reya shouted. "I'll kill this woman if you try."

Jared and Reed remained quiet and in the shadows.

"Show yourselves or I kill her." Reya jammed the gun into Bristol's head. "I mean it. Step out now or she hits the porch just like the man in the driveway."

Hoping Reya didn't know there were two of them, Jared signaled for Reed to hold his position, and Jared stepped out. "I'm over here. Please don't hurt Bristol. You could take me instead and let her go."

"No."

"That's Jared Wolfe," Bristol said calmly. "He's an FBI agent, and the man I love."

"Love." Reya flashed her eyes wide.

Jared was equally as shocked. Not just by her confession, but why she felt a need to say it now.

"I actually met him when I was in college. We worked at a middle school camp that summer. Fell in love. But he'd already joined the Navy and had to go serve our country, so we couldn't be together."

Bristol took a long breath and locked gazes with him.

281

"Now we reconnected, and I would really like the chance to find out if he's the man for me."

Reya simply grunted.

"Remember when you fell in love with your husband?" Bristol asked. "Wouldn't you have wanted to do just about anything to be with him? To have his child?"

Reya's expression softened, and her arm loosened a bit. Likely Bristol's plan. Make herself and him more human to Reya. Not law enforcement officers bent on ruining her dream, but a couple in love.

Was that Bristol's only goal, or was she trying to tell him she loved him in case Reya killed her?

No. He wouldn't let that happen. Not as long as he had breath in his body.

"Do you remember the feeling, Reya?" Bristol asked.

"Yes." Reya's voice was barely loud enough for Jared to hear her. "I remember. But it ended. Now we only fight and blame, so we had to break up."

Reya seemed distracted. Jared took a step forward.

"Stop!" Reya waved her gun at him.

Bristol's eyes widened and a baffled look crossed her face.

What? Was she signaling something? Had he done the wrong thing? Had his actions put her life in danger?

"I'm sorry." Jared held up his hand. "I won't move again. I promise. But I need to tell Bristol I love her too. I never stopped. I can see that now. Clearly. Please don't take her life. Take me instead."

Reya returned the gun to Bristol's head. Bristol met his gaze and smiled.

What in the world? Smiling with a gun at her head? Had she lost it?

"Nothing to fear." She calmly reached up and grabbed the gun barrel.

"No! No! Bristol, no!" Jared charged toward them.

Bristol wrestled the gun out of Reya's hand.

Jared's heart refused to beat, but somehow he kept moving forward.

Bristol aimed the gun at Reya. "On the ground, now!"

Reya flashed her gaze up to Bristol but then dropped to the ground.

"Of all the foolish things to do." Jared wrenched his handcuffs free and jerked Reya's arms behind her back. He secured the cuffs and turned her to face the drive where Reed was jogging over to them.

"I'll put her in the car." Reed grabbed Reya's cuffs and directed her off the porch.

Jared took Bristol by the shoulders then drew her into his arms for a quick hug and released her. "Does she have Luna? Is she here?"

Bristol smiled. "Safe inside."

"Thank you, God!" He held her gaze. "You shouldn't have taken such a risk. Reya could've fired. Hit you. Me. Reed."

"Actually, she couldn't." Bristol smiled. "It was impossible."

"I don't understand."

"When she started waving the gun at you, I saw the answer to our problem."

"That's when you smiled at me."

She nodded and held up the gun. "This is a Springfield XDS 9mm. One of my favorite carry guns so I know it well, and it has a live round indicator that you can see and feel."

She pointed at the top of the slide. "It's flat right now, but if I chamber a bullet." She pulled back the slide, dropping a bullet into the chamber, and a metal piece popped up on the slide. "You can see the indicator now shows it's loaded."

"So she didn't have a bullet in the chamber and couldn't

fire on us." Jared shook his head. "I didn't know about the indicator."

"And neither did Reya. The gun belongs to her twin."

"Valerie Zupan."

Bristol flashed her eyes wide. "How did you find out about her?"

He explained about the fingerprint. "That's how I knew to go to Reya's to look for you. Then the team found this cabin. Made sense she would come here." He jerked a thumb over his shoulder. "Who's the man in the driveway?"

Bristol's smile fell, and a haunted look darkened her eyes. "A man Sonya Pratt had an affair with, and he believed he was Luna's father. He tried to take Luna, and Reya shot him."

"Could he be the father?"

"His story rang true. We'll have to question Sonya, but hopefully not tonight." Bristol took his hand and led him into the cabin.

Bristol gently lifted the baby from her carrier and turned her over to check for the birthmark to confirm her identity though Bristol really had no doubts. "Looks to me like the picture the Pratts' took."

"Me too," Jared said, sounding choked up.

Bristol cradled the sleeping newborn and smiled up at him. "Tonight is the time to take Luna home to her family and let everyone who had a part in finding her relish in the successful outcome."

22

***

"We have Luna," Bristol said into Jared's phone perched between her ear and shoulder as she settled Luna's seat into the car. "She's fine."

Mrs. Pratt cried out. "My baby. You really found my baby."

"Yes." Bristol secured the seat in the base Jared had moved from Reya's car. "And we'll be able to reunite her with you within the hour."

"Hurry," Mrs. Pratt begged. "Oh, please hurry."

Bristol ended the call and gave the phone back to Jared, purposely keeping her gaze away from Glenn Bates where he lay on the driveway. Reed had looked at the deceased man's wallet to discover his ID, and he did indeed work for the same company as Mrs. Pratt.

"Thanks for letting me be the one to call the Pratts," Bristol said.

"Of course." He stroked a hand over her hair.

She ignored it the best she could. She couldn't give in to her emotions now, or she would fall apart, and she had a baby to deliver to her parents. "I'll sit in the back with Luna in case she needs a bottle again on the drive."

She climbed in, and Jared closed her door.

Bristol buckled up and took the baby's soft little hand in hers. She had to keep touching the infant. Feel the warmth on her skin. The life flowing through her veins. And offer prayers of thanks. Copious prayers of thanks.

Jared got the car moving down the drive, and he waved at Reed who would go with a local deputy to drive Reya back to Portland for booking.

Jared flipped on his lights to get them through traffic faster so Luna could be checked out by a doctor. Bristol wanted to talk to Jared about her declaration of love and his responding claim, but she wouldn't. Not until after Luna was safely in her parents' arms. Jared must have felt the same way as they didn't speak on the drive at all.

She settled for holding Luna's hand and breathing in and out. Letting the subduing adrenaline out with each breath. Hoping it would stop her hands from trembling too. She'd never been taken at gunpoint before. Hoped to never be taken again. Leaving law enforcement should help.

Outside the hospital, Jared turned off the lights, parked, and got out. He removed the car seat, and she ran around to his side.

He handed the seat to her. "You saved Luna. You should be the one to give her back to her parents."

"It was a team effort." Bristol took the baby and marched for the door. She didn't want to waste a second longer before reuniting the family and having Luna's blood sugar checked.

"But you kept at it, and your gut took you to the right place," Jared said. "Plus, your extensive knowledge of weapons allowed us to subdue Reya."

The door swished open. "You would've gotten there too."

"But I wouldn't have known about the indicator like you did. And the outcome could've been far different."

"Are you kidding? I wouldn't have let you go to the cabin

alone." She allowed herself to smile for the first time since being taken. Her heart was filled to brimming with love for this baby and relief and gratefulness.

They hurried across the lobby to the elevator. Jared summoned the car and held the door for Bristol. They boarded, and the *swish* of the doors felt final somehow in their success. Tears wetted Bristol's eyes, and she swallowed them down. She didn't want to arrive all weepy-eyed in front of the Pratts.

But try as she might, the tears kept coming. By the time she reached the Pratts' room, where Adair stood waiting outside, she was nearly sobbing and had to swipe at the tears to not embarrass herself.

"I updated the Pratts on the situation, leaving out Glenn Bates. That's best revealed when we question Mrs. Pratt in the morning after she and her husband have a night with their baby." Adair held out his hand and shook Jared's and Bristol's hands. "We'll debrief you both after you settle Luna with her parents."

Bristol pushed the door open. Mr. Pratt ran to her, and she handed Luna over to him. Jared followed behind and pressed a hand on Bristol's lower back. She concentrated on the warmth of his touch to stem her tears. Agent Byrd remained to the side where she'd been through this whole ordeal. A doctor and nurse both wearing pink scrubs stood by the window. They were likely the ones who would check out Luna's vitals.

"Thank you, oh, thank you," Mrs. Pratt said as her husband extracted Luna from the seat and placed her in his wife's arms. "Oh, my precious, precious little girl. You really are fine."

"She ate just before we left, and she gulped down the formula," Bristol said. "I think the woman who had Luna, took good care of her."

"She thought she was her daughter, right?"

Bristol nodded. "Which is why she took such good care of her."

"We should give Luna a quick check-up." The doctor flipped her ponytail over her shoulder.

"I'm not letting her go," Mrs. Pratt said. "You'll have to do it while I hold her."

The doctor smiled. "I can do that."

"We'll just be going," Jared said.

"I'd like to check back in with you later if you don't mind," Bristol said.

"Please come here." Mrs. Pratt held out her hand.

Bristol crossed the room and took the beaming mother's hand, surprised to find it cold.

"I will never be able to thank you enough," she said. "I was rude and mean, and yet you did your job and brought Luna back to us. Know that I thank you for all you did. Both of you. And the many others who helped too. Please offer our thanks to them."

"We're glad we could help." Bristol squeezed and released the mother's hand then backed out, nodding at Toni on the way.

Bristol expected to find Adair in the hallway, but he'd departed. She looked up at Jared and worked hard to hold her emotions in check as they stepped out of the birthing center. The elevator doors opened, and her family poured out. Her mom and dad rushed up to her.

Bristol wasn't surprised to see her dad, her sisters, and all three of her cousins as they'd been working in the training room, but they had to have called her mom once they'd heard Bristol was missing.

Her dad, his eyes moist, scooped her into a hug. "We were terrified, Baby Girl."

His tender use of her nickname tore at her heart. After

losing Thomas, such a scare had to have taken them to nearly unbearable pain again. "If I'd known Reya was alive, I wouldn't have gone alone to the house."

"You still shouldn't have gone alone." Her dad pushed her to arm's length and frowned. "You never know when a killer might return to the scene of the crime."

"My fault," Jared said.

Her dad eyed Jared.

"I was in charge, and I let her go." Jared's eyes narrowed. "It was a rookie mistake I shouldn't have made, and I take full responsibility. Honestly, I let losing a child in an abduction a few years ago push me to move faster than I should, and it could've ended badly."

"Takes a good officer to admit his mistake," her dad said. "Now promise you'll learn from it."

"I will. Have." Jared looked at Bristol, and the depth of his affection for her warmed her body clean through.

"So it's like that, huh?" Her dad crossed his arms.

"Now, Gene," her mother said. "We all make mistakes, and you will not hold that against Jared."

"I won't if you say I won't." Her father smiled at her mother, a loving, I-aim-to-please kind of smile.

"Then while we're confessing," Jared said. "I'm the guy who bailed on Bristol at summer camp."

"Aha!" Teagan pumped her fist. "I knew it!"

Bristol looked at her older cousin. "Did Grandad tell you?"

"Grandad?" Her eyes creased. "No. You two have some major unspoken vibes going on. Vibes that were too strong to develop so quickly, and your camp guy was the only one you ever felt so deeply about. So I put two and two together and shazam. Jared is camp guy."

"I thought we did a good job of hiding it," Bristol said.

"In a family of law enforcement officers?" Teagan grinned. "Not possible."

Her father lifted his shoulders and eyed Jared. "Which means, if you hurt my daughter again, I'll know about it, and I'll be all over you."

"Dad," Bristol warned. "Don't scare him off before we even have a chance to find out if we have a future."

"No worries," Jared said. "I don't plan to hurt her."

Her dad kept his gaze fastened to Jared. "See that you don't."

"Yes, sir," Jared said. "Now if you'll excuse us, we have a debrief we need to attend."

Bristol couldn't be any more thankful for the change in topic. "And you all can go home."

"We're headed to your grandparents' house," her mom said. "Your gran and grandad are waiting for us, and if I know Gran, she's making breakfast for everyone." Her mother looked at Jared. "Will you join us?"

"If Bristol wants me to."

"Of course." If she weren't in uniform and on her way to the debrief she would take his hand.

She started off.

He came alongside her. "I hope you don't mind me confessing to your family."

"Not at all."

"Your dad took it better than I thought he would, but I'm glad to have it over with."

"Actually," she looked up at him. "It's not over. You still have to tell my grandparents, and they'll be the hardest sell of all."

~

Thankfully, Adair took charge of the debrief as Jared couldn't concentrate. His mind wandered between thanking God for the positive outcome, remembering the sight of Luna snuggled in her mother's arms, and thinking about Bristol's last comment about her grandparents.

There would be hours and hours of paperwork to do to close out this investigation, and he would be the one who would compile it all. He could claim that he needed to do the work now, but he also knew Adair would give him time to get some sleep before finalizing the reports that would flood in from every person in this room.

And then there would be questioning of Sonya Pratt and Reya, something Jared would insist on doing himself. He couldn't allow Bristol to join him when she was an active participant in the altercation with the man. Jared would also have to write his own statement, something he and she should do right away before any facts were forgotten or misremembered.

"No. No," Piper whispered and grabbed Jared's arm. "I think my labor has started."

"C'mon." Jared stood and took her arm to lead her into the hallway, signaling for Bristol to join them.

By the time Piper reached the hallway, she had her phone to her ear. "It's time, Nick. The baby is coming. I'll wait in the lobby for you." Piper listened. "Love you too."

She hung up. "This isn't our hospital. Nick's on his way to pick me up."

"Do you have enough time to go somewhere else?" Bristol's voice rose as if she didn't want another child to be in jeopardy.

"Contractions are just starting." Piper grimaced and bent over.

Jared had no clue what to do. He looked at Bristol for help, but she was intently watching Piper until she stood back up. "That seemed really strong. Why not just have someone check things out before getting on the road?"

"I'm fine. We just need to find a place to sit in the lobby and time the contractions. Then I can decide if I stay or go."

Jared took Piper's arm again and led her down the hallway. He didn't know if this was the right thing to do, but she didn't shake off his hand so he kept moving.

"Over there." Bristol pointed to a seating group in a secluded alcove.

They made their way across the large space and sat.

"We were taught to follow the 5-1-1 rule in our birthing class," Piper said. "Labor may be active and we should go to the hospital if contractions happen at least every five minutes, last for one minute each, and have been happening consistently for at least one hour."

"Were these your first contractions?" Bristol asked.

She shook her head. "Been having them for an hour. Probably longer. But they weren't within the five-minute range, and I didn't want to interrupt the meeting. Then it got bad, and I had to do something. Even if it meant walking out on Adair, which one does not do lightly." She braced her feet and planted her hands on her knees. "Here comes another one. Time the length."

Bristol got out her phone and set a timer running. She stared at the screen likely watching the numbers count up.

Jared let his mind wander, imagining he was in this situation with Bristol as his wife and having his child. Something he now knew he wanted for sure. But had she been truthful at the cabin when she admitted her love for him? Sure, she'd told her family that she wanted to find out if they had a future, but that didn't necessarily mean she loved him.

"Oh my." Piper breathed deeply and let it out slowly while running her hands over her belly. She obviously knew what she was doing and appeared calm, though her face was contorted with pain.

Come on, Nick. Hurry.

"Okay." Piper panted. "It's over."

"Sixty-nine seconds," Bristol said.

"I'll time the break between them." Jared tapped the timer on his phone.

"Thank you." Piper sighed. "Not something I ever thought I would be doing with task force members."

"I kind of thought it could happen." Jared smiled at Piper. "But you're one of the best so I had to ask for you. Luna deserved the best."

"Even if you hadn't asked, I would've insisted." Piper smiled. "I'm so relieved Luna was found, and she seems healthy. Who knows, maybe I was holding out until that happened then let my body relax and labor set in."

Her phone dinged. She looked at the screen and frowned. "Nick's stuck in traffic."

"We could drive you to your hospital," Jared said. "But not until we're sure you're not too far into your labor."

As if her body had heard him, another contraction set in, and her face tightened as she started breathing.

"Only three minutes thirty seconds between," Jared said. "I'm calling Coglin to get you a room now."

Piper nodded as she gripped the edge of her chair and moaned. Jared dialed his phone and glanced at Bristol. Their gazes held for a long moment, transmitting what, he didn't know, but it felt warm and incredible.

"Coglin, good," Jared said and explained the situation.

"Hold on while I check on room availability." Jared watched Piper, his heart racing. "We have a suite. Head up to the birthing center, and I'll call ahead to let them know to expect you."

Jared ended the call and updated the women.

Piper continued to breathe in shallow even breaths through her contraction, then got her phone out again. "Texting Nick to tell him where to find me."

"Ask for his location," Bristol said. "I'll try to get an officer to him to transport him here faster."

"We need to move before you have another contraction." Jared took Piper's arm. "We can contact Nick once we get you settled in a room."

"With you directing my steps, I can text as I walk. Just don't let me plow into any walls." She laughed and tapped in her message.

Jared admired her good mood, and his respect for her internal strength grew. He led her to the elevator. Thankfully, the car was on the ground floor waiting for them. They got in and started up. Jared tapped his foot and wished he could make the car move faster.

"Nick's phone number and location." Piper held out her phone to Bristol. "Do you think you really can help?"

"I'll do my best." She thumbed Nick's number into her phone and looked at Jared. "You get Piper settled, and I'll call dispatch."

He nodded, though he honestly wished it were the other way around. He knew nothing about helping a woman in labor and feared he was about to get a crash course in an area of life he wasn't ready to see.

23

Dispatch located a Portland police officer in Nick's area, and Bristol had him patched through to Nick. Dispatch thought the officer should be able to get Nick to the hospital in fifteen minutes after they were able to meet up. The officer was a mile or so behind Nick and could ride the shoulder to reach him.

Was this request strictly within protocol? No. Was it something the officer was willing to do because of the sacrifices Piper had made to find Luna? Of course.

Bristol swiped her pass at the birthing center door and waved her ID card as she passed the nurse on duty. Jared had texted Piper's room number so Bristol started down the hall.

She approached the Pratts' suite, where Patrick, one of the Steele Guardians' guards stood watch. The family might not be in any danger, but Bristol would keep a guard on the suite until the family went home. That was, if her family kept the hospital contract that long. She would have to meet with Coglin first thing in the morning. What happened to Aaron and Osborne could happen to a guard in any company. Hopefully, Coglin and the board would see it that way.

"Hey, Patrick," Bristol said. "Everything quiet here?"

He nodded. "Unless you mean nurses and doctors coming and going."

Bristol got a hitch in her heart. She had to check to see if Luna was okay. She knocked on the door and then entered.

Mrs. Pratt held Luna, her expression dreamy while Mr. Pratt stood over her. Toni was no longer in the room nor were any medical staff. The lights had been turned down and soft music played in the background.

The way it should be with parents and their newborn.

Thank You. Thank You. Thank You.

Tears flooded Bristol's eyes, but she quickly swiped them away.

Mrs. Pratt looked up. "Oh, good. I hoped you would stop in."

"I don't want to interrupt your reunion." Bristol stepped closer to get a good look at Luna. "One of our task force members went into labor, and I have to get down to her suite, but I wanted to check on Luna. See if all is good with her examination."

"She's just fine. Blood sugar is great." Mr. Pratt beamed a smile. "Thanks to you."

"Finding her was a team effort," Bristol said, as she was uncomfortable under the praise when she should've found Luna sooner.

"From what we heard, your knowledge of guns saved the day," Mr. Pratt said. "In any event, we can't express our thanks enough."

"No need." Bristol smiled. "I'll be going. But I'm so happy to see you all reunited and Luna's blood sugar is good."

"Thank you." Tears wetted Mrs. Pratt's eyes.

"Don't cry, honey." Mr. Pratt patted his wife's back.

"These are happy tears." A wide grin spread across her face, and she bent down to kiss the sleeping baby's forehead.

"I'll check in with you tomorrow." Bristol's heart filled with such a rush of happiness, that tears beaded up, and she hurried out of the room before she started sobbing. Or before she felt compelled to ask about Luna's real father.

She gave Patrick a forced smile and marched down the hallway, swallowing her tears with each step. She knocked on Piper's door then entered. Piper had already dressed in a gown and sat up in the bed with Nurse Raney at her side. Jared stood on the far side of the bed.

He uttered a soft, "Thank you," and came rushing around the end of the bed. He gripped Bristol's hand like a lifeline. "I'm so glad you're here."

"I can tell." She smiled and turned her attention to Mary and Piper. "An officer should have Nick here in fifteen minutes or less."

"Thank God!" Piper smiled. "And thank you for arranging that."

Bristol freed her hand and stepped closer to the bed. "We'll stay with you until Nick gets here. Just tell me what to do."

Nurse Raney looked at Bristol. "Other side of the bed. Hold her hand if needed. Ice chips as needed and cheer her on."

Bristol circled the end of the bed and looked at Jared. "You can probably go back to the debrief if you want."

He rubbed the back of his neck and kept glancing at the door. "I can stay as long as Piper wants me here."

Piper locked her gaze on him. "No offense, but the fewer people here, the better, and it seems like Bristol's determined to stay."

"I am," Bristol said.

"Then go, Jar—" Piper jerked forward in a contraction and grabbed onto Bristol's hand with such intensity that Bristol couldn't hide the pain from her expression.

Piper had the strength of ten men in her grip, and Bristol was already rethinking her desire to stay. But Piper needed someone, and Bristol had already committed to stay.

"I'll be in the waiting area," Jared said to Bristol and mouthed *Thank you* again.

She dredged up a smile, and he fled the room. She didn't blame him. But Piper had given her all to finding Luna, and Bristol could return the effort and give her all to helping Piper.

Jared was sure the unsettled feeling in his gut had to be much like an expectant father. He'd been pacing the waiting area for over ten minutes, not knowing what to do. Not that fathers these days waited on the sidelines. At least he didn't think they did. He wouldn't. Sure, he'd bolted from Piper's suite, but he wouldn't do the same thing at the birth of his own child. Or if any child went missing in the future. He didn't want or expect that to happen, but if he was called upon to work such an investigation again, he would be right up front asking to lead.

He could handle it. No matter the outcome.

God was indeed at his side. Jared now knew that. And just because they'd had a bad outcome with Wyatt didn't mean that every outcome in the future would be bad. God had a plan for Wyatt. A plan Jared didn't understand. Would never understand. But it was a perfect plan that only God could craft. Jared could now live with what happened to Wyatt. Better than that, Jared could let go of the trauma. Move on. Live as God intended him to live. Open. Alive.

Fully alive. And ready for a relationship with the woman he'd loved for years.

The door opened, and Bristol stepped in.

"Nick arrived?" Jared asked.

"He did." She crossed the room, collapsed on a chair, and let out a long noisy breath. "The nurse said Piper was progressing very rapidly through labor and to expect her to give birth any time now."

"Wow." Jared sat next to Bristol, the tightness in his gut lessening. "Good thing we didn't get into traffic with her. Do you want to wait for the baby? Seems like we should, but then it also seems like this is very personal, and we shouldn't."

She pivoted to look at him. "Nick said he would come out to tell us when the baby arrives, so it sounds like they're expecting us to stay."

"What about your family?" he asked. "They're expecting us for breakfast."

"I called them from the suite and told them we weren't coming."

"Phew," Jared said, half in jest but a hint of truth lingered in his tone.

Bristol's eyebrows went up. "You don't want to eat with them?"

Did he? "You kind of scared me when you said I had to win your grandparents over."

She waved a hand. "I was mostly joking."

"Mostly?" His mouth suddenly dry, he swallowed hard.

"Their good opinion of the man I choose for life is a must for me." She took his hand and looked him in the eye, but his chest tightened. "I have no doubt they will see you for the wonderful man you've become and forget that you dumped me."

"You think so?" The tightness in his chest eased some.

"Once I tell them about your fine qualities, and they see them for themselves, I know they'll approve." She smiled, the soft smile he'd always believed was meant just for him. "What about meeting your family?"

He groaned. "I don't care what they think about you."

"Translated, you don't think they'll approve."

"Do you come from a wealthy family? Have social status? No." He shook his head. "They won't understand my choice any more than they understand me. But I would honestly worry if I brought a woman home to meet them and they liked her on the spot. That would mean I didn't choose very well for myself." He chuckled.

She tilted her head and studied him. "You really sound okay with that."

"Took me years to figure it out, but yeah. I'm okay with being who God wants me to be, even if my family doesn't like it. I am who I am." He held tightly to her hand. "And I'm finally okay with losing Wyatt. God has a plan. I just have to trust in it and live it the best I can."

"That's one of the things my grandparents are going to love about you." Her smile stretched ear-to-ear. "I had a revelation myself."

"And?" he asked, hoping she'd also found a way to trust, as that was the only way the two of them would get together again.

"You get taken at gunpoint by a half-crazed woman and you come to the end of what you can do on your own. It's then you realize you have to fall back to God. And you figure out that faith means finding a way, no matter what's happening, no matter how hard or tough it is, to know that God is real. That He's in control and fighting for you." She sat back, contentment on her face.

"I hate that you went through this, but I'm glad you

restored your relationship with God." He was about to tug her close when his phone rang. "It's Reed."

Jared answered. "Bristol is with me, and I'm putting you on speaker."

"Everyone at Veritas wants to know how Piper is doing and if Nick arrived," Reed said. "He's not replying to texts so we hoped you were there with them."

"Nick arrived, and the labor nurse says Piper will have the baby anytime now," Bristol said.

"Wow. That was quick," Reed said. "Sierra was in labor for almost a day."

"The nurse thinks Piper went into labor much earlier, and the seriousness of the investigation distracted her from contractions," Bristol said.

"She has a laser focus, so I can see that happening." Reed chuckled. "I'm also calling to tell you Holloway and Melissa are both in custody. Holloway ran a red light, and the officer who stopped him remembered the BOLO."

"We need to interview them," Jared said, seeing his plans disappear as they had so many times before. He wanted to take Bristol home after the baby was born and veg out together until sunrise. But on the other hand, he wanted to look Holloway in the face and figure out the part the crooked attorney played in this investigation.

Jared looked at Bristol for her reaction.

"I feel like we need to be here for Nick and Piper. But we'll definitely grill Holloway after we hear about the baby."

Jared nodded and turned his attention back to the phone. "We'll head to the detention center soon. No one's life is in danger so we'll let Holloway sit and stew for a bit. Who knows? A little time behind bars might make him more ready to talk."

Bristol sat in the interview room next to Jared as they waited for Holloway to be brought in for questioning. She both dreaded interviewing the man and looked forward to it. Either way, it ruined the joy of sharing the birth of Piper and Nick's son. A healthy eight pounds and six ounces, they named the little guy Carter, and they couldn't be happier.

"Talk about a contrast in tasks." Jared shook his head. "Going from a baby's birth to this."

"I was thinking the same thing," Bristol said. "At least we know Holloway won't be separating any more babies from their parents."

The door opened, and Holloway was escorted into the room. He dropped onto the chair and leaned back, his cocky expression belying his appearance. A five o'clock shadow darkened his face and matched the dark circles under his eyes. He hadn't changed into jail garb yet and was dressed in khakis and a red polo shirt looking like the country club guy that he was. Minus the handcuffs circling his wrists.

"So." His eyebrows arched as he stared at them. "Not the loving couple who sat in my office, I see."

"FBI Agent Jared Wolfe." Jared displayed his credentials. "And Deputy Bristol Steele."

"I hate to admit it, but the pair of you fooled me. I bought into your story. Guess undercover is your specialty."

"First time." Bristol met his challenging gaze as she wanted to let him know that even as rookies in the under-cover business, they'd fooled him. Of course, she and Jared were in love so that part had been easy. At least subconsciously.

"Then shame on me for being a fool." Holloway frowned and lifted his cuffed hands to scratch his face. "But then what difference did it make? I didn't do anything wrong."

"Not with us," Jared said. "You didn't have time. But we

know that you ordered Valerie Zupan to kidnap Luna Pratt for her father."

If he was surprised at the comment, he didn't show it. "You have no proof of that."

"Actually, we do," Jared replied calmly. "We have a witness who can confirm you asked Valerie to take the baby."

"Valerie? She won't say a word against me."

"No, not Valerie. She was murdered."

"Really? When did that happen?"

"We found her in Reya Isaac's house yesterday."

He snorted. "Some cops you are."

"We weren't the only ones who fooled you," Bristol said. "I have to assume you think Reya died and Valerie double-crossed you. But Reya killed her sister then impersonated her so she could take Luna to replace her deceased daughter."

"No." He sat forward, his eyes narrowing. "She looked and acted just like Valerie."

"That's because Reya changed her looks to match Valerie to fool others. Reya was tired of all the negative publicity and wanted to get away from it for a little while."

Holloway shook his head.

"Reya has stated that you were behind the kidnapping. With her testimony, you'll go away for a very long time." Bristol smiled with satisfaction though she knew Reya couldn't testify in her mental state.

Holloway's face paled.

"And if that's not enough," Bristol continued while she had him uneasy. "The women you had stashed in your house can pin you to other illegal adoptions. As can Olive Wallace."

He smirked.

"Oh, right," Bristol said. "I should say Pam Vogel."

His smirk evaporated.

"Not to mention Melissa." Jared sat back and draped his arm on Bristol's chair. "Nelson Osborne has identified her as the woman who paid him off to take Aaron King hostage and impersonate him at the hospital. She was more than happy to tell our associates that you were the one who gave her the money for his payoff."

Holloway shrugged, but his eyes held unease. "Her word against mine."

Bristol ignored his comment. "Add it with the other testimonies, and you're going to go away for a long time."

"Go easy on yourself, Holloway," Jared said. "Time to cop to your role and maybe the DA will take that into consideration."

That revolting smirk was back on Holloway's face. "You really don't have enough on me."

"Glenn Bates could tell a different story." *If he was alive.* "You didn't think we'd find Luna's biological father, did you? But we did, and he admitted to being Luna's father and to you arranging to kidnap her."

"He's lying."

"But you know him?"

Holloway let his gaze wander the room. "No. Of course not. I just know any man who says I had a child abducted is lying."

"The video at Reya Isaacs's house doesn't lie though," Jared said. "The doorbell camera caught you quite clearly as you carried a woman who was at death's door. You could go down for murder too."

"Nah," he said. "If I was there, which I'm not saying I was, I wouldn't show my face, and I would never have anything to do with killing someone."

"Don't need to see your face these days," Jared said. "Our

forensics staff can use photogrammetry and image comparison to prove it was you. So you see, we've got you."

"Not yet or you wouldn't be begging me to confess." His snide smile returned. "I'll take my chances."

Bristol resisted growling at Holloway. As an attorney, he knew what to say and what not to say. Didn't matter. Bristol wouldn't give up on this investigation, and she knew Jared wouldn't either until Holloway was charged and convicted of kidnapping Luna and as many other children as they could prove.

24

Four weeks later. Labor Day.

Jared listened to the tires of his vehicle crunch down the driveway of the Steeles' farm. Her grandad was hosting his famous end-of-the-summer barbecue. Surprisingly not fish, but burgers and chicken.

Jared's nervous stomach would likely stop him from eating a bite until he talked to Bristol's dad. Maybe to her grandad too. Today he would ask for her hand in marriage. He'd never done anything like that, and it was far too important to screw up. He and Bristol had been inseparable since Luna's investigation concluded. Even though Bristol had left her deputy job, they'd worked tirelessly to bring together enough evidence to charge Holloway with kidnapping and an accessory to murder. Now the man awaited trial.

And they also interviewed Sonya Pratt, who confessed to having a one-night stand with Glenn Bates. Her husband insisted on a DNA test, which proved he wasn't the biological father. He chose to stay with Sonya, but for how long, Jared didn't know as the huge rift between them seemed almost insurmountable.

Jared had been praying for them and offered another

one now as he slowed in the drive. A lineup of cars stretched toward the barn, and he pulled in behind the blue VW Bug at the rear. Not only were family invited to this event but friends too, and Bristol warned fifty or more people could attend.

He got out, and the eighty-degree heat of the summer day hit him in the face. The blazing sun baked into his body, but he didn't care. It was a perfect day to ask the woman he loved to marry him. Perfect if her dad approved, and if she said yes, that was.

His breakfast churning in his stomach, he strolled down the drive counting the cars to keep his brain occupied. He laid eyes on Amelia in a tree swing holding her baby girl. Her contented expression said it all. She'd moved into a hired hand's house on the property along with Fae and her son. Amelia and Fae shared a job as a housekeeper for a local vintner. They alternated caring for each other's child when they didn't work. A perfect short-term solution until they could figure out how to move forward. Katana did indeed give up her child and moved back home.

He waved at Amelia. "Beautiful day."

"Every day is a beautiful day with this little one." She smiled at him.

He felt that way about being with Bristol. He didn't know how he could've left her in the first place. But he was about to rectify that.

He strode down the hill to the barn where the haymow doors were flung open and the large space held folding tables and chairs. Party lights twinkled above and balloons with curly streamers bobbed around them. The thick wooden floor had been swept but pieces of hay clung to the cracks. The space smelled like hay mixed with a tangy barbecue sauce.

He searched for Bristol and found her at a bar near the

back of the space. He wound through the guests, greeting the people he knew, but not stopping for anything. He would soon hurl from nervousness if he didn't get this out of the way. She wore shorts, a T-shirt and flip-flops. Yes, this was his Bristol. The woman he'd met at camp. She was filling red plastic cups with iced tea and lemonade for guests. She handed a cup to a little boy then looked up.

Their gazes locked. She smiled, the one that sent his heart racing. He moved even faster toward her. Her dad stepped in his path.

"Glad you could make it, Jared," Gene said as if oblivious to Jared's path.

Jared had hoped to say hi to Bristol before talking to her dad, but he also wanted to get talking to this very intimidating man over with. "Sir."

"Seriously, it's Gene. Not sir."

"Could we talk for a minute?" Jared asked, but it came out in more of a croak. "Maybe away from everyone. And it might be good if your dad came too."

"Ah, that kind of talk." Gene grinned. "With the way you and Bristol have been inseparable lately, I figured this would be coming soon. If you went in for that sort of thing, that is. I'm glad to see that you do. Shows respect."

"Yes, sir, I mean, Gene." Jared pointed across the room. "I see Mr. Steele going out back. Maybe we could join him."

"He's going for another platter of meat, so your timing is perfect." Gene clapped Jared on the back and urged him through the crowd.

The trip out back was a blur, but Jared glanced to the right to confirm the cooler he'd arranged to have made by Bristol's mother sat just where she said she would leave it.

Bristol's grandad stood at one of three large grills, his tongs holding a chicken breast seared in grill stripes and covered in barbecue sauce. "Just in time to help."

Gene took the platter and held it out to his father. "Jared has something he wants to talk to us about."

"'Bout time." Artie plopped the chicken onto the platter.

"I'm not sure if you know what I want to talk about," Jared said.

"'Course we do." He tonged a chicken thigh. "You can't fool law enforcement or former law enforcement officers very often."

"At least not good ones, like us." Gene grinned.

Jared looked at Gene. "Then you know I want to ask for your daughter's hand in marriage."

"What?" Gene's voice shot up. "I thought you just wanted to ask about dating her."

Jared's heart dropped to the pit of his stomach. "No. No. I—"

"Just kidding, man." Gene jabbed Jared in the arm. "I knew this is what you wanted."

"Me too," Artie said. "And it isn't any of my business, but I approve. Figured the girl would end up marrying someone in law enforcement, and I'm glad it's a fed like you who won't be patrolling the streets every day."

"Agreed," Gene said. "Not with the way our city is struggling with the increase in crime."

Not an answer Jared had expected. "I hope it's more than that. That you know I will be by Bristol's side in everything for the rest of our lives."

Artie put down his tongs and closed his grill. He gripped Jared's shoulder. "You're a fine man, that's clear, and I don't think you'll ever hurt Bristol again. But if you do…" He tightened his grip.

Gene nodded at the grill. "We won't be grilling just chicken, if you get our drift."

Jared swallowed. "I do and you have nothing to worry about."

Gene held out his hand and gripped Jared's. "Then welcome to the family, son."

"That is if she says yes." Artie laughed and strode off with his platter.

Jared swallowed again, his throat dry. "I guess there's nothing left but to find out if she will."

~

Bristol handed a glass of iced tea to one of her grandad's friends and scanned the crowd for Jared. She'd seen him disappear with her dad, and a few minutes later, the pair followed Grandad back to the barn. She had to figure Jared had just asked for her hand in marriage. At least she hoped he had. She'd let go of her final obstacle to marrying Jared. Her fear of marrying a law enforcement officer. If she truly trusted God, then she could accept that God put this man in her life again and that being with Jared was God's will.

She and Jared had spent nearly four weeks together, confirming their feelings for each other. A short time, some people might say, but after once having been head-over-heels in love with him, it wasn't hard to fall for him again.

But this Jared wasn't a boy. He was a man. A fine man who she hoped to build a family with. Just like the one her parents and grandparents had built. She was now firmly a part of the family business. Especially after she succeeded in keeping the lucrative hospital contract when the board had wanted to throw them under the bus as the scapegoat for the kidnapping.

Not a week after the kidnapping, their guard Damon took down a man with an assault rifle in a bag. Without Damon's quick thinking, the man would've shot up the hospital. Impressed with Damon's diligence, Coglin appealed to the board, and Steele Guardians was given a six-month trial period. She'd assigned Zeke to work full-time out of the hospital, and she spent a few days a week there herself. The rest of the time she worked on landing new accounts and had been quite successful, if she said so herself.

Jared broke through the crowd to approach her. He wore khaki tactical pants and a black polo shirt that deepened his already dark coloring. He could wear pretty much anything, and her heart would kick into high gear when she saw him.

He stopped in front of the table and winked. "Could I get an iced tea, ma'am?"

"Of course, kind sir." She played along and poured the drink.

"Are you tied to this bar or might you be able to take a stroll around the grounds?"

"My boss allows breaks for sure." She waved at Teagan who was passing by.

Teagan, wearing a flowery sundress, slipped through the others to join them. "You don't even need to ask me to take over. The looks you two are sharing could start tonight's bonfire."

Bristol swiped a hand at her cousin, who ducked away before Bristol could connect.

"Thank you," Jared said to Teagan.

Teagan smiled. "Don't worry, she'll say yes."

Bristol eyed her cousin as she moved around the counter. She hated that Teagan put Jared on the spot. What if he didn't plan to propose to Bristol?

He didn't seem to mind the comment, but took Bristol's hand and led her to the back door.

He grabbed a blue cooler sitting next to the wall and held it up. "From your mother. She was really good at keeping my secret. At least I think she was."

"I didn't know a thing about this, which in this family amounts to a near miracle." She laughed.

He laughed along with her and led her to a meadow with tall grass and wildflowers just waiting to bloom. He shook a plaid blanket out. "Sit. I'll get out the food."

"What did my mom make?" Bristol took a seat and curled her legs under her.

"She said you loved dill egg salad sandwiches on home-made honey wheat bread, chips, and dill pickles on the side. Plus, your gran brought over peanut butter cookies, and your mom included a few of those."

He handed her a glass container holding the sandwich, and she quickly prayed then dug into it. "Umm. I was hungry. Been pouring tea and lemonade for hours."

Jared settled on the blanket, crossing his legs. "Your grandad puts on quite the party."

Memories of the past came to Bristol's mind. "He's done it since before I was born. I remember how fun it was when the night ended with fireworks but the laws have gotten too restrictive for that. Now if we aren't in a drought, we have a big bonfire."

"Like your grandad planned for tonight." Jared took a bite of his sandwich. "This is good. Never had egg salad with dill."

"It's another thing I can make so maybe you'll have it again." She couldn't come right out and say she would make it for him for the rest of their lives if he proposed, though the meaning lingered there.

"Speaking of again." He set down his container and dug into his pocket then helped her stand and got down on one knee.

Butterflies fluttered in her stomach and a burst of joy so immense, so amazing, swamped her, and she struggled to contain it before she got lightheaded. But she did hold it back. Just barely.

"I know you suspected I was going to do this and knew what was coming. But it's good that it's not really a big surprise because we both know how we feel about each other. I mean, I love you, Bristol. Everything about you. The way you wrinkle your nose. Do your very best at everything you try. Your loyalty. Your sense of family and commitment to them. Your big and generous heart. Your sense of humor. I could go on and on, but I'll end by saying I want to spend the rest of my life with you."

He opened a ring box revealing a French-cut diamond that caught the sunlight and glittered like a star. "Will you marry me?"

"Absolutely." She drew him to his feet and threw herself at him.

He caught her up in his powerful arms and held her tight, but then moved back and kissed her. His lips were warm and tasted of dill. She clung to him and deepened the kiss, wanting him to know in a single kiss that she loved him as much as he loved her. But she had to tell him too.

She leaned back. "I love you too, of course. More than I ever imagined I could love someone."

He released her and gently took her hand to slide the ring on her finger. It fit perfectly. How, she didn't know and didn't care. She turned her hand and admired the sparkling center diamond and the rows of smaller diamonds on the white gold band. "The ring is just beautiful. You have very good taste."

"I chose you, didn't I?" He smiled at her.

"Perfect answer." She linked her arms around his waist. "And proves what an amazing husband you're going to be."

"I'm not sure I'll get it right all the time." His brow furrowed.

She ran a finger over it to make him relax. "Don't worry. I'll be sure to help you."

He tossed back his head and laughed. "Have a seat. I have a bottle of sparkling apple juice to toast with."

He helped her sit, and she held out her hand and twisted it again, capturing the light on her ring from all angles. "I feel like a very special princess. As more of a tomboy, I don't often feel that way."

"You're a princess to me." He popped open the juice.

She smiled at him. "You're on a roll today."

"I know, right?" He poured two glasses of juice, the bubbles rising up the side of the fluted glass as he handed one to her. "To our future together. May we have everything your parents and grandparents have and a lifetime of creating memories together."

She clinked glasses with him and looked around. "Have you ever considered living in the country?"

"Never." He cocked his head. "Is that something you might want to do?"

She shrugged. "Only if we have kids. Then I think it might be great."

"I can see that." He set down his glass and picked up his sandwich. "You know my hours can be erratic and the drive from the Bureau office could be a problem."

"I can see that. Just a thought. Not like we've even talked about where we'd live once we got married."

"I know one place we won't live. In the house with your sisters and cousins." He made a sour face. "It's been enough of a challenge to get you alone these last few weeks. If we lived there, we'd never have children."

She laughed and clutched her side. "I would never ever propose that idea."

She took a sip of the juice and sat back to eat the rest of her meal, just enjoying the time with Jared in the beautiful sunshine with the soft breeze playing over them and whispering through the grass. She wanted to stay here for the rest of the day, but her grandad was counting on her help.

"We should go back," she said. "Would you mind helping me with my chores?"

"Not at all, unless you're talking about chores like mucking out a stall or something farmy like that. Then I have to draw the line."

"City boy," she taunted.

"And proud of it." He grabbed her hand and pulled her to him.

Their lips met again in an explosion of love. The kind of love she knew was forever. Much deeper and grander than when they'd first known each other. And she had to believe in the love that God put in her life when He brought the two of them together.

Jared released her, his gaze reluctant, but he quickly packed up the cooler and stood to help her up. "How do you want to handle the announcement? Tell people today or wait until we can tell your family alone?"

"Wait, I think."

"Then wait it is. But you'll have to hide your ring."

"Hmm, that I don't like." She turned it around. "There. No one will notice this."

"I wouldn't count on that. Not with your family." He folded the blanket and picked up the cooler.

He took her hand, and she clung to him, already thinking about their life together. Even planning that wedding and the honeymoon as they walked hand in hand toward the barn.

At the barn doors he looked at her. "I should take the cooler up to the house and clean it out for your mom."

"Ah, yes, the considerate man I'm going to marry." She

grinned up at him. "I'll come with you, and then we need to relieve Teagan with the drinks."

They'd gotten six feet into the barn when her grandad whistled to stop the boisterous conversations.

"Well?" he called out.

Jared glanced at her and shrugged.

"Go ahead." She felt for her ring to turn it right side around.

"She said yes." Jared dropped the cooler, grabbed her up in a hug, and swung her around.

A whoop went through the crowd, and Bristol shook her head. "You can hardly ever keep a secret from this family."

"Hard to do with all the law enforcement officers." Jared set her down. "And one secret I don't ever want to keep is that I love you and am so grateful that you said yes."

"Hey." Bristol stroked the side of his face. "I think if I'd said no, this group would've harassed me until I did say yes. Looks like you already have them wrapped around your finger."

He frowned.

A spear of concern stabbed her. "What?"

"Your dad and grandad weren't and never will be wrapped around my finger," he said.

"No worries." She grinned. "It's the Steele women who run this family, and you might as well know it before we say our 'I dos.'"

He laughed. "That was another secret that was never well kept, and it's not going to stand in my way of saying 'I do.' Nothing will stop that. Nothing at all."

STEELE GUARDIAN SERIES
Intrigue. Suspense. Family.

A baby kidnapped from a hospital. A jewelry heist. A man with amnesia. An abducted socialite. Smuggled antiquities. Murder. And in every book, God's amazing power and love.

Book 1 – Tough as Steele – February 1, 2022
Book 2 – Nerves of Steele – May 1, 2022
Book 3 – Forged in Steele – August 10, 2022
Book 4 – Made of Steele – November 1, 2022
Book 5 – Solid as Steele – February 1, 2023
Book 6 – Edge of Steele – May 1, 2023

For More Details Visit -

www.susansleeman.com/books/steele-guardians

NIGHTHAWK SECURITY SERIES

Protecting others when unspeakable danger lurks.

A woman being stalked. A mother and child being hunted. And more. All in danger. Needing protection from the men of Nighthawk Security.

Book 1 – Night Fall
Book 2 – Night Vision
Book 3 – Night Hawk
Book 4 – Night Moves
Book 5 – Night Watch
Book 6 – Night Prey

For More Details Visit -
www.susansleeman.com/books/nighthawk-security/

THE TRUTH SEEKERS

People are rarely who they seem

A twin who didn't know she had a sister. A mother whose child isn't her own. A woman whose parents lied to her. All needing help from The Truth Seekers forensic team.

Book 1 - Dead Ringer
Book 2 - Dead Silence
Book 3 - Dead End
Book 4 - Dead Heat
Book 5 - Dead Center
Book 6 - Dead Even

For More Details Visit -
www.susansleeman.com/books/truth-seekers/

The COLD HARBOR SERIES

Meet Blackwell Tactical- former military and law enforcement heroes who will give everything to protect innocents... even their own lives.

Book 1 - Cold Terror
Book 2 - Cold Truth
Book 3 - Cold Fury
Book 4 - Cold Case
Book 5 - Cold Fear
Book 6 - Cold Pursuit
Book 7 - Cold Dawn

For More Details Visit -
www.susansleeman.com/books/cold-harbor/

ABOUT SUSAN

SUSAN SLEEMAN is a bestselling and award-winning author of more than 50 inspirational/Christian and clean read romantic suspense books. In addition to writing, Susan also hosts the website, TheSuspenseZone.com.

Susan currently lives in Oregon, but has had the pleasure of living in nine states. Her husband is a retired church music director and they have two beautiful daughters, two very special sons-in-law, and two amazing grandsons.

For more information visit: www.susansleeman.com

Made in the USA
Columbia, SC
02 September 2022

66518928R00195